DEATH'S
REVENGE

ALSO BY STAN WILCZEK JR.

The Kept Secret

The Soma Man

DEATH'S REVENGE

STAN WILCZEK JR.

PYRAMID PUBLISHING INC.
UTICA, NEW YORK

Printed in the United States of America

First Printing: November 2012
10 9 8 7 6 5 4 3 2 1

ISBN 978-1-886166-34-9

Library of Congress Cataloging-in-Publication Data

Wilczek, Stan.
  Death's revenge / by Stan Wilczek, Jr.
  p. cm.
  ISBN 978-1-886166-34-9 (alk. paper)
  1. Revenge--Fiction. 2. Greed--Fiction. I. Title.
  PS3623.I534D43 2012
  813'.6--dc23
2012029995

Pyramid Publishing Inc.
PO Box 8339
Utica, New York 13505

www.pyramidpublishing.com

For Rose

Thank you for all those nights . . .
You know the ones I'm talking about.

ACKNOWLEDGMENTS

I know . . . I know . . . this book has taken forever! Thanks to all of you who kept asking, "When is the next book coming out?" Well, here it is! My only excuse is, life got in the way.

Many thanks to those who took the time to read and comment on the draft manuscript: Pam Bryant, Marcia Benson, Marion Lucas, Gail Perrin, Elaine Russell, Sharon Vining and Robin Wheeler. A special thanks to Leslie Morelli, Frank Baran, and Gary Boyer for their detailed editorial comments and suggestions. All of you made a difference and I hope you see your suggestions in the final product

A very special thanks to the staff at Pyramid Publishing, specifically Zach Steffen. None of this would happen without you.

To those who think you see yourself or others described in this book (you know who you are), let me assure you that you do not. Also, because this novel is totally fictitious, nothing in it is true, except of course for the parts that are!

Finally, I want to thank all of you who took the time to read and then provide me with such great feedback on *The Kept Secret* and *The Soma Man*. I hope you again find this book clutched in your hands when you know you should be doing something else.

As a final note, any and all mistakes contained herein are mine.

DEATH'S REVENGE

PROLOGUE

He was invisible, sitting across the room in the shadows at the far end of the dark, crowded, muggy bar, cocksure his ex-wife wouldn't notice. In his years of observing her, though he knew some might call it stalking, not once had she seen him. She was in a new life now. He had been part of the old. The one she had long forgotten. The one he was still in. The one he would soon remind her of.

"Excuse me." Hot breath fell on his right ear as a stranger's voice suddenly blocked out the dozens of conversations surrounding him. Nudging sideways into the small space next to the stool, her breasts rubbed against his clammy upper arm. He instinctively leaned left. "A little crowded in here tonight?" Without saying a word he turned his head and refocused on the woman across the room.

P. J. Dorsey's was one of a dozen bars in the renovated Armory Square district of downtown Syracuse, New York. Now home to upscale apartments, restaurants, bars, and trendy boutiques, the crowds that flocked here nightly were a stark contrast from the rats and homeless people that had roamed the area just a few years before. When he followed her in earlier, he knew it would be just the right place to 'observe' her.

"Thanks for the space." The woman slipped away from the bar, two sweaty cold bottles of Coors Light in each hand, this time with a more deliberate rubbing of her body onto his, which he ignored.

He gazed across the room again. That familiar contagious smile was clearly visible, even at this distance. She was holding a freshly mixed drink, Absolut and orange no doubt, and seemed to be carrying on two conversations at once. How could she just block out her past like that? His hands tightened on the large glass mug in front of him. And look at the way she was dressed. "Slut," he mumbled aloud. Now he had something else to add to his list of reasons for hating her.

It didn't really matter, though. His list was already long enough. After all, she was the one he blamed for their daughter's death. Their only child, gone forever. She was the one who walked out on their marriage. Had he known at the time that the only thing she really wanted from him was her freedom, he wouldn't have given it to her. But he didn't, so he did. She's now in her new life, while he's still grieving the old. Even today's news—cancer, less than six months, the words had hit him like a punch in the stomach— he blamed on her.

It's all her damn fault, he thought. He started shaking as he gulped for a deep breath of heavy air. It wasn't right. She should be grieving for their daughter too.

He lifted his mug and downed the rest of the beer. It was still ice cold. He pushed the glass and a twenty toward the back of the bar, catching the bartender's eye.

It would be so easy to kill her, he thought as he looked over at her again. To snuff out her life as she had done his and their daughter's. But no, death, even a slow, gruesome one, was too final, too irreversible. Just because she had blood on her hands, didn't mean he needed to. Anyway, he wanted her to suffer just as much, if not more than he had. Death was too much of an end.

He thought he heard her voice. Then her laugh. The one that had been so familiar to him. His eyes closed as they went blurry. He wiped the drop with his fingers as it slid down his cheek.

He squeezed the freshly poured beer with both hands, watching the white frost disappear from the outside of the mug. How could his life have come to this? Not long ago, things were so perfect. Now his life would soon be over. Why? No matter how hard he tried, he knew he would never find the answer to that question. Not here on earth, anyway.

Not here on earth . . .

A smile, requiring less energy than the one a minute ago, spread across his face. Every cloud does have a silver lining, he thought. In six months he would see his daughter again. In six months he would be done with his suffering. In six months . . . his eyes opened wide. "Six months was not enough time," he whispered. "She needs to suffer more than six months."

Then, like a vision, it came to him. Death may be the end, but the dead can still affect the future. When that happens, you have little control over the events that transpire. In fact, you have no choice but to succumb to the dead's wishes.

A calm came over him, one he hadn't felt in years. He sucked down the rest of his beer, left a generous tip on the bar, and started toward the door. As he snaked his way through the crowd, his heart pounded in his chest. With one more step, he was touching her, back to back. He started to turn, but hatred stopped him.

He continued down the steps, stopped in front of the door, then turned and stared back at her. In an instant, their eyes met. It was less than a second. He pushed his way out the door, but not before he saw her smile disappearing from her face. He knew she had seen him. Or maybe she just thought she had seen him. He wasn't sure which was worse. He smiled. It didn't matter, he thought. The look on her face told him that he had found death's revenge.

1

As the car door opened, Dan could feel the suffocating blast of hot, humid air against his face. It felt so thick he had to force himself to suck in a deep breath. Even though it was seven thirty in the evening, the sun was still above the trees, keeping the temperature hovering near ninety. The unexpectedly warm June weather for upstate New York was a welcome relief from the bitterly cold winter that seemed to end only a few weeks ago. No one was complaining about the heat today, although that wouldn't last long.

As he stood next to the car he glanced at the blinding orange ball, still high in the sky, then at his watch. The puzzled look on his face soon disappeared as he remembered that this coming Saturday was the longest day of the year.

He leaned over and reached back into the car to grab the ticket that was lying on the center console and the black canvas bag that was on the passenger seat. The air in the car still felt cold. He took a deep breath before standing back up. Closing the car door, he pushed the lock button on his remote, then pushed it again, each time listening for the muffled clicking sound from within the car. Then he lifted the car door handle to make sure it was locked. Glancing from side to side, he walked briskly down the well-land-scaped path to the alcove of his apartment building.

As he pushed on his apartment door, the cold air from within washed over his now sweaty, damp body. A shiver jolted him as he stepped inside. He leaned his head back out into the alcove to make sure no one had seen him, then quickly closed the door, being careful not to let it slam. He locked the two dead bolts, then turned and leaned back against the freezing metal door.

He stood there for several minutes, as if in a hypnotic trance, motionless, with his eyes staring at nothing and everything. Then, suddenly, he raised the ticket that was still clenched in his fingers and read the itinerary. Mohawk Airways flight 2145, departing Syracuse on Thursday June 19 at 7:10 a.m. from gate 44, arriving Washington Reagan at 8:30 a.m.

Another shiver jolted him. "I can't believe I'm going to meet with him," he mumbled aloud. "Maybe I shouldn't have agreed to meet on such short notice. Then I could have driven instead . . . I can still back out. I don't have to get on that plane tomorrow. And even if I do get on the plane, I don't have to show up for the meet-ing . . . so I am still in control of this." Convinced he was, he placed the bag and ticket on the counter, then remembered he had a six pack of Coors Light and leftover pizza in the refrigerator.

"That hit the spot," Dan said aloud, as he sat down in his well worn but comfortable leather recliner, holding a beer in one hand and his black canvas bag in the other. He reached into the bag and, without looking, pulled out the SONY micro cassette recorder, pressed the rewind button, and placed it and the bag on the coffee table in front of him. Then he reached for the hard covered black and purple journal that was laying on the table. He opened it to the page where his silver Cross pen was clipped, the same page he had finished on the night before.

It had taken his counselor years to convince him to start keeping a journal. "It would be great therapy," she'd say. But for Dr. Daniel Lockwood, it had turned into an addiction, one he didn't even realize he had. Although he had diligently written his thoughts down every evening since his wife had left him five years ago, often spending hours doing so, he rarely read what he wrote. If asked how many of the identical hard covered journals there were, Dan wouldn't be able to tell you a number. He only knew he was up to the letter P.

Collecting his thoughts, he took a deep breath and started writing. Almost an hour later, he reached down, switched the cassette player on, and began to meticulously transcribe the phone conversation he had recorded earlier in the day, just as he had done for the previous fourteen calls over the past six weeks. When he was done, he rewound the tape and listened to it again, double checking to make sure he had captured every word in the journal. Then he repeated the process.

Finally, he clipped the pen to the page in the journal, closed the book and threw it back on the coffee table. He leaned back in his chair and gazed at the shadows on the ceiling. "I don't have to meet with him tomorrow," he again repeated aloud to himself. "But if I don't, then the last three months of my life will have been a waste of time. And time is something I don't have a lot of. Maybe I am crazy after all."

Somehow saying those words out loud, though no one was

there to hear them, seemed to calm him down.

"I AM CRAZY!" he yelled out. "Step one of the twelve step AA process . . . admit you have the problem."

Crazy or not, for a man who had only months to live, he appeared to be totally in control of himself and what he was doing. It had been three months since he learned of his pancreatic cancer. Fourth stage. Already spread to the liver. He had decided against any treatments, reasoning that months of sickening chemotherapy, in exchange for a few months more life, and even that wasn't a guarantee, was not worth it. Luckily, he had been able to control what little pain he experienced so far, though he knew it would get worse, with daily doses of Tylenol and a few beers.

Admittedly, his mind had been focused on something else in these intervening months. He was on a mission. It had totally consumed him. Knowing he only had months to live gave him the incentive, and balls, he needed to put his revenge plan into place. And so far, everything was proceeding exactly as he had planned, including tomorrow's meeting.

Dan smiled to himself, something he had done more of in the past three months than in the previous ten years. The most difficult part of his plan, at least he had originally thought it was going to be the most difficult part, was finding someone to play along with him. Someone who would unknowingly carry out his plan long after he was gone. Fortunately, money had solved that problem. He now understood why greed was called one of the seven deadly sins.

"I've got to meet with him eventually . . . tomorrow is as good a time as any." Again, talking out loud made it sound more convincing to him.

Although he knew his meeting tomorrow was a necessary part of his plan, it would also be the most daring thing he'd done so far. Of course, he also realized it could turn out to be the most stupid. Another smile came across his face.

He got up, walked to his bedroom and fell belly first onto his bed, just like he did when he was a kid. Suddenly he was reminded of the dull pain deep in his gut. Laying motionless, with his eyes closed, he realized how exhausted he was. He turned his head and slowly opened and focused his eyes on the clock. The blue-green numbers—10:18 p.m.—came into view. He reached over and pushed the alarm button. It was set for 4:00 a.m. That would give him plenty of time to get to the airport, through check-in, and to the gate for his 7:10 a.m. flight.

As he lay there, staring at the clock, his stomach started to tighten. He could feel his heart pounding hard and fast. He was still concerned about flying tomorrow under his own name, but in this post-911 world of heightened airport security, it was the surest way of guaranteeing there would be no mess ups. The last thing he needed was to be arrested by airport personnel for impersonating someone who didn't exist. His other identity was carefully concealed in his briefcase. He would replace the appropriate items in his wallet upon his arrival in Washington tomorrow.

He suddenly turned his head and caught sight of the briefcase on the chair in the corner of the room. Taking in a deep breath, he tried to reassure himself that he was ready for this meeting. He had accounted for every detail, every possible problem that could arise, checked and double checked everything. He was certain all was in order. He turned back to look at the alarm clock, reached over once again and pushed the alarm button, still set at 4:00 a.m.,

9

then dozed off, fully clothed, with the lights on.

He stared out the window as the runway started to move below him. He glanced at his watch in time to see the digital readout change to 7:13 a.m.

"Perfect, perfect, perfect! Everything is right on schedule," he mumbled to himself.

"Pardon me?" said the older, but obviously not hard of hearing, woman sitting in the seat next to him.

Ignoring her, he turned his head back toward the window. Seconds later, he felt the force of the speeding plane push his body back into the seat, then his stomach bounced, as the plane nosed up and leaped into the air. He closed his eyes. His heart started racing as he thought about the day ahead of him. He couldn't believe it was finally happening. He smiled.

Moments later, as if she could sense something before anyone else, the woman next to Dan reached over and grabbed his arm. As he turned to look at her, he too heard the deafening noise, like fingernails on a chalk board, only infinitely louder. In this case, though, it was the sound of metal bending and twisting.

From the ground, all that could be seen was the plane banking hard to the left, then heading nose first to the earth. A huge fire-ball erupted from the trees just beyond the runway.

2

One. Two. Three. Reannon counted to herself as she heard each tone. She then took the cell phone from her ear and pressed the one button three times, repeating a one-one-thousand between each movement of her finger. Even though she was holding the phone in front of her, she could still clearly hear the tone each time she pressed the button. She put the phone back up to her ear just in time to hear the single beep. Then the phone went silent.

She placed the cell phone back in the charger cradle and filled in the blanks after line one hundred and forty on the page, putting her initials and the date in the last space. She glanced at her watch. It was only 10:46 a.m. She had this task down pat.

Reannon had just completed her first year of accounting at Boston College and was grateful she again had a summer job working at her uncle's wine, beer, and liquor distributorship in Syracuse. Like last summer, she worked in the small business office, filling in for whomever happened to be on vacation that week. The work was easy, the pay was good, and with Friday afternoons and weekends off, she still had time to enjoy her summer respite from college.

She closed the yellow folder and eyed the words written in bold letters on the cover, New Demand and Projection Project. She wasn't exactly sure what the project was, only that her uncle had dreamed it up, and until it was proven viable, he wasn't willing to share the details with anyone.

Her task was actually quite simple. Each day, precisely between 10:00 a.m. and 11:00 a.m., calls were placed to the next ten phone numbers on the list. With a total of two hundred numbers, it took the entire month to get through the list.

Reannon had strict instructions to never speak over the phone. The only form of communication was via the push buttons, which she concluded was somehow linked to a computer at the other end.

Her only other instruction had been, if the tones ever came back other than what was specified in the instructions, she was to notify her uncle immediately.

"I'm all done Uncle Nick," Reannon said, after she knocked once on the oak door jamb of the office and strolled up to the large, old, but well-maintained mahogany desk, where her uncle was sitting.

Nick was a huge man, even considering that over the past year or so he had shed a hundred pounds of flab from his body. His weight loss, unfortunately, was not from dieting, but from stress. Consequently, any positive affect this had on his appearance had been overshadowed by how much he'd also aged, some said at least ten years. Add to that the recent mood swings, from a man whose jovial personality once rivaled that of Santa, it was no wonder even his closest friends thought he was dying, of what, they

12

didn't know for sure.

As Nick looked up from the papers on the desk in front of him, a smile grew on the lower half of his face. He glanced at his watch. "Finished within the hour again. Great job Reannon." He reached for, and she handed him, the yellow folder. "Any problems?"

"No, nothing. Everything worked perfectly." After three weeks of phone calls, one hundred and forty in all, her uncle's system seemed to be working just fine. "You know Uncle Nick, I took a computer programming course last semester and I might be able to program a PC to automatically make these phone calls for you."

Nick stared at her. Though he was straining, some of the smile had noticeably vanished from his face. "Let me think about it. I'm still not sure if this project is giving me the information I'm looking for. I might end up scrapping it anyway."

"Maybe I could take a look at the project. I might be able to make it do what you want it to." Reannon's excitement was now evident in her voice. Though she was grateful for the summer job, most of the tasks she was assigned were far below her intellectual capabilities. She was hungry for something more challenging.

"Let me think about it honey."

"Okay . . . just let me know."

Nick watched her as she walked out of his office. He knew he had just lied to her. It was one of a dozen lies he had already told today. It didn't bother him in the least.

As he glanced down at the yellow folder, Reannon's voice echoed through his mind. "Everything worked perfectly. Everything worked perfectly. Everything worked perfectly." If only she knew, he thought to himself, his face now devoid of any smile.

Two years ago Nick's life had taken a turn for the worst when someone walked off with a bag full of his money. The cash, collected from his upstate New York network of small time drug dealers, was being delivered to him when three inexperienced couriers botched a transfer. Though the couriers paid for their mistake with their lives, the cash was never recovered. His suppliers, who were even more ruthless than he, still got their money, though it had taken some creative accounting on the company books to manage it. A hundred-year-old family business, one that had survived the Great Depression and Prohibition, was now on the verge of bankruptcy.

Nick had not given up on finding his money. He had assumed that a passerby had found the red duffel bag and, with their new found fortune, would eventually expose themselves by living a lifestyle well above their means. When that happened, he was hoping his network of eyes and ears, mostly local politicians and law enforcement, spread across upstate New York, would pick up on the spending spree and report back to him.

Unfortunately, after two years of quarterly calls, subtle reminders to remain vigilant to their task, and compensated by his campaign contributions and bottles of top shelf booze during the holidays, he had nothing to show for his effort. He was even losing enthusiasm over the project when several months ago he delegated the calls, something he would not have thought of doing during the first year and a half, to his trusted, non-questioning, assistant. With her on vacation for the month of June, the task had fallen to Reannon.

"I'll give it another quarter," Nick said aloud, as he placed the yellow folder in the top left drawer of his desk, the only thing he kept in that drawer, and locked it. It would be a fitting time to stop, he thought, almost two years to the month since the money was

14

taken. If a spending spree hadn't shown up by then, the culprits were either well outside of the area he was monitoring, or they were smart about spending their new found treasure. Besides, after two years, his network of eyes and ears were getting tired of playing his little game. He sensed a "don't call me, I'll call you" attitude emerging from some of them.

Nick leaned back in his chair. "How could I have been so stupid?" It was a phrase he had repeated to himself thousands of times in the past two years. That and, "Two million dollars fuck'n gone!"

3

Roger Stone sat motionless in the high back chair, eyes locked on the red expandable folder on the desk in front of him. It was almost six o'clock in the evening, and he had just spent the past three hours reviewing and then re-reviewing every piece of paper in the three inch-thick folder.

"Son of a bitch!" he said out loud, then looked up at the open doorway to his office to make sure no one was around to hear him.

This morning Roger had woken up believing he was going to be a very rich man by the end of the day. Clasping his hands behind his head, he leaned back in the chair, trying to figure out what had gone wrong.

For over forty years the only pay checks he had ever received had United States Treasury printed on the top of them. He had retired from the Army with over twenty years of service, including two tours of duty in Vietnam, although he would never voluntarily admit that he saw no real combat. Roger was an excellent details man. An organizer. A strategic planner. For these skills he was awarded administrative assignments in Vietnam, and afterwards, at the Pentagon, although he did spend one tour of duty at NATO's Supreme Headquarters in Brussels.

Another skill he had been fortunate enough to acquire during his stint in the Army was computer programming. The Army wasn't quick to pick up on the merits of information technology, but when it did, Roger was positioned to ride the wave of promotion associated with it. That skill alone made him a sought after commodity in the Defense establishment.

His reputation and many connections fostered during his years in the military made it easy for him to land a job in the Defense Department when he retired from the Army. Ironically, his new office at the Pentagon was only a few hundred feet from the military one he retired from.

Over the years Roger had been content with following orders. He was never one to aspire to the next higher position and therefore never a threat to any boss he worked for. This reputation had afforded him the opportunity to move on to different assignments whenever he got too bored doing whatever it was he was doing. He liked the change associated with jumping from assignment to assignment. He also liked the lack of accountability that came with never being held responsible for getting anything done.

Several years ago Roger landed a project manager position in DARPA, the Defense Advanced Research Projects Agency of the Defense Department. DARPA was a research and development group known mostly for its imaginative, out-of-the-box thinking. Among its many accomplishments, the agency has been credited with creating the forerunner to the Internet.

Roger's job was not to think up new ideas, but to manage

bringing other people's ideas to fruition. The latter required the planning and organizational skills he possessed. He was currently responsible for researching and evaluating the feasibility of ideas sent to the Defense Department by ordinary citizens. Most of the ideas that landed on his desk got there because they were so far-fetched that no other agency wanted to deal with them. But in this post-911 environment, resources were being spent to evaluate even the most bizarre ideas, to make sure no stone was left unturned in the war on terrorism. Although his work was necessary, it was not seen as being very important. For the most part, his boss left him alone.

Roger liked change, not only in his work life, but in his personal life too. He had survived three failed, childless marriages and more short-term relationships than he cared to remember. At fifty-nine he had a younger, distinguished look about him, almost movie star like. He was tall, just over six one, had a rugged handsome face that was always tanned, and a full head of meticulously styled salt and pepper hair. His thin physique was more a byproduct of his usual happy hour dinner entree of scotch on the rocks, than any kind of regular exercise, which he had given up long ago. He attracted more than his fair share of women, but recently had become content with paying for any pleasure he might desire, knowing that way his fantasies would be totally met.

Though he never aspired to be in charge, recently he felt he deserved more than his current GS-12 grade salary of $95,000 afforded him. He had always put off any serious planning for retirement, instead living for today. Except for his townhouse in Georgetown, a 2008 Z06 Corvette, and two government pensions, he had little to show for his forty years of "sacrifice to his country" as he would always say to himself whenever he was feeling sorry for the cards he had been dealt in life.

Over the years he had seen many of his colleagues take jobs in the private sector at purported salaries two to three times more than what they were making working for Uncle Sam. It seemed the private sector was willing to pay the right individuals for their knowledge of, and relationships with, the Uncle. If only he could stumble onto one of those once-in-a-lifetime opportunities, he might yet be able to attain his dream of retiring to endless days of warm Jamaican beaches, before he was too old to enjoy it.

Until earlier today, Roger thought that he had stumbled over one of those opportunities. It had started six weeks ago when an anonymous phone call was transferred to him by a totally inexperienced employee in the Department of Homeland Security. The Department was still experiencing growing pains, especially with the recently implemented hotline it had set up for reporting potential terrorist threats. Overwhelmed with input from a shaken public, they found it difficult to keep up with the call volume coming in. Other agencies, including DARPA, were asked to provide support until the public's fascination with the program wore off.

Roger would have normally been more abrasive to the employee transferring the call, since he didn't like it when others dumped their work on him. But in this case, Vanessa's throaty but soft spoken voice convinced him to help out, especially when she gave him her number and said she owed him one.

The caller introduced himself as Mr. Timer, which he readily admitted was an alias. The government, fully aware of the public's fear of retaliation since 911, was much more receptive of anonymity than it had been in the past. It had finally concluded that it was more important for a terrorist act to be thwarted than to know who the informant was. Monitoring chatter over the Internet had taught them this.

From the beginning, there was something about Timer that piqued Roger's curiosity. Timer was very articulate, always choosing his words carefully, almost as if they had been rehearsed beforehand. Yet there was an underlying tone of fear in his voice. To Roger, it meant the man was truly afraid of what he had found. More importantly, it also told him that what he had found was probably real.

"I think I uncovered a terrorist plot."

"Is the public in any imminent or immediate danger?"

"No, I don't believe so."

"Do you know when or where this act of terrorism will take place?"

"No."

"Is it something that will take place on American soil?"

"Yes . . . that I'm certain of."

"What exactly do the terrorists plan to do?"

"They plan to destroy the public's confidence in our monetary system."

"Do you know how they plan to do this?"

"Yes."

"Can you tell me?"

"They plan to flood the economy with counterfeit money."

"How do you know this?"

"I accidentally found some of the money."

"How much did you find?"

"Several mill . . . let's just say a lot of money."

20

When Roger first heard these words, his heart pounded so hard his chest ached. He honestly thought he was having a heart attack.

Unfortunately, Timer too sounded distressed over sharing the information he had uncovered. He confided to Roger that he was not confident that the governmental bureaucracy could protect him. Since there did not appear to be any imminent danger, he asked Roger to keep their conversation confidential until he was ready to come forth officially. He also requested that Roger use his personal cell phone for all future communications. Roger was more than willing to keep any record of these conversations out of the Uncle's purview.

Over the following two weeks, Roger spoke with Timer four more times, each call traced via his caller ID to rural phones in Blue Mountain Lake and Woodstock, New York, Kennebargo Lake in Maine, and Picton, Ontario, Canada. No pattern to the locations and untraceable to the actual caller.

Although Roger was having no luck identifying who Timer actually was, he was making considerable progress in gaining his trust. Timer had sent, to his Georgetown address, a copy of the documents he had found detailing the terrorist's plan. Roger had a difficult time interpreting the documents the same way Timer had, but decided to play along with him anyway. Then, during that last conversation on the second week, Roger decided to ask the burning question he had been holding back.

"I believe you told me during our first phone conversation that you had some of the counterfeit money."

"Yes . . . I do."

"I have a close friend at the Treasury Department. I'd like to pass some of the money by her. Have her assess its quality. That way we'll know what kind of a threat we are really up against. Do you think you could send me some samples?"

"How well do you know this woman?"

"Extremely well. Don't worry. She'll keep it on the QT."

"I'll get a package out to you tomorrow."

A week had gone by and Roger had neither received a package nor heard from Timer. Convinced Timer's finding had been nothing but a hoax, albeit one that someone went to an awful lot of time and effort to perpetrate, he decided to enjoy happy hour a little more than usual that evening.

When he arrived home, he found an eleven by fourteen inch manila envelope, lined with plastic bubble wrap, folded but sticking out of his mailbox.

He sat at the desk in his study staring at the envelope in front of him. There was no return address, but it was postmarked Raquette Lake, New York. He took a deep breath and picked up the envelope. His hands shook as he slid his fingers under the seal along the end flap. He spread open the end of the envelope and peered in. There were three stacks of bills, twenties, fifties, and hundreds, each held together with money straps.

He removed each bundle, one by one, and counted the bills without removing the strap. There were a hundred bills in each stack. Seventeen thousand dollars in all. Although he was no expert, it all looked real to him.

4

Anticipating what was coming next, Sue smiled to herself.

"There's a three dollar cover charge tonight."

She just didn't get it. Why would a bar charge a woman admission? Especially a topless bar. They should be paying her to come here. More women means more men. And three dollars, come on. Only a dive would think about charging three bucks. She handed him the bills that were clenched between her fingers. She'd been here before.

The lights were turned down low. She was convinced part of the reason was to hide the identity of those there. The air inside felt cold, but was a welcome relief from the hot and sticky night she had just walked in from. There weren't a lot of people considering it was a Friday night, one of the more popular nights of the week for businessmen to frequent the place. Heading for an open bar stool, she glanced to her left at the mirror covered wall. Not bad for a fifty year old broad, she thought.

Judging by the stares she was getting, from not only men, but also the few women there, she knew all the preparation earlier in the evening had been worth it. Her low-cut black see-through top was just sheer enough to expose her slightly tanned skin. Although she was a thirty-four B, the black Victoria's Secret push up bra, clearly visible through her top, provided an attention getting cleavage. The small rose tattoo on her left breast helped too, even though it was fake. Her black silk skirt was just long enough to cover the garter belt straps holding up her seamed black stockings. Even in the dimly lit bar, her heavy makeup was strikingly noticeable.

Normally five-five, she stood taller than six feet with her seven inch black stiletto platform heels. With the body of a thirty year old, thin, flat belly, petite rear end and legs that wouldn't quit, she liked the reflection she saw in the mirror. She was even having a great hair day.

More confident in herself, she slid onto the bar stool and crossed her legs, purposefully exposing the black garter belt straps.

"Hi Sue . . . haven't seen you here in quite a while. What can I get you?" The cute twentysomething blonde bartender was dressed in a tight black body suit that showed all it legally could of her thirty-eight D's. Although Sue knew they had to be fake, she still felt inferior to the little bitch.

"Oh, hi Tina," responding as if not noticing her. "I'll have a peppermint schnapps on the rocks."

"With a splash of water, right?" Tina interrupted, then turned away before Sue could respond.

Sue felt a hand slowly glide along the right side of her ribs and then across her belly, brushing along the bottom of her right breast. With a rush of excitement and without even bothering to turn around she whispered, "What took you so long?"

24

The hand slowly moved up and gently caressed her breast. She felt her face go hot with embarrassment knowing several pairs of eyes were watching. Reaching for the hand, her feeling of embarrassment turned to excitement as she felt long slender fingers and nails. Turning her head to the left, a soft warm pair of lips met hers. She froze as she grew tingly all over, like a teenager experiencing her first kiss. Her breath deepened and heart pounded. Finally, their lips separated, but, as if in a trance, their eyes didn't.

"I didn't see you come in, otherwise I would have come over sooner. Actually, I hardly recognized you. You look hot tonight. I take it you're expecting someone . . . and by the looks of it, a bottom?"

"I was, but after that greeting, maybe I'll change my mind," Sue said jokingly, hoping she was convincing enough. The tingling was getting stronger. "Can I get you a drink, Nikki?" Without waiting for an answer, she reached with her hand, picked up a twenty from the bar and waved it at Tina, all the while her eyes still locked on Nikki's.

"Sure, but I can't visit long. I'm up in a few minutes." Nikki glanced at the stage, then turned back, her arm still around Sue's waist. "So who's the lucky man . . . or should I say person." Nikki's arm tightened. "And . . . whoever it is . . . I'd love to try to change your mind."

Sue felt her face go hot again. They silently stared into each others eyes.

"Well . . . at least I've got you thinking about it." They both laughed, then embraced, this time with their arms wrapped around each other.

"Thanks for the drink, but I gotta go. Why don't we do lunch next week?" Nikki whispered softly into Sue's ear.

A tingling sensation swept through her body again, from her ear to her toes, and without thinking her head moved up and down, slowly.

"Great . . . I'll call you on Monday."

Sue nodded again, this time holding back a shiver.

As Nikki slowly pulled away from her ear, Sue felt those warm lips again, as they first brushed across her cheek, then met her own. The kiss lingered long enough for Nikki to run her fingers along Sue's thigh, up under her skirt, touching her bare skin. Then Nikki abruptly pulled away, reached for her drink, winked, and walked toward the door leading to the back room.

Sue took a deep breath, downed her drink and motioned to Tina with her glass. This would be her second drink in less than five minutes.

"Can I get that for you?" she heard a familiar voice behind her say.

This time she turned in her stool to make eye contact before she spoke. "I thought you might have forgotten about our session tonight?"

"Not a chance. I've been thinking about this all day and I'm very much looking forward to being yours tonight. You look great by the way."

"Thank you . . . so do you." Her hungry stare moved down his body then back up to his eyes. Although dressed in a suit, he didn't look like the typical businessman standing around the bar. He looked too young, too tanned, his hair too long, and his black silk suit too stylish for a corporate board room. He also lacked the paunchy gut most of the men there seemed to wear proudly in front of them. She felt the tingling again.

26

"And I am very much looking forward to tonight, too." She slipped her arm under his coat and around his waist, pulling him against her body.

He put his arm on her shoulder, kissed her on the cheek and took a deep breath. Her scent excited him. "Isn't she the one who was just talking to you," he said, as he motioned with a nod of his head to the dancer up on stage.

Sue turned and made eye contact with the dancer just in time to see the slinky top fall to the floor. She tried to remember the last time she had seen Nikki's naked body, and maybe the mood she was in had something to do with it, too, but she had to admit, Nikki looked hotter than ever.

"You mean Nikki . . . she's just an old friend of mine." Sue turned and looked at him as he kept his eyes locked on the stage. "She's pretty hot, isn't she," she finally spoke up, tightening her arm, pulling him a little closer to her.

He turned and refocused his attention on Sue. "She isn't bad."

She knew he was lying. She also knew she'd get the truth out of him later.

He waited in the bedroom, naked, except for a leather thong, while Sue freshened up in the downstairs bathroom. He had made them fresh drinks, doubles in tall glasses. The stereo was turned down low. The only light was from two dozen candles scattered around the room. It would have been romantic were it not for the black leather whip, hand cuffs, assorted surgical clips, and two hundred dollar bills on the corner of the bed.

He heard foot steps, then watched, as she entered the room and stood in the doorway. Her hair was pinned up and she had removed her top and skirt. His pulse quickened as she walked toward him, then stopped. She whispered softly, "Are you ready for me?"

He answered by dropping to his knees.

5

When the phone rang, Jim reached over and hit the snooze button on the alarm. It was 3:00 a.m. before they had finally fallen asleep, exhausted but totally satisfied. He had set the alarm for 11:00 a.m., not wanting to sleep the entire day away, and was confused as to why it was going off at 10:17. Finally realizing it was the phone, Jim answered it. "Hello . . . just a minute. Sue. Sue!" Nudging her, "Sue, it's for you."

"Who is it?"

"I don't know, here." Jim turned away and quickly dozed off again.

"Jim . . . Jim! You know that plane that crashed a few days ago? Dan was on it."

"Dan?"

"My ex-husband. That was the FBI. They wanna talk to me."

6

At 10:30 a.m. the temperature was already approaching eighty-five. Roger dropped the back of the lounge chair down another notch and pushed his feet, which straddled both sides of the chair, deeper into the soft white sand, still cool from the night sea breeze. What a way to spend the first day of summer, he thought.

"One frozen Bloody Mary," he heard a voice say, just as he was opening his eyes to see what had blocked the hot rays of the sun from his face.

As his eyes adjusted to the brightness of the cloudless blue sky, they quickly focused on the young woman holding a tray with the drink he had ordered minutes ago.

"Would you like it on the table sir," she spoke again, after a long pause, sensing the man was much more interested in her bikini clad body than the drink.

"A . . . sure, that would be great," Roger stuttered, as he sat up.

"Room 226, right?" she said, after placing the drink on the small table next to his chair and writing something on the pad on her tray.

Puzzled at first, he suddenly remembered who she was. "Good memory. Yes . . . 226. Thanks." He stared at her as she walked away, thinking it was probably his generous tipping during yesterday's happy hour that she remembered more than him. Then, when she suddenly turned around and winked at him, as if she was certain he'd be looking at her, he wasn't so sure.

Roger was glad he had decided to take yesterday afternoon off and get an early start on the weekend. He had beat the DC traffic on his four-hour drive to Virginia Beach and was able to catch a few hours of sun before happy hour. He needed to unwind after the week he had just experienced.

He was still depressed over what had happened, or in this case, what hadn't happened, on Thursday. For the past six weeks, Roger had worked very hard to gain Timer's confidence. Each phone call, there had been fifteen in all, most occurring on Mondays and Wednesdays, with an occasional surprise call on several Fridays, provided Roger with more and more of the details about how Timer had stumbled upon the terrorist plot. Although fascinating, the actual plot was secondary to Roger's main interest, the money.

He did in fact have a contact in the Treasury Department, and she confirmed his initial observation that there was nothing counterfeit about the bills he had provided to her. It was a piece of information he had not shared with Timer, and one he likely never would, at least not if his own plan to get Timer's fortune succeeded. Roger saw this as his once in a lifetime opportunity. It was almost too easy, as if it was being handed to him.

But so far, Timer had left few clues for Roger to use to uncover his true identity. He had deduced, based on the rural phone booths Timer had used, scattered across New York, Pennsylvania, Massachusetts, Vermont and Canada, that Timer lived in that general area, but other than that, he had little else to go on. Timer had been very careful to keep his identity a secret. Roger knew that unless he could find out Timer's true identity, he had little hope of getting the rest of the cash. That's why, when Timer agreed during their Wednesday telephone call to meet that very next day in Washington, Roger thought he was on his way to becoming a very rich man.

He knew what he was doing was unethical, but, he reasoned, no more so than his coworkers moving to private industry and taking with them the knowledge and information they had picked up from the Uncle. Everybody did it. Even ex-presidents used their past experience with the Uncle to write multimillion dollar books or give one hundred thousand dollar a pop speeches. Besides, if something did happen and he was called on the carpet for what he was doing, it was only because he was doing what Timer wanted. Keep this whole issue out of the official government files until he was ready to officially come out with it. For years the Uncle had been preaching for a more friendly, customer focused government. Hell, even the IRS was on board. Roger reassured himself that the worst that could happen to him was he might be accused of using bad judgment.

That was all before Thursday, though. Roger thought he had worked out every detail for their meeting. He was exactly where Timer wanted him to be at 10:00 a.m., sitting on the fifth step up from the bottom, in front of the Lincoln Memorial, about five feet from the left as you were facing it from the Mall. As instructed, he wore a black and orange Baltimore Orioles baseball cap and carried a twenty-ounce bottle of diet Pepsi.

Roger had sat there for four hours straight, afraid to budge for fear of missing Timer. The temperature quickly climbed into the low nineties. Hot and thirsty, he finished off the diet Pepsi by noon, even though it tasted strange without its usual mixers of Bacardi and lime. Then, an hour later, he was sorry he had drunk the entire bottle without considering the affect it would eventually have on his bladder. By two o'clock his squirming had become far too obvious, forcing him to leave his post. He went back to the office, hoping he would at least hear from Timer, but didn't.

"Something had to have gone wrong," Roger again mumbled to himself for the tenth time today, as he relived the past six weeks events over and over again in his mind.

"Can I get you another rum swizzle Roger?" the now familiar voice asked.

"That sounds like a great idea to me, Sheila," Roger responded, staring at the tall silhouette standing at the foot of his chair.

Over the past few hours, actually six to be exact, with each visit by the beach-tender, as he found they were called, little by little Roger was able to find out what he needed to know about his leggy servant. She was in her mid-thirties, divorced, not serious with anyone at this time, and most important, free for dinner.

"Since my favorite beach-tender is leaving in a while, I think I'll just take that drink up to my room and get ready for dinner," Roger said, as Sheila returned with his drink. "Are we still on for tonight?"

"Absolutely. How does seven thirty sound. I'll meet you here at the bar. Okay?"

"Perfect . . . I'll see you then," Roger said, as he turned and walked away.

"Hope you recognize me dressed in something other than a bikini," he heard her say, as he continued walking, hoping he would eventually see her in something less than that.

Even though he had spent the entire day lying in the sun, he felt exhausted as he unlocked and opened the door to his room. "Perfect," he said, as he glanced at the clock next to his bed. "I can get a power nap in before dinner." More importantly, he wanted to make up for sleep he hopefully would not be getting later that night.

He stripped off his bathing suit and closed the curtain on the sliding glass door to the balcony that over looked the ocean. He turned the TV on CNN, set the volume low and fell back on the bed, drifting into a light sleep within minutes.

Suddenly his whole body jerked, a reflex from a dream no doubt. A few seconds later he realized where he was, panicked and tried to get his eyes to focus on the numbers on the alarm clock next to his bed.

"It's not even seven yet," he said as he let out a heavy sigh. Missing dinner with Sheila would have been on par with the way the rest of his week had gone.

As he let his body relax again, he laid on his side and half listened to the TV.

" . . . Federal authorities have ruled out terrorism as the cause of the crash of flight 2145 shortly after take off on Thursday morning from Hancock International Airport in Syracuse, New York. The plane was headed for Washington's Reagan Airport. All forty-four passengers and four crew members were killed."

Roger had been so focused on Timer these past few days that he had tuned out what was going on in the rest of the world.

34

Listening to the news, his brain was subconsciously churning the facts he had been going over for the past forty-eight hours, and just now, as if finding and assembling the last piece of a puzzle, he sat up and stared at the video clip of the crash site on the TV.

"Could Timer have been on that plane?"

7

The kettle on the stove began to whistle. Sue turned off the burner and poured the hot water into the large ceramic cup. The caffeine from the two previous cups of coffee was starting to give her a little buzz, but she still had the urge for another. As she lifted the cup, it shook in her hand. She wasn't sure if it was from the call earlier this morning or last night's partying. She smiled. "Last night's partying!" she whispered.

She and Jim had dated less than two months before they decided to move in together. That was almost two years ago, and since then life seemed to only get better. They were compatible in almost every way, especially when it came to sex. There wasn't anything they wouldn't do to bring pleasure to each other and they both had fun doing it. "Sex is supposed to be fun" they'd often say together, and last night's domination fantasy was one of Sue's favorites.

They were mature enough to know it wasn't just the sex, but also old enough to know not having to have to worry about that part of their life together took a lot of pressure off the rest of the relationship. They were madly in love with each other, which was apparent to anyone who knew or even saw them. Someone once told them they acted like fifty-year-old teenagers.

Sue glanced at the clock above the kitchen table, wondering if she had enough time to wake up Jim, when the sound of the doorbell made her jump. "What the hell am I so scared for?"

"Mrs. Lockwood?" The man looked confused.

"Yes."

"Susan Lockwood?"

Sue nodded.

Looking flustered, he fumbled with his pad. The woman standing in front of him looked nothing like the fifty-year-old he had expected. "I'm Jack Nelson from the FBI." He reached into his shirt pocket and handed Sue his ID badge. She took the badge and looked at it closely. Then she looked up at the agent.

She couldn't remember if she had ever seen an FBI agent in person before, so she had no idea what one was supposed to look like. But to her, Jack Nelson did not look like one. He was too young, too short, too skinny and black. Also, the midday heat, along with the dark suit he was wearing, caused beads of sweat to roll down his face. She didn't think FBI agents were supposed to sweat.

"Thanks again for agreeing to see me on such short notice. I only have a few questions, so this shouldn't take too long."

"No trouble at all, although I'm not sure how much help I can be. Please, come in. Can I get you a cup of coffee?" she asked, leading him to the couch in the living room.

"Actually a glass of cold water would be great."

By the time she returned to the living room, Jack had removed his coat and was using his handkerchief to wipe the beads of sweat from his forehead. He had placed a yellow note pad and what appeared to be several sheets of typed questions on his lap.

"Thanks." He reached for the glass and gulped down half the water in two swallows. "They weren't kidding when they said it was going to be hot in Syracuse this week."

"After the winter we just had, I don't think a lot of people are complaining. I take it you are not from Syracuse?"

As if purposely ignoring her, Jack continued to write, filling in blanks and checking off several boxes. "Just give me another second . . . there." He put his pen down on the papers and looked up at her. "Actually, I just moved to Syracuse two months ago. For six months before that I was on assignment in Quantico, Virginia, so I missed winter this year. Well, I can't say as I missed it that much. I'm from northern New York, so I know what the winters can be like around here."

As if sensing that he was getting a little too friendly, Jack picked up the glass of water, took a small sip, cleared his throat, and began speaking in a noticeably more professional tone. He repeated what he had said on the phone earlier, but this time Sue was able to be a little more attentive. Although she remembered hearing the same words before, it wasn't until now that she understood the seriousness of them. To think that following a plane crash, the FBI, in coordination with The Department of Homeland Security, had been assigned the responsibility to expeditiously conduct a background check on all of the passengers, to determine if there was any link to a terrorist organization, didn't give her a very comfortable feeling about flying. It was too late then.

Although her ex-husband may have been a little crazy, he certainly wouldn't do anything like blow up a plane, of that she was certain. But, she was still relieved to hear Jack say that the FAA had already preliminarily determined that a mechanical problem, not a terrorist act, was the cause of the crash. "If they've already determined it wasn't terrorists, why is the FBI still investigating the passengers? And how did you know to talk to me anyway?"

"The FAA's results are still preliminary, and regardless, we are required to complete our investigation."

"And how did you find me?"

"Through your ex-husband's landlord. Apparently when he moved into his apartment he put you down as someone to contact in the event of an emergency. The application was five years old, but we have our ways of tracking people down."

They stared at each other as if to see who would be the first to blink.

"Actually, we looked up your name in the phone book and gave it a shot."

Sue forced a smile. "We've been divorced for five years. It was kind of ugly back then. In fact, I haven't even spoken to him in years."

"So, you have no idea why he was on that plane?"

"No. Quite frankly, I'm surprised that he even got on a plane. We flew a few times when we were married, but he was never really comfortable with it. Plus, over the past couple of years, he just hasn't been himself."

Jack looked up, waiting for her to say more.

"Dan had been an associate professor at Syracuse University. About two years ago, he took a sabbatical and never returned to the classroom again. He ended up taking an early retirement package. I guess he just couldn't get up in front of his students any more. Some of our friends said he was slowly going crazy. I'm not so sure. He might have just been playing the system."

"Do you know of anyone else who might know why he was going to Washington that day?"

"No. Dan had turned into a loner. Any friends he had deserted him long ago. I don't think he was happy with his life. But, I'm glad to see that he was at least getting out and doing something. I guess he was just in the wrong place at the wrong time."

Sue noticed how Jack seemed to be writing down her every word. Initially impressed with his interest in what she was saying, it suddenly dawned on her that he probably had not been in the FBI very long. This interview was a necessary, but unimportant task that was given to the new junior agent to handle. He wanted to make sure he got an A on the paper, regardless of its usefulness.

"That's all I have Mrs. Lockwood. Is there anything else you can think of?" He handed her his business card. "If anything does come up that you think might be important to our investigation, please don't hesitate to call me. I work out of the Federal Office Building in downtown Syracuse."

Jack gathered his papers, stood up and draped his coat over his arm. As they walked to the door, Jack stopped and turned to Sue. "Oh, one more thing. When I spoke to the landlord at the apartment complex yesterday, he was wondering who would be taking care of Dr. Lockwood's things. Since your name was on the application, I believe he was going to try to contact you, although I asked him to give me a day or two before he did. So you can probably expect a call from him. If you know who Dr. Lockwood's lawyer is, you might want to give him a call. That way you can turn the problem over to him."

40

"Thanks for the heads-up."

"You're welcome. Thanks for your time."

They shook hands. She stared at his backside as he strutted down the walkway toward his car. "Not bad." Her first impression of him may have been a little too harsh. From the back you could definitely see how broad his shoulders were, how thin his waist was, and "nice tight ass." That sight, along with the warm outside air, excited her. She turned back into the house and remembered Jim upstairs, still in bed. "Wake up time!"

"Good afternoon. Mitchell, Mitchell, and Haggas. Can I help you?"

She had purposely called on Saturday afternoon, expecting to get an answering machine. She debated hanging up.

"Hello. Is anyone there?"

"Yes, is Steve in?"

"Yes he is. Can I ask who's calling please?"

Damn it, she thought. "Susan Lockwood."

"One moment please."

"Sue, what has it been, five years? How are you?

"I'm doing great Steve, how are you?"

"Fantastic, what can I do for you?"

"I don't know if you've heard, but Dan was on the plane that crashed last week. Since he has no other relatives, I was wondering if you still handled his legal affairs . . . Steve, are you still there?"

"Yes, sorry. I'm just in . . . at one time we were the best of friends. My God. I haven't seen him in years, but as far as I know, I have his last will. If you hold on a minute I can . . . "

"No that's okay. I really just wanted to know that you were the one to handle his affairs. The landlord in the apartment complex where he was living has already left me a message on my answering machine, and I'd rather not get involved with any of this."

"Sue, I think you are going to have to be involved to some extent. As I recall, Dan's will names you the executor and sole beneficiary."

8

Roger set the cruise control on his bright yellow Corvette at seventy-five as he left the ramp onto Interstate 64 west. "Twelve fifteen," he said, as he glanced at the clock. "I'll be there by four o'clock."

Although it was forecast to be one of those picture perfect summer Sundays, and he would have normally spent the entire day at the beach, Roger had decided to head back early. His curiosity about Timer being on that plane was getting the better of him. The more he thought about it, the more sense it made to him. When Timer failed to show up on Thursday, Roger's first thought had been that something must have gone wrong. Terribly wrong. Whatever had happened, it must have been totally outside of Timer's control.

Over these weeks in dealing with Timer, the one thing Roger had concluded about him was he was very deliberate in his actions, from the words he chose, to how he said them. He seemed to have an exact purpose in everything he did. He seemed to always know why he was doing what he was doing then, how it related to what he had done in the past, and how it was going to impact what he wanted to do in the future.

"If Timer said he was going to be at the Lincoln Memorial at ten o'clock, only something totally outside of his control would have stopped him from being there," Roger said confidently to himself, sounding as if he had known Timer for years. What didn't yet fully register with him, though, was that if his current hypothesis about Timer was right, Timer was dead.

Roger leaned his head back against the headrest. For the first time he noticed the lack of other cars on the highway. Another benefit of leaving early, he reasoned, trying to justify why he was in his car instead of soaking up rays on the beach. Of course, if Sheila hadn't been scheduled to work today, he knew there was no way he'd have left early. Their dinner date last evening went perfectly. It seemed natural for them to spend the night together, although Roger had been taken aback at how demanding Sheila had been in bed. He was also pleasantly surprised to have had his needs totally met by her. Just before he left, he stopped by the beach-side bar where she was working to say goodbye, something he normally would not have done. In this case though, he was lining things up for his next visit to the beach.

It was 4:15 p.m. by the time Roger arrived at his office at the Pentagon. As he had anticipated, the place was deserted. He switched on his computer, unlocked the top desk drawer and retrieved the familiar red folder he kept there.

"Here it is," he said to himself, as he pulled out a folded eleven-by-seventeen piece of paper from the folder. He opened the paper and laid it on the desk in front of him. It was a map of the northeastern US and southeastern Canada, covered with green dots, showing the locations of the fifteen phone booths and two post offices Timer had used to contact Roger over the past six weeks. Roger stood up and backed away from the desk. What wasn't apparent up close suddenly became obvious as the brain focused the eyes on the colored dots and not on the lines and words on the map. The dots seemed to be randomly scattered across the piece of paper, except for an area in the very center, where there was an empty space, devoid of any dots. Roger stepped toward the map and placed his finger on that spot. He moved his finger and let his eyes focus on the exposed letters on the map. Syracuse.

Roger stared at the map in disbelief. Why hadn't he seen this before. What other clues were there hidden in the red folder. He was now beginning to think that he had over estimated Timer's abilities. If Roger was right, he had just narrowed down his search for Timer from one in a population of millions of people through-out the northeast, to one in forty-four passengers on Flight 2145.

9

One of the findings from the post-911 inquiries was that it was difficult, if not impossible, to cross check data among the hundreds, if not thousands of databases that existed in the information world we live in. Without this capability, it was an onerous task to try to determine an individual's true background and identity, as well as what activities they had been engaged in, something critically important for fighting terrorism.

To help solve this dilemma, DARPA had been charged with trying to come up with a way to mine information from the myriad of computer databases, collecting a cross section of information such as medical, credit, financial, travel and criminal, and to develop a way to analyze the resulting information. Because of his computer savvy, Roger had been temporarily assigned to work on the Total Information Awareness program, or TIA program as it was called. He had enjoyed the notoriety of being selected for the project, as well as the change, since his assignment at the time was beginning to bore him. Unfortunately, this effort was short-lived when Congress, worried about privacy concerns, prohibited the program from being used against Americans and reduced funding for it.

Although the research had been scaled down significantly, the basic program that had been developed and the links that were established to query thousands of databases were never destroyed. With access to these databases, Roger was hoping he might be able to find out who Timer really was.

The FAA had always been meticulous about storing data electronically for later retrieval, but after 911, all governmental agencies were being held accountable to not only collect more data, but to also enter it into their respective databases as quickly as possible, so current, relevant information could be shared among the various agencies, real time. Even though the crash of Flight 2145 occurred only three days ago, Roger knew the file would contain a wealth of information on the passengers onboard.

"Well . . . he didn't use his alias," Roger said aloud, as he finished reviewing for the second time the names of all the passengers onboard the flight.

It had not taken Roger long to access the database set up by the FAA for their investigation of the crash. Since he had access to almost every government database in existence, as well as hundreds in the private sector, he was hoping it wouldn't take him long to find Timer's real identity. Although he knew it was a long shot, he had decided that he would first review the passenger list for the obvious, Timer's name. Roger wasn't surprised that the name didn't appear. He had always suspected Timer was well educated and doubted he would have risked using an alias, no matter how well documented, to board a commercial airliner in this post-

911 environment. But he felt it was still worth a try. It would be the first of many things he would try.

Roger glanced at his watch. It was late, just before ten. He had been at it nonstop for almost six hours. No wonder he was exhausted. His back was killing him and he had a splitting headache, which he knew was from hovering over the computer terminal all evening. Other than the abuse to his body, he had little to show for his effort.

His gut told him that Timer had been on that plane, yet none of the thirty-one male passengers had a profile or background that even remotely suggested they could be the alias he was looking for. By now Roger could recite the names, addresses, occupations, reasons for being on that particular flight, and a whole host of other attributes associated with each of them.

Initially, he had analyzed each male passenger by querying the databases with a search engine DARPA had started to develop prior to the program funding reductions. This search engine could not only look for data using key words, but it could also analyze the information in a multitude of various databases based on bounding parameters inputted by the user. For example, Roger had initially surmised that Timer had purchased his ticket within twenty-four hours of Thursday's scheduled meeting, since they had agreed to and finalized the plans for their meeting during a phone conversation on Wednesday afternoon. He used the search engine to find out when each of the male passengers had bought his ticket, initially concentrating on those that bought them first in the twenty-four hour period before the flight, then forty-eight, and then seventy-two.

Although five of the male passengers had purchased tickets

within forty-eight hours of the flight, none of them fit Timer's profile. For instance, Roger had guessed that Timer was in his late forties or early fifties. Of these five, one was twenty-two, two were twenty-five, one was seventy-four and the last was twelve, a boy whose father had decided at the last minute to bring on a business trip he had in Washington, one that he had purchased a ticket for a month prior.

That was the first of more than a hundred different combinations of questions Roger asked the DARPA search engine to analyze. But no matter what combination of questions he asked, he could not find a passenger that would closely fit his profile of Timer.

Since there were only thirty-one male passengers onboard the flight, and he was getting nowhere with the search engine, Roger decided to read all of the information that had been collected on each of them in the past three days. He found the most interesting report to be one that had been assembled by the FBI, which contained a detailed profile of every passenger on the plane. Although voluminous and in some cases totally irrelevant, such as with the twelve year old boy, he still read every page of the document for each male passenger. Again he came up empty handed.

Roger was now more frustrated than ever. Timer had agreed to meet, hadn't shown up, hadn't called to explain why, and the only logical explanation Roger had, that he had been on Flight 2145, he couldn't prove. He now wished he had stayed in Virginia Beach.

"I need a drink," he said as he rose up from his chair, first grinding his thumbs into the small of his back, then stretching his arms straight up and balancing on his toes. Leaning over and reaching for the mouse, he moved the cursor to the END SEARCH box and clicked on it. Expecting the program to shutdown, he started to turn away when he noticed a message pop-up on the screen.

Would you like to run ARTI now?

Yes.   No.

"What the hell is ARTI?" he said, staring at the screen with a blank look. Too exhausted to remember if he had even seen the word ARTI before, he reached for the mouse, clicked on no, and continued to shutdown his computer.

Before he left, he scribbled ARTI on a yellow Post-it note and tacked it to the now dark computer screen.

10

"Why didn't he change his will!"

The meeting with Steve Haggas this morning had confirmed that Sue was executor and sole beneficiary of her ex-husband's will and estate. She had closed out that portion of her life years ago. Now it was back to haunt her.

"Estate? What a joke."

Sue had tossed the ball back in Steve's court. "You take care of everything. Charge whatever you think is fair and take it from the estate. If there is anything left over, let me know."

She could tell he was already expecting her to tell him to handle the whole thing. They both knew the estate wasn't going to amount to much. Maybe there was an up-to-date insurance policy. Steve would be lucky to get his actual expenses covered. But Dan had once been a close friend, so Steve felt obligated to abide by Sue's request. At least there weren't any burial expenses to deal with.

Steve did request that Sue go through Dan's apartment to see if there was anything of a personal or sentimental nature that she might want to keep. Reluctantly, she agreed. Although she dreaded going there, she knew deep inside that Steve was right in asking her to do so. Representing Dan in the divorce, he knew better than anyone how bitter and painful the process had been for the both of them. But he had to put his personal feelings aside and do what he was legally charged to do, regardless of how much it might hurt Sue.

On her way to the apartment, Sue had made up her mind that she was going there to do two things. First, Steve was right, even though it was a remote chance, there could be something of a sentimental value that she might want. Sue had been the one to move out of the house. She had wanted to leave her past behind and start over again. Her new life started with whatever she could stuff into her minivan. Over time, she had come to realize that she couldn't completely ignore her past. There were a lot of happy memories that often brought her much joy. She wasn't sure what Dan might have kept when he moved out of the house, but in hindsight, she should have taken her share of those memories. Perhaps this was her second chance to do so.

Her second reason for going there was purely financial. When they were married, Dan had kept meticulous records of the family finances. She couldn't imagine him not doing so now, crazy or not. If they existed, it would shed some light on Dan's financial situation. She was hoping she would find Dan had enough savings to at least pay Steve for his services, and, if she was lucky, a little left for her and Jim to take a vacation next year on spring break.

Traffic was light, and it only took her a few minutes to arrive at his apartment complex. Standing at the door and expecting the worst, she took a deep breath, closed her eyes, turned the key, and pushed open the door. "Well at least he was sane enough to use the air conditioning." She opened her eyes and stared into the apartment. "Clean." Stepping in to close the door, she immediately noticed the two dead bolts. She flipped the switches and several lights came on. She slowly turned and surveyed the apartment. "Very clean."

A chill went through her. She wasn't sure if it was from the cool air in the apartment or seeing the familiar furniture they had both purchased so many years ago. Then, as if being drawn to it like a magnet, her eyes fell upon the large leather recliner tucked into the far corner of the room. For a moment she thought she saw Dan sitting there with a baby in his lap. She blinked. They were gone. She realized this was going to be even harder than she first thought.

11

"Actually, a drink would be great."

"You really want a drink in the middle of the afternoon?"

"Screwdriver, if you have it."

"You must be having a bad day."

"Bad isn't a strong enough adjective to describe my day."

Nikki handed Sue the drink, then pointed to the large, over stuffed, white sofa. "Come . . . sit. Lunch can wait. Tell me about the worse-than-bad day you are having."

It wasn't until Sue had heard Nikki Larson's voice on the telephone earlier this morning, that she remembered their conversation at the bar on Friday night about having lunch sometime this week. She also hadn't been fast enough to think of a response, other than nothing, to Nikki's inquiry about her plans for the afternoon. Her reluctance to meet was gone, now that she had been to Dan's apartment. For the one person, other than her counselor, who she could talk to about her ex-husband, was Nikki.

Sue had met Nikki shortly after she moved out on Dan. Over

time, their friendship grew close, fueled in part by the similar abuses each had endured from their ex-spouses. Though there were more differences than similarities between them, including twenty years of age, they ended up spending more and more time together. When Sue decided to invest in a two bedroom condo, she had welcomed Nikki's suggestion to room with her, not so much for the financial support, as for the companionship.

They grew very close in the year that they lived together, sharing every secret of their past with one another, and, even more.

"You're having problems with Jim?"

"No. No. Not at all. That part of my life is perfect."

Though she didn't show it, Nikki was not only jealous, but more importantly, disappointed to hear her say that.

"Well, almost perfect," Sue added a moment later.

That comment sent a shiver down Nikki's back.

"Although, that's not why I'm having a bad day . . . it's my ex-husband."

"I thought that bastard was out of your life."

"He is now." Sue took several sips, emptying half of the glass of its cold orange mixture. "Well . . . physically anyway."

"I know what ya mean. They never stop fuck'n with your head. In some ways it's worse than physical abuse. They don't even have to be here. Hell, my fuck'n ex lives three thousand miles away in California and he can still play mind games on me!"

"Well, I gotcha beat on that one Nikki." Sue clanged her glass against Nikki's and downed the rest of the drink. "My ex is dead, and he's still mess'n with me."

Both women sat silent staring at one another, neither moving. Nikki finally reached for Sue's empty glass and without saying a word, got up to mix fresh drinks.

Nikki had spent the entire weekend fantasizing about how she would sweep Sue off her feet. She couldn't wait for this morning to finally arrive and hyperventilated when Sue said she would be there for lunch. She planned out every detail of the afternoon. After all, she was going to accomplish in a few hours what it had taken her months to do, years before. During that prior courting, no matter how much Nikki teased, flirted, touched, or even confided, first her curiosities, then her experiences, she finally realized Sue was not going to willingly step into that part of her world. So, one Friday evening, after growing weary of the same old singles bar rituals, Nikki introduced Sue, albeit forcibly at first, to pleasures she had only embarrassingly read about. An awkward week followed where the two women barely spoke. On the following Friday, Nikki again became the aggressor, but this time found a much more willing participant in Sue.

Nikki remembered how vulnerable Sue could be at emotional times like these and smiled as she wondered if she could now use it to her advantage. Perhaps this afternoon's seduction was going to be easier than she thought. She mixed doubles for both of them. Before lifting the full glasses, she reached up to the loose fitting, silky and somewhat transparent white blouse she was wearing and undid first one, then a second button. As she walked back toward the sofa, she glanced at her jiggling breasts wondering how long it would take for Sue to catch her own glimpse of them.

12

"It doesn't get any better than this," Jim said aloud, even though he was alone in his car. Talking out loud was a habit he had developed when he first started driving, to calm himself. Prior to the advent of hands free cell phones, he would often find fellow motorists staring at him as he babbled away. Now, no one seemed to pay attention.

Looking up, Jim mumbled, "Look at that sky." It was still a bright steel blue, without a cloud to be seen. It had been that way all day. He had debated putting the top down for the ride home. It would cool down quickly as the sun set, but he reasoned that the night air would feel good after being in the hot sun all day. Then there were the June bugs to contend with. The large, hard shelled, beetle-like insects filled the evening sky along the lake during the month of June. The front of the car and the windshield were going to be splattered with the dead creatures. With the top down, hope-fully there wouldn't be too much of a mess on the back seat. He didn't care though. With the cool wind blowing through his hair, he knew he had made the right choice.

He squinted. The rays from the setting sun stung his face as it poked through a clearing in the tree line ahead. He leaned up in his seat to look at his reflection in the rear view mirror. The stinging seemed to get worse when he saw how pink his skin was. "I should have used more suntan lotion." He stepped on the gas pedal, kicking in the four barrel. After a slight hesitation, the car rumbled and lurched ahead. He thought he heard the tires screech. As the speedometer needle passed ninety, the sun disappeared behind the tree lined road again. He pulled his foot back, let the car coast back to sixty, then glanced in the rear view mirror again, this time to make sure his illegal act went undetected.

"You need to floor it every once in a while to blow all the crap out of the engine," he remembered his father would say. As a boy he liked looking out the rear window to watch the dark smoke trail behind the car. Although no longer appropriate for today's computer controlled, anti-pollution-laden cars, Jim still followed his father's advice for his '67 Firebird.

He had purchased the car ten years ago as a fortieth birthday present to himself. Advertised as a fixer upper, it was really a junker. But following his divorce, he felt restoring the car would be a great father-son project and help him to reconnect with his then twelve year old. It worked. For the next year, that car became the distraction they both needed. Then, on his son's sixteenth birthday, Jim handed him the car keys. "I know you'll be careful with it because you know how much effort went into fixing it up." The strategy worked. His son always drove that car like a little old lady out for a Sunday drive.

On Jim's fiftieth birthday last fall, his son put a huge red bow on the convertible top and handed Jim the keys. "I expect it back when I turn fifty," was all he said.

"It doesn't get any better than this." He couldn't remember when he felt so good about life. Back in college? The day his son was born? Whenever, it had been a while ago. His divorce had been the low point in his life. But during the past two years, the glass had been more than half full. In fact, it was overflowing. He didn't even mind turning fifty last fall, although he hated the barrage of junk mail he was now receiving, almost daily, reminding him of his age, which he suspected was all being coordinated through AARP.

Luckily, he didn't look his age. He had always taken good care of himself, and especially so since his divorce. Coaching the high school wrestling team helped keep him in shape, but he knew his genes, more than his occasional exercising, had a lot more to do with it.

Jim even had what he considered to be the perfect job, a high school technology teacher, in the perfect place, Baldwinsville, a small rural community outside Syracuse, New York. Although he wasn't going to get rich, unlike in the private sector, his tenured position was secure, the hours were great, and most important, he had the summers off. With twenty-nine years of teaching under his belt, he couldn't believe he was close to retirement.

And every time he thought it couldn't get any better, a day like today came along to prove him wrong. He had just spent the day with his four closest friends celebrating graduation day, an unofficial holiday thought up by them after they had all completed their first year of teaching. The stress of having to act like real adults, for nine whole months, had been too much for them. At the end of that first year they rented a beach house on the Cape for a week and partied until they dropped. It became their reality check on life.

New priorities, like wives and kids, had, over the years, reduced the week-long bonding event to a single day. Amazingly though, since that first get-together, the five had perfect attendance at graduation day, which had been held at Henderson Harbor for the past twenty years, ever since Jim had bought his first boat.

The harbor was on the northeastern end of Lake Ontario, about an hour's drive from Syracuse. Jim kept his boat docked there, a 1976 forty-four foot Chris Craft motor yacht, the renovation project he and his son took on after the Firebird. An equivalent new boat would go for a half million. But two years of sweat equity and a lot of TLC had turned another junker, which was a kind description since the owner was about to torch it, into a prized possession. The Obsession was the biggest, most well kept boat in the marina, and always attracted her share of attention, wherever she went.

Everyone had arrived on time earlier this morning and by eleven they were anchored in Dutch John Bay, a perfectly half moon shaped bay on the northern end of Stony Island, about ten miles from the harbor. With no sign of civilization for miles, they could be as loud and obnoxious as they wanted. It was the perfect place for graduation day.

None of them was accustomed to drinking before noon, so the alcohol kicked in quickly, and as their voices got louder the debates and discussions, from reminiscing about their college days to how to solve the world's problems, ensued. Jim knew from past experience that it was important to provide a steady stream of food to keep the alcohol in check. He was amazed that five guys could consume two pounds of shrimp, a gross of fresh clams, and a couple pounds of hamburger by early afternoon.

In their younger days, by three they'd be planning the rest of the day's festivities. That usually meant which bars were they going to stop at on the way home. Now that they were all over fifty three o'clock meant an hour or two nap in the sun, before a leisurely dinner at one of the lakeside restaurants in town.

As was the case at every graduation day since the first, the end of the day topic of discussion always seemed to turn to marriage and sex. With a total of ten marriages and six divorces among them, everyone experiencing at least one of each, on paper they were experts on the subjects. For some reason, this year Jim became the focus of the others' attention. At one point, he even accused them of coordinating this ahead of time, which they vehemently denied. It was because he was the only one who was single and had been that way for ten years, they reassured him.

During the first few years following his divorce, Jim had focused on his son and had rarely even gone out. Gradually, he started dating, but most of the eligible women were either old enough to be too set in their ways, or young enough to still want to have kids. No way did he want to be rolled in on a wheelchair to watch a future son's little league game. In his late forties, he realized it was going to be difficult to find someone who had the same likes, wants, and needs as he did, and who would also excite him for the rest of his life. He reasoned that was why second marriages failed just as often as first ones. He was not excited about going down that path again.

Then, two years ago, he met Sue.

Jim smiled to himself as he thought about the day's roasting. "They're all jealous," he said aloud. "JEALOUS!" he screamed at the top of his lungs. And they should be, he thought. From the true confessions that were shared on graduation day, Jim knew he was in one of those once-in-a-lifetime story book romances. He and Sue were compatible in every way. He couldn't remember when he was so happy with any woman.

But the comments from earlier in the day kept echoing in his mind. "If you're so happy, why aren't you making it legal? There must be something she's not doing to satisfy you? Is she too old for you? If you find someone younger, you'll have no idea what she will look like when she's older . . . at least you do now!" And on, and on, and on.

Jim wasn't sure if he was afraid of getting married again, or the high probability of the marriage turning into another divorce. The thought of either made his stomach turn. His mouth watered for a drink.

His friends appeared to be happy with their current marriages, although it was their second and in one case, third try at it. But he sensed some of the same anxieties surfacing in the day's discussions that he had seen in their previous marriages and breakups. Were they all just progressing through another cycle and wanted him to join them? He wondered.

Jim turned onto Route 3 south, heading toward the village of Mexico, the half-way point on his drive home. His windshield was covered with bug guts, but with the top down he didn't dare try to clean it off. Besides, he was now heading away from the lake and the worst of the swarms.

He had driven this road a thousand times before. It was straight and deserted for the next several miles, so he stepped on the gas until the speedometer was just shy of seventy. It was pitch dark, except for the oblong shaped moon that periodically appeared through the trees. The night air now felt cold. He reached for his hat on the bucket seat where he had thrown it earlier. Not feeling it, he glanced to his right and saw it sticking out between the seat and the door. He leaned over further and was just barely able to grab the brim between his out-stretched fingers.

Straightening up, his eyes refocused on the road. Without thinking, his hands quickly turned the steering wheel to the right. But being a forty-plus year-old car, it didn't react like today's steel belted, anti-lock brake, variable power steering, high tech models.

"SHIT!" Jim yelled, as he saw out of the corner of his eye whatever it was in the middle of the road that he had just hit with the left front end of his car. He heard a dull thud as the car bounced wildly upward. Instinctively, he slammed his foot on the brakes so hard his body pressed back into the seat. With the brakes locked, the tires screeched, and the car began to spin out of control, gliding over the pavement as if it was on ice. Jim sat there, his body frozen in the seat, as the car seemed to move in slow-motion, the headlight beams moving in and out as they passed by trees, then open road, then trees again. Eyes closed, he braced himself for the impending impact.

13

"Daniel E. Lockwood . . . who the hell is Daniel E. Lockwood?"

Roger frantically shuffled the papers on his desk until he found the passenger list from flight 2145.

"That son of a bitch."

There it was, in plain sight, staring him in the face.

He grabbed the mouse, quickly closed out the screen on the display, then searched for and loaded a new file. He typed in a few letters and pushed enter. He felt his heart pound when a second later up popped the file from the FBI report for Daniel E. Lockwood. He read the first few sentences in the summary section at the beginning of the report.

"You incompetent bastards . . . it wasn't a typo. He did this on purpose. He wanted you to think it was Danielle!"

It was the second evening in a row Roger found himself sitting in his office past 9:30 p.m., something he rarely did. In fact, except for the frantic weeks following 911, when he was swept up with the rest of the country in a patriotic frenzy, he couldn't recall ever working late for the Uncle. But tonight was different. Tonight he was on a mission.

Yesterday, he had spent hours searching through the FAA database on the crash, initially confident that the secret to Timer's real identity was hidden there somewhere. But no matter what he tried, none of the passengers seemed to match the profile he had developed for Timer. He left feeling depressed, drove directly home, and drank himself to sleep watching "The Sting" on TNN.

He had arrived at work this morning more determined than ever to prove his theory about Timer, as if the previous night's alcohol had provided him with a shot of adrenaline. This time, he was prepared to work late into the night, if needed. His initial enthusiasm was thwarted when he remembered the all-day training session he was scheduled to attend on sexual harassment in the workplace, the same one he had canceled out on twice before. This time he decided to attend, hoping to catch-up on some needed rest, which he did.

He didn't get back to his office until after four. The first thing he noticed was the yellow Post-it note on his terminal. "I'll get to that later," he said, anxious to re-review the FAA file again, hoping to find something he had missed the night before. But after re-reading everything he had looked at the day before, he found nothing about any of the male passengers that he didn't already know.

By nine o'clock, Roger was not only getting upset at himself for not being able to find the proof he was looking for, he was also getting drunk. Knowing he might be working late and not wanting to forgo his nightly happy hour buzz, he had brought two liter bottles of Schweppes tonic water to work that morning and placed them in the break room refrigerator down the hall from his office.

But before leaving for work, he had replaced a quarter of the contents of each bottle with vodka. Since the incident last year where someone had borrowed some milk from the refrigerator for their coffee, which was actually breast milk from a woman on her first day back from maternity leave, Roger reasoned that the refrigerator was the best place to hide his cocktail. Besides, it also kept it cold.

As he sucked the last mouthful of liquid from the second plastic bottle, he cursed at himself for not bringing three. With two empty bottles in front of him, he was now ready to admit defeat, at least for this evening. His hand reached for the mouse, clicked on the END SEARCH box, then instinctively started to move the cursor to close down the program. Just as his index finger was pressing down on the mouse, the message popped up on the screen again and he froze.

Would you like to run ARTI now?

Yes.   No.

"ARTI, ARTI, ARTI," he repeated aloud. "What is ARTI?" He slowly leaned back in his chair, lifted his arms and clasped his hands behind his head, all the time staring at the word ARTI on the screen.

Although Roger had worked on the development of the program, so did a score of other people, including outside contractors. As a module or subroutine of computer language was completed, it was inserted into the main program library, in some cases even before the programmer had a chance to properly document its purpose. With the funding cuts that had ensued, resources were shifted and program operating manuals were never completed. Roger reasoned that the only way for him to find out about ARTI was to try to track down the program manager in charge of it and ask him directly. He quickly concluded that would draw too much attention to what he was doing.

He had been careful over these past several weeks to keep everything associated with Timer from the Uncle. If confronted, he always had an alibi ready as to why he was doing what he was doing, one that had nothing to do with Timer. He now sat there staring at the computer screen not knowing what ARTI was or what would happen if he clicked on yes. His dream could be lost with one simple click of the mouse.

He quickly reached down and clicked on yes, his decision to do so obviously driven by the alcohol he had just consumed.

ARTI Program Running.

The screenpop looked innocent enough. Although relieved, he anxiously waited for what was coming next, and again wished he had mixed a third liter.

ARTI was actually an adaptation of a concept that was originally developed by the nuclear industry to analyze the things that could go wrong in a nuclear power plant. It used a programming logic called Artificial Intelligence to try to determine what the user was looking for, if there were links to other data or information that he had not accessed, and to bring it to his attention.

For the investigation Roger had been performing, ARTI had quickly determined that he was interested in reviewing the data associated with all male passengers on Flight 2145. ARTI also found that Roger had looked at the data available for all male passengers, except one.

You have not accessed data for one male passenger:

Daniel E. Lockwood

When the message appeared on the screen, Roger blinked in disbelief, then read it again. His first thought was that whatever ARTI was, it had somehow made an error. He was certain the passenger list did not have that name on it.

One of the first things he had done when he had arrived on Sunday night was to print out a copy of the passenger manifest for flight 2145. He had then crossed off the names of the female passengers and placed a number in front of each of the thirty-one remaining male passengers. For the past two days that was the list he had used to access the rest of the data in the FAA file.

He went back and looked at his original list again, this time looking at the names he had crossed off.

"That son of a bitch," was all he could say as he read the second name he had crossed off, Danielle Lockwood. He then went back into the FBI file and typed in Lockwood. Up popped the file of Daniel E. Lockwood. In the summary section of the report, the investigating FBI agent had made a notation.

The original passenger manifest contains a typographical error. Danielle Lockwood should be Daniel E. Lockwood. Have reviewed video footage of the passenger boarding and verified it was Lockwood, a male, who boarded Flight 2145. Have verified said male lived at the above address.

Roger carefully reviewed the rest of the file on Lockwood, his heart racing all the while. Each piece of information matched exactly the profile he had developed for Timer.

"Daniel E. Lockwood, alias Danielle Lockwood, alias Mr. Timer . . . gotcha!" was all Roger could say as he looked at the computer terminal in front of him.

His feeling of success and accomplishment however was short-lived as it finally hit him that it meant Timer was dead.

14

The silence told Jim the car had stopped. His heart was thumping in his chest. His hands were gripping the steering wheel so hard that he thought he was going to break it. As he opened his eyes, he first saw the haze in the headlights, then smelled the pungent odor of burning tire rubber. Miraculously, the car had come to a stop dead center in the middle of the road, but facing in the opposite direction from where he was going just a few seconds ago. Jim relaxed and let out the breath of air he had been holding. "Thank you!"

His sigh of relief turned to panic as he remembered, "What the hell was that in the road?" He lifted his foot off the brake pedal and the car slowly moved to the shoulder of the road. He shifted into park, reached over and opened the glove box door. The flashlight rolled onto the floor. "I hope it," he started to say as he reached for the flashlight, pushed the switch on, and the car filled with light. He fumbled for a few seconds for the emergency hazard flashes before he realized that the car was too old to have them.

Leaving the car running and the lights on, he slowly got out and started walking back down the road. His knees were shaking. He waved the flashlight beam back and forth over the road ahead. The swirling skid marks disappeared into the darkness, beyond the range of the light beam. As he walked a few steps farther, the two skid marks straightened, then suddenly stopped. He forced his legs to move faster and lifted the flashlight up above his head, following the beam as it raced up the road ahead of him. Then, the light beam seemed to stop by itself as it reflected off something in the middle of the road. Jim froze. The flashlight now felt like a fifty pound weight as he tried to steady his shaking arm.

"Blood," Jim said aloud, finally admitting that's what it was he was looking at in the road ahead. He slowly moved forward. As he got closer, the light beam followed the trail of red toward the side of the road. Jim stopped and stared at the mangled lump in front of him.

"A turkey . . . I hit a fuck'n turkey!" Relieved, he just stood there staring at the dead bird. He turned and looked at his car. "Shit!" The driver's side headlight was out. He started walking back toward the car. As he got closer to it, he pointed the flashlight at the drivers side fender. "Lucky, lucky, lucky!" The only damage appeared to be the broken headlight and a spattering of blood and feathers. He decided to leave the feathers, in case he was stopped by the police for the headlight.

It wasn't until Jim pulled into the driveway and saw Sue's car that he remembered why he was in such a rush to get home. "Be home by ten thirty and you get whatever you want!"

"Yes . . . ten twenty-five."

He heard the music playing in the background as soon as he

opened the door. The lights were turned down low, so he stood there a few seconds to let his eyes adjust to the darkness.

"Hi . . . I'm home." He heard the floor creak above him.

As he walked toward the stairs he felt something beneath his feet. Instinctively, he looked down at the carpeted floor, then stopped. He couldn't quite make out what it was, so he bent over to get a closer look.

"What the hell?"

He stood up and looked down the hall to the foot of the stairs that led up to the bedroom loft. The floor was covered with money. Twenties, fifties, even hundred dollar bills. He walked toward the stairs. The money trail continued. Halfway up the stairs, he stopped and picked up one of the bills, a hundred, and held it to his nose. That's when he saw her standing at the top of the stairs.

"Don't worry . . . it's real," was all she said.

15

Jim was lying on his back, hands above his head, eyes closed, wallowing in ecstasy. As she had promised, the past two hours had been totally about him. He had gotten anything he wanted and then some. He smiled.

"I take it that smile on your face means I made you happy?"

Startled, Jim opened his eyes to see Sue standing next to the bed, illuminated only by the flickering candle flames.

"I believe you ordered a Jack and diet, pint glass, single-shot, lots of ice," Sue said, while handing him the drink.

Jim propped himself up on his elbow and took a sip from the frost covered glass. "Happy wasn't exactly the adjective I was thinking of," he said, staring into her eyes.

Sue reached down and touched him between his legs. "How about totally satisfied," she said.

Jim flinched. "Watch it, your hands are cold!"

"Funny . . . it doesn't seem to mind."

"Man, what has gotten into you tonight?"

Sue knelt down next to the bed and put her drink on the night stand. She leaned over and while kissing Jim, reached down to the floor. "This!" she said, as she dropped a hand full of money on Jim's bare chest.

Jim had been so focused on what Sue had been doing to him for the past two hours that he had completely forgotten about the trail of money he had found when he walked in the door earlier.

"And of course . . . this." She squeezed her other hand.

Jim sat up and looked around the room. There were more bills scattered around the floor of the bedroom. "Have you gone off the deep end? Tell me this is all part of some fantasy."

"Well if it was, at least I found out where your priorities are. It took you about two seconds to completely forget about that hundred dollar bill you were sniffing coming up the stairs. Not that I'm saying that's a bad thing, mind you." She squeezed again.

Jim pulled her hand away from him. "Sue, where did all this money come from?"

"My ex-husband."

Sue went on to explain her morning visit to the lawyer's office, then Dan's apartment. Initially thinking she would only be there for a few minutes, she ended up staying for several hours. It was a small, one bedroom apartment, and Dan had furnished it with furniture from their previous home. Except for a few books, photo albums, pictures and knickknacks, there seemed to be little else that Dan had saved from their marriage. She placed the things she wanted to keep on the kitchen table. Some things, like the photo albums, she couldn't look at just yet. She didn't have time to go through all of the books on the bookshelf then, so she resolved to make a second trip tomorrow. Besides, it looked as if she was

74

going to have to bring back a box or two to get the things gathering on the table to the car.

"What the hell does that have to do with all this money!"

"I'm getting there, I'm getting there!"

After her quick once through of the apartment, she ended up in the bedroom sitting at Dan's' small antique oak roll-a-desk. She remembered the day she gave it to him. It was their six-month anniversary. Her heart jumped when she tried to slide the desk top back, and found it to be locked. During happier times, although the desk top was always closed, the only time it was ever locked was around birthdays and holidays, when Dan needed a safe hiding place for a gift. Sue instinctively reached and slid her hand down along the right back corner of the desk. Her fingers hit against the nail sticking out and she removed the key that was hanging on it. She smiled knowing Dan had no idea how many times she had peeked at her presents.

As she put the key into the lock and turned it, she hesitated. Why had Dan locked the desk? As far as she knew, and the apartment manager seemed to confirm when Sue got the key from him earlier, he had lived alone. Taking a deep breath, she rolled up the desk top and stared in near disbelief. Everything seemed to be the same as it had been five, ten, even fifteen years before. Papers, pens, Post-it notes, everything, neatly tucked away in their little cubbyholes. Out of curiosity, she opened the small drawer on the upper right hand side of the desk, the place where past presents were hidden, and found it empty. Even the familiar shoe boxes were tucked under the shelf along the back of the desk top. Dan would store the papers he wanted to keep—important correspondence, bank statements, bills, credit card receipts—in old shoe boxes. Once filled, the box would be placed in storage, and a new one put in its place. He had reasoned this method took up the least amount of space. Twenty years of records could fit on the shelf of a closet.

Hoping the boxes had the financial records she was looking for, she reached for the one on the left side of the desk and slid it toward her. She sat there staring for a moment at the open desk. A chill came over her again. Forgetting what she had learned in ten years of counseling, feelings of guilt, pain, loss, and depression seeped back into her thoughts. She needed to get out of there. She reached for the second box and slid it toward her. Hoping these were the records she was looking for, she picked up both boxes and left the apartment, making sure not to make eye contact with the leather chair.

It was late afternoon before she got up the nerve to go through the boxes, she told him, leaving out the details of her luncheon with Nikki, something she promised herself she would share with him at some time in the near future. She poured herself a double screwdriver, sat down on the couch, and stared at the two boxes on the coffee table in front of her. The events of the past few days were taking a toll on her emotionally. It had taken her years to get to where she was, and days to erase all that progress.

With her left hand, she reached for one of the boxes, picking it up by the rubber band that held the cover on. As she moved the box to her lap, the rubber band broke, and the box fell to the floor, knocking her drink from her right hand. "Damn it!" She jumped when the cold ice and liquid fell onto her legs, ran into the kitchen, and quickly returned with a roll of paper towels. Kneeling down, she tipped up the glass, placed the ice back into it, and began to blot the liquid up with a handful of towels. As she moved the box out of the way, it tipped over on its side, spilling its contents. She stared in disbelief at what she saw. Twenties, fifties, hundreds, all neatly banded together with money straps, like you'd see at the bank.

16

Jim always suffered from a hangover after a graduation day get together. This one would have been much worse, but the three Tylenol he had taken before collapsing on the bed last night had done the trick again. The sex had helped too. So had the excitement over Sue's discovery.

He was several minutes into his steamy-hot shower, when he remembered last night's accident. The headlight, damaged in the run-in with the turkey, turned out to only be a loosened wire. Now the only thing he had left for the remainder of the morning was giving his car a good cleaning, including removing the layers of dead bugs that covered the front-end and windshield, and the blood and feathers on the driver's side fender.

The whole thing looked much worse in the daylight. As he bent down to clean the front grill, his head began to pound, reminding him of the previous day's partying. Sweat started dripping from his forehead. Of course, he blamed it on the early morning heat.

The red Silverado pickup pulled up in front of the townhouse on the wrong side of the road. With the trailer on the back and the steep incline of the driveway, it was safer to park there. The mangled license plate was proof of that. Besides, Cadys Arbor was a residential street, about a football field in length, with a cul-de-sac at the end. The illegally parked truck was not going to cause a traffic jam at this hour of the morning.

Hearing the loud thud from the cab door slamming shut, Jim looked up to see who had interrupted his work. The startled look on his face turned into a huge grin as soon as he saw who it was. "Hey . . . Tripy-boy, did you come to mow your dad's lawn?"

Trip walked briskly up the steep incline of the driveway smiling to himself. Although he would never admit it to his father, at twenty-two, he liked being called Tripy-boy by him. It provided at least one constant in his life. Trip, a nickname his parents had planned years before he was even born, stood for triple or the third, as in James Calihan III. In his younger days, he hated the nickname. "Why couldn't you have given me a normal name like everyone else?" he'd often say. His father would tell him that someday he would think it was cool and it would also be a great icebreaker for picking up women. He wasn't very old when he realized that his father was rarely wrong.

They met at the top of the driveway just outside the garage and hugged, their usual greeting for one another. The bond between them was apparent, and they weren't afraid to show this kind of affection for one another in public.

Following the divorce ten years ago, Jim had focused hard on being a good father, which at the time was driven by the guilt he felt over both not spending enough time with his son and abandoning his mother. Regardless, he had done his best over the years to build a strong relationship with his only son.

"I didn't think you could afford me to cut your lawn. Besides, you look like you could use a little exercise." He reached out and pinched the skin on his dad's belly.

"Be careful."

Jim stepped back and stared at his son. Standing on the upward slope of the driveway, he still had to look up to make eye contact. At six-foot-two and one hundred and eighty-five pounds, Trip did not have an ounce of fat on him. Jim was envious.

Trip had been a big boy from the start, weighing in at nine pounds fifteen ounces. Growing up, he tried playing every sport there was at least once, except hockey of course. Too expensive for a three month trial. Though athletic, he really never had that competitive, win-at-all-cost spirit, and if he couldn't play for just the fun of it, he didn't want to play at all.

He spent every summer, from age six on, at his mother's uncle's farm about a hundred miles southeast of Syracuse, in Harpersfield, New York. In mid-July he'd leave a little boy, and six weeks later return looking like he was a year older, at least physically anyway. This was especially true during the summers before his junior and senior year in high school. The previous ten months of Nintendo, couch potato fat, would be gone, his waist would be slimmer, his shoulders broader and his biceps noticeably bigger. Any clothing left in the closet at the beginning of summer was donated to the Salvation Army when school started.

The farm was where Trip "grew up," not just physically, but emotionally too. When he was twelve his parents sat him down one day to tell him they were getting a divorce. Although he knew what divorce meant, and lived through many of his cousins' and friends' parents breakups, he never thought it would happen to his family. He wished that summer at the farm would never end, because he knew when it did, he would not be returning to the same life he had left.

There was another reason why Trip dreaded returning home at the end of the summer. It meant he had to go back to school. He hated school. He began counting down the days to his high school graduation in his sophomore year. Although he dreamed about going to college to study agriculture, he knew deep inside his C average would never get him there. After high school, he worked several jobs, until one day he went to his father with a makeshift business plan to start a lawn maintenance business. Jim lent him the money, and now, three years later, the business was doing well. More importantly, Trip was proud of his success, was having fun, and even taking an accounting course at Onondaga Community College in the evening.

"Dad, when are you and Sue going up to the boat?"

"We were planning on leaving early Friday morning, but that depends if I can reschedule a course I have to take. Plus, now Sue has this whole mess with her ex-husband. It has kind'a screwed things up too."

"Man . . . Sue was telling me about it yesterday when I stopped by. The whole thing sounds a little creepy to me." Taking a deep breath, Trip then asked, "By the way . . . can I bring a friend on the boat this weekend?"

Jim looked puzzled. "I thought you stopped seeing . . ."

"Don't worry, it's not Joyce," Trip interrupted. "I haven't seen her in two months. You and Mom were right about that one."

Prior to turning twenty-one, Trip's girlfriends were his age.

Once he turned twenty-one, though, the bar scene opened up a whole new population of eligible women, some much older. Joyce, eight years older, latched onto Trip, and it wasn't long before he was spending every evening at her apartment. It wasn't this part of the relationship that led Jim to finally lay down the law with Trip. It was a late loan payment. Trip had let Joyce borrow some money.

"So, who is she?"

"Her name is Brandi. She just finished her third year of Pharmacy at Albany State. She's home for the summer. Her parents live in Liverpool. I met her a few weeks ago during happy hour at the Retreat. It was the weekend you wanted to go fishing and I couldn't go because I had to work . . . remember? Anyway, we've gone out a few times. In fact we're going out again tonight."

"Okay, okay, but how . . . "

"She's twenty-one."

"No, that's not what I was going to ask you. With all your babbling, you didn't tell me what she looked like."

"Drop-dead gorgeous! Five-ten, with the longest legs I've ever seen. Long blond hair, blue eyes. You're gonna love her. So, is it okay?"

"When have I ever said no to you to bringing someone on the boat?"

"Never . . . thanks Dad. You still plan on heading out on Friday afternoon?"

"Weather permitting, we're pulling away from the slip at five sharp, so don't be late!"

"Don't worry, you know I wouldn't miss a weekend in the Bahamas-of-the-North."

17

"I don't suppose you happened to count the money before tossing it all around the house, did you?" Jim asked, in a sarcastic tone, as he turned the SUV onto John Glenn Boulevard in the direction of Dan's apartment complex.

"Exactly $22,000, banded up in thousand dollar money straps. Eight hundreds, ten fifties, and four twenties. I counted every one just to make sure it wasn't some kind of a joke, like putting real bills on the outside and fakes in the center. They were all real," Sue said confidently.

"How do you know they're all real? They could be counterfeit!"

"You're right, they could be. I thought the same thing at first. So yesterday I filled up my car at the Sunoco station on the corner of fifty-seven and thirty-one and paid for it with one of the fifties. They always check the bills with one of those marker pens. No problem. Then I went to the liquor store. A hundred dollar bill passed there."

"Wait a minute. You went and used the money suspecting it

wasn't real. What if it turned out it wasn't?"

"No . . . I used the money to confirm it was real. It looked like it was real and felt like it was real. I just got two independent sources to verify that it was real. Actually, I now have three independent sources. After all, it passed your sniff test last night, didn't it?" Sue said in her own sarcastic tone.

"Wait a minute," Jim interrupted, as he pulled the car into the parking lot of the apartment complex and came to an abrupt stop directly across two parking spaces, just inches away from a silver Lexus. "First of all, you, me, the kid at the Sunoco station, and the guy in the liquor store, are not experts on determining if a bill is counterfeit or not. What you did yesterday was stupid. What if it had been counterfeit . . . how the hell would you have weaseled your way out of that one?"

"I had already thought about that. I went to the bank just before they closed and took three hundred dollars out of my account. Two hundreds and two fifties. I had them put the money in one of those little envelopes. I switched two of the bills and I made sure the cashiers saw me take the money out of the envelope when I was paying. If it had come up counterfeit, I would have explained where I had just gotten the money from and asked for it back."

"So you could take it right back to the bank like a good little law abiding citizen," Jim interrupted.

"Exactly."

"Sue, that's one of the oldest con tricks around. My guess is, had those bills been counterfeit, right now you'd be having another meeting with your FBI friend, only this time it wouldn't be as friendly a meeting as your first one!"

Sue was visibly shaken by what Jim had just said. It wasn't just the words he spoke, but the way he said them. During the past two years together she could count on one hand the number of times Jim had gotten even a little upset about anything. He just didn't let things he couldn't control affect him. So to see him act like this was frightening to her.

Jim reached for Sue's hand and in unison, they leaned toward one another over the console, embraced, and held each other tightly. Sue began to cry.

"Promise me, that until we figure out what the heck is going on here, you won't pull another crazy stunt like that."

Sue nodded her head against his chest.

Jim pushed her away far enough to look into her tear filled eyes. "I love you. You are the woman of my dreams. I don't want anything to ever happen to you. I'm sure there's some logical explanation to all of this, but until we find out what it is, I think we should err on the side of caution. Okay?"

"I'm sorry . . . that was stupid."

"Well . . . maybe not stupid . . . no, it was stupid." Jim leaned over and kissed her, then they both hugged again. "Come on . . . let's go see if we can find your ex-husband's printing press. Kidding!"

Sue pointed Jim to the other end of the apartment complex and they parked in one of the many empty parking spots normally available during the midday. Jim's initial hesitation to help Sue turned to reluctant acceptance, when she reminded him that their summer vacation might not start until they solved this mystery. Besides, now his curiosity had gotten the better of him. The thought of finding more money excited him. It was like winning the lottery, only better. Even lottery winnings were taxable.

Sue turned the lock to the apartment door, opened it and switched on the lights. "We need to find a paper trail of his finances. From there we can probably figure out where this money came from."

"How do you know there is going to be a paper trail?"

"Because I know my ex-husband. Dan was meticulous about keeping records. That second shoe box I took from his desk was essentially empty except for a few bills from June. My guess is, there is a filled box somewhere, with bills from May on back."

"You said this is a one bedroom apartment, right?" Jim asked as he glanced around. "So it can't be that big . . . where do you suggest we start?"

"The bedroom."

"My favorite room," Jim looked at Sue with a sparkle in his eye.

"Don't even think about it." Sue turned and started for the bedroom. She jumped when she felt Jim's pinch.

"Shoot! Sue, give me the key to the apartment. We left the empty boxes in the car. I'll go back and get them."

Sue turned and tossed him the key. "Nice catch," she said, as she watched Jim close the door behind him. Turning toward the bedroom, her eyes were again drawn to the leather chair and she froze. She suddenly felt cold, very alone, and scared. The vision of Dan and the baby reappeared. She blinked, but this time it did not go away. She could hear a voice softly singing, "Rock-a-bye baby in the tree top."

Sue jumped and spun around. "Don't sneak up on me like that!"

"Sorry, I thought you heard me come in."

Sue wrapped her arms around Jim.

86

"Sue . . . you're shaking. Are you okay?"

"Just hold me for a second."

Sue leaned back and looked Jim in the eye. "Thanks for helping me with this. I know it's not your problem, but I don't know what I'd do without you."

Jim followed Sue into the bedroom and stood behind her as she sat down in front of the roll-a-desk. He watched as she reached for the key, unlocked the desk, rolled back the top, and moved her head back and forth, scanning the small cubbyholes.

"Bingo," she yelled out.

"What?"

"His checkbook." Sue opened the worn leather case and stared at the blank check.

"What is it?" Jim asked, as Sue sat motionless.

"My name is still on his checks."

"Are you sure you're divorced? I haven't been sleeping with a married woman have I?"

"Not unless you've been sleeping with someone else besides me, you haven't."

"I can't handle you, how could I . . . "

"He must have another checking account," Sue interrupted.

"How do you know that?"

"Look." Sue showed Jim the check register. "In the past six months Dan only wrote seven checks. Six to the cable company, and one to a Mr. Drummins. What about his phone bills, electric, rent. He's gotta have another checking account, but I don't see anything here," she said, as she searched through the rest of the desk.

"Where would he keep those other shoe boxes you were talking about?" Jim asked.

"Check the closet. I didn't get to it yesterday."

Jim walked to the closet and slid open the louvered wooden door. There on a shelf, about eye level, along the left side, were rows of shoe boxes stacked to the ceiling. "I think I found the files."

Sue was there in a second, nudging up beside Jim and wrapping her arm around his waist. "He was a creature of habit . . . lucky for us. Let's see." Sue glanced up at the boxes, familiar with what she saw. Dates, written in bold black ink, on the end of each box. "The top box, on the right," she pointed. "And the one next to it. And the two below it. Grab those boxes. That will cover the last four years."

They each took a box, sat on the bed, removed the rubber band holding on the lid, and started reviewing the documents.

"Something happened about two years ago, around July or August," Jim finally spoke up.

They had been so focused on reviewing the contents of the boxes, they hadn't spoken a word for the past thirty minutes. Now they sat there staring at one another, Jim waiting for Sue to reveal what had happened.

"Two years ago . . . that was the last time Dan was in front of a classroom," Sue began speaking slowly. "He started a one year sabbatical in the summer, supposedly to write a book."

"Supposedly?"

"I'm not sure of all the details. By that time we hadn't seen or even spoken to each other in years. But I had a friend in Administration and she kept me up to date on things.

"Anyway, there was no way Dan was off writing a book. He hated writing. He never published anything. It's the reason why he never made full professor, which was fine with him."

"What happened after the year?"

"He retired. Never went back to teaching. A lot of people thought he had finally fallen off the deep end. I thought . . . I thought he just gave up on life. I know I almost did."

There was a long silence. Sue sat with her head down.

"Why, what did you find?"

"Well . . . I'm not positive, but that same summer, two years ago, it looks like he started paying for everything in cash. He rarely used his credit cards. He rarely wrote a check. All of his receipts, electric, phone, are all stamped paid, but it looks like he paid for them at the grocery store. He even started paying his rent in cash." Jim handed Sue a receipt marked paid from the rental property office.

"Well," Sue stared at the receipt, "lots of people pay in cash. Lots of people don't even have checking accounts. For some reason, he suddenly didn't trust the banks."

"Do you have his latest bank statement, probably from May, in your box?" Jim asked.

"Yup, it's right here," Sue fumbled for a minute then pulled out the bank envelope. She pulled out the statement. "April 28th through May 27th. He only wrote two checks. One to the Cable company and one to a Mr. Drummins. Here is the statement with the two canceled checks," she said as she handed them to Jim.

Jim did not reach out for it.

"What's the balance in his checking account?"

Sue glanced up and down the statement, then looked up at Jim. She looked back down at the statement. "Current balance as of May 27th . . . $47,327.48."

18

Yesterday evening, Roger had been on an emotional high. He had persisted. He had proved his theory. His gut had been right again. He had found out who Timer was. He could feel the Jamaican sun warming his body as his mind drifted to thoughts of retirement. But like a pleasant dream that slips away as you begin to awaken in the morning, the euphoria quickly turned to depression when he realized Timer was dead.

Although he had left the office with a happy-hour buzz, his depressed emotional state drove him to finish what he had started. He went straight to his favorite bar. When his alarm went off this morning, his first thought was one of surprise, since he couldn't recall how, or when, he had gotten home. His pounding head told him why.

As he lay there staring at his alarm clock, contemplating calling in sick, he started to recall the plan he had formulated while sitting at the bar, in his inebriated state, only hours ago.

Although confident of Timer's identity, Roger knew the evidence was circumstantial at best. Before he could proceed further, he needed more corroboration. He was also confident Timer had more cash. He wasn't going to let something as minor as Timer's death, or a hangover, stop him from finding out how much more.

"I guess you aren't as smart as I thought you were," Roger said, as he dropped his pen on the yellow pad he had been writing on, rocked his head downward, touching his chin to his chest, stretching the muscles in the back of his neck. "Thank you big brother."

One of the more startling revelations Roger found while working on the TIA program was how much of what we do in the digital society we live in is kept track of by someone. Whether it be Walmart, whose computers record everything we buy from them by matching the bar coded merchandise against our credit cards, the cell phone companies who keep track of every phone number we dial, the banks who know our disposable income by our direct deposited pay checks, or the hotels that know where we vacation, how many drinks we take from the minibar in our rooms, and what X-rated movies we watch, more and more of what we do, and where we go, is being documented for someone to view at a later date.

For the past six weeks Roger had kept meticulous notes and had performed a significant amount of research trying to determine Timer's identity. He had documented the dates and times of each of the fifteen calls Timer had made to him. His caller ID had identified the phone numbers, and by tapping into the phone company databases, he was able to find the exact location of the phone booths Timer had used. They were randomly scattered across the northeastern US and Canada. Lake Placid, New York; Bennington, Vermont; Westborough, Massachusetts; Tunkhannock, Pennsylvania; Niagara Falls, Canada; Gananoque, Ontario; and a host of others.

No two places the same, no rhyme nor reason as to the sequence of the locations picked. What eventually became apparent was that the locations were at some distance from, and centrally located around, Syracuse, New York.

Knowing Timer might actually be Daniel E. Lockwood, Roger now searched Lockwood's financial records, credit card purchases, canceled checks, phone bills, and anything else the TIA program would access, to see if he could place him in, or near, any of the towns on the dates and times that the phone calls were made.

Initially he came up empty handed, not even a gas credit card receipt to place Lockwood in the physical location of one of the phone booths. As a last resort, he decided to once again use the TIA search engine. He asked it to identify any data bases having to do with traveling, that Lockwood may have used. One hit came up.

New York State Thruway Authority E-Z Pass

The New York State Thruway, which was actually Route 90 of the interstate highway system, traversed east-west across the center of the state. It was one of the last remaining toll roads on the interstate and the only way to efficiently travel across the state.

To reduce costs and congestion at the toll booths, an automated electronic payment system had been installed several years ago on the roadway. With an E-Z Pass device installed in your car, a commuter could pass through the toll booths without stopping. A sensor would record the toll owed, and debit your account accordingly. But the system also did something else. It kept track of the date and time that you entered and exited the roadway.

Roger pulled the E-Z Pass file for Daniel E. Lockwood. He

then looked for a phone booth that Lockwood had used that was in close proximity to the Thruway, reasoning he would have used the toll road to get to that location.

Roger looked at the map with the locations of the phone booths Timer had used for his calls to him. One of them was located right on the roadway at Exit 30, in Herkimer, a town about sixty miles east of Syracuse.

That call was made on May 20th from 12:43 to 12:58 p.m. Lockwood's E-Z Pass account showed, on that day, that he had used the Thruway twice. First, he entered at the Liverpool toll booth, just north of Syracuse, at 11:14 a.m. and exited at the Herkimer toll booth at 12:23 p.m. He then got back on the Thruway at Herkimer at 1:10 p.m., exiting at Liverpool at 2:36 p.m.

Checking the dates of each of the fifteen phone calls, he found similar E-Z Pass matches for eight more, all of which were at locations necessitating traveling the toll road. The remaining six calls were at locations requiring travel in a north-south direction from Syracuse, where the thruway would not have been the pre-ferred route.

He now felt he had his corroborating evidence. Timer was in fact Daniel E. Lockwood. It was now time to find out who Lockwood really was, and more importantly, how much he had been worth.

19

"Have you been able to figure it out yet?" Sue said, as she stood behind Jim and massaged his shoulders.

Jim had been at it for almost two hours. They had cleaned off the dining room table, and, one at a time, Jim meticulously reviewed every envelope in what was now six boxes. This brought him back six years into Dan's past. Every monthly checking account statement for the past six years was neatly stacked in piles in front of him. Next to that was a pile of income tax returns. To the right of that was a pad covered with dates and numbers that Jim had scribbled down in a way legible only to him.

"Are you sure you haven't found another checkbook around somewhere?" Jim questioned.

Besides packing the items she had previously placed on the table into the cardboard boxes they had brought over, Sue had gone over every nook and cranny of Dan's desk, as well as his dresser drawers and closet. She was certain she wouldn't find any more records, but went through the exercise anyway. The only thing left was the dozen or so boxes left on the closet shelf, all labeled with dates from the time she was married to Dan.

"Nada, nothing. I told you," as she tapped her finger on the top of one of the boxes on the table, "this is where Dan kept his files. All of them."

"Well something doesn't make sense. Up until two years ago everything seems normal. His pay checks are direct deposited. Ten to fifteen checks are written every month, to about the same places. He spends about what he takes in. Then look what happens here." Jim pointed to one of the checking account statements. "In August, only four checks are written, rent, cable, a car payment and Visa. From what I can tell, he paid all his other bills, but in cash. A few months later," Jim picked up another statement and handed it to Sue, "it looks like he starts paying his rent in cash too."

"Okay, so he starts paying for things in cash. Weird, but I don't think there's a law against it."

"You're right, but look at the next few months. He writes two or three checks, yet his monthly balance continues to grow. Where is he getting the cash from to pay his other bills?"

"Maybe he won some money in the lottery or he had a good night at Turning Stone Casino. I don't know?" Sue said as she realized she was defending her ex.

"Good ideas. He could've won some money at Turning Stone without having to report it to anyone, and it could have been in cash. The lottery is a possibility too, but I believe any winnings over a thousand dollars have to be processed directly from the state, and they send you an earnings statement at the end of the year. I don't see anything on his tax return for that year," Jim said, as he placed his hand on the pile in front of him.

"Even if it was at the casino, or he had won the lottery, taking a guess at his annual expenses and the cash in that shoe box, he would have had to have won this much money to have lived for the past two years on it." Jim flipped over the page on the pad and pointed to a figure written in large numbers at the bottom of the page.

"One hundred thousand dollars!" Sue said, almost choking on her words.

"A hundred thousand, tax free, untraceable dollars," Jim added.

"There has got to be some logical explanation for this," Sue said as she shook her head back and forth. "We're missing something, somewhere. There must be another account somewhere."

"Sue, even if there is, where is he getting the money to put into it. He hadn't touched a pay check or retirement check in years! He paid for things in cash."

"Cash from where!"

"I don't know," Jim shot back.

There was a long silence.

"Why are we yelling at each other?" Sue finally spoke up in a low, calm voice. "Looking at this coldly, my ex-husband died and left me everything. It turns out to be more money than I can explain. But to be honest, I don't think it is my responsibility to explain it either. I can think of a lot of ways he could have gotten that money, all perfectly legal. But I may never find out the truth. He's the only one who knows for sure and he's dead! It's not like it's a million dollars."

"You know something, you're right. Hell, we should be, I mean, you should be, celebrating," Jim said with a smile. "It's certainly not something we should be arguing about."

Jim stood up from the table, stretched his arms straight up above his head, touching his finger tips on the ceiling, then reached for Sue and pulled her body against his. They searched for each others lips and kissed, gently at first. But as the seconds passed, their tongues met, breathing got deeper, and slowly a fire seemed to ignite within both of them.

Sue pulled away, but let her lips brush against Jim's as she spoke. "Let's finish up here, go home, make love for the rest of the afternoon, and then I'll take you out to dinner."

"That sounds great to me," Jim said jokingly, in a high pitched voice, as he backed away holding his legs together.

"Do you know how much I love you. Thank you for helping me with all this," Sue said, as a tear fell down her cheek.

"No problem . . . especially now that I know you can afford my bill."

Jim reached for Sue's hand. "Why don't I clean up this mess, and why don't you go through the rest of the boxes in the closet, just to make sure it's all old stuff from when you were married. I think it would be good for you to go through that today, while I'm here."

Jim was just finishing up putting an envelope in the last box when he heard Sue walk up behind him. "Perfect timing," he said, without looking up. "I'm almost done. Did you find anything?"

Not hearing a response, he turned in his chair. "Sue, did you?" He stopped when he saw Sue's face. Her skin was milk-white, like she had just seen a ghost.

"Are you okay?"

Still staring at her face, he hadn't noticed she was holding something in her hands.

"Sue . . . what's wrong?"

Staring into Jim's eyes, Sue removed the cover to the box she was holding and dumped its contents onto the table.

"If I counted it correctly, here's another fifty thousand!"

20

"What if Timer, I mean Lockwood, was telling the truth . . . what if he really did have proof of . . ."

Roger thought about what he had just mumbled to himself. He couldn't even bring himself to finish the sentence, to say the words.

Although he had never met the man, Lockwood had been able to take him on the emotional roller-coaster ride of his life over the past six weeks. Each depressing low point, lower than the one before it, was followed by a high point, infinitely higher than the previous. Of course, Roger didn't realize that Lockwood was only the catalyst for these mood swings. His own obsession with finding a get-rich-quick scheme, one that he had hoped would set him up for the rest of his life, was the real driver. That, along with the physical and neurological effects of a lifetime of alcohol.

Greed was now subconsciously dominating Roger's every move.

Roger recalled his first phone call with Lockwood and how he had almost written off the whole thing as a hoax. Of course, that all changed a few weeks later when the money arrived in his mailbox and Roger confirmed it wasn't counterfeit. Although he kept that fact away from Lockwood, he still wanted to know where the cash came from. So one day he just asked him.

"How did you happen to find out about the terrorist plot?"

"It was all by accident. I happened to be in the right place at the right time."

"Where did you find the money?"

"At the bottom of a river."

"Excuse me?"

"I found it at the bottom of a river. Actually, the St. Lawrence River."

"Is that where you believe the terrorists are going to bring the money into the country?"

"Why not? If the rumrunners did it during prohibition with liquor, why couldn't someone do it today with money."

"So how did you find the money?"

"I was on a boat, scuba diving, in the St. Lawrence, in early May. It was a clear, windless day, very rare for that time of year. I was resting between dives when a boat, with three men, probably a mile away, coming from Canada toward the US, came to a sudden stop. It was calm enough that their voices easily carried across the water. Their cursing told me their engine had died.

"I was about to pull up anchor, in response to their yelling and hand waving, when I caught sight of a boat headed in their direction. I quickly recognized it as the Coast Guard, so I abandoned my rescue plan. As the Coast Guard approached the boat, I saw one of the men lower a package over the side of the boat into the water.

"The Coast Guard was along side the boat for an hour, then

100

eventually towed the boat away. By that time, they had drifted far down river. My curiosity got the better of me. It took me less than half an hour to find the package. I haven't been back to the river since."

The only problem with the story was that Roger had learned that the money wasn't counterfeit. And if the money wasn't counterfeit, the rest of the story didn't make sense either. Why flood the market with real money? Although he found this perplexing, his goal was not to solve the riddle, but to acquire the rest of the money.

Roger had just spent the entire afternoon reviewing every financial database TIA could find on Daniel E. Lockwood. Although he wasn't much of a numbers person, he understood enough about accounting to quickly determine that the numbers were not adding up when it came to Lockwood's finances.

"He has either got an account I can't find, or . . . undocumented cash coming from somewhere," the later idea being the most intriguing to Roger.

Roger had determined that Lockwood had about fifty thousand dollars in cash in his bank accounts. Although nothing to sneeze at, it wasn't close to what he had been expecting to find. This was not turning out to be the once-in-a-lifetime opportunity he thought it was going to be.

"Dave, got a minute?"

"Sure Roger, come on in . . . sit down. What's up?"

"You know I am on vacation next week."

"The week of the fourth, got it right here."

"Right, well, I'd like to take tomorrow, Thursday, and Friday off too, if that's okay with you. Get an early start on my vacation."

"Sure, no problem. Things have been kinda slow around here anyway, and with this weather, I don't blame you for getting out of here."

"Great, thanks."

As soon as Roger got back to his office, he brought up the maps.com web site. In seconds he was printing out the directions from Atlantic City to Syracuse, New York.

21

There was something about having sex in the middle of the afternoon that always made it more erotic for Sue, as if doing it in the daylight was somehow dirty and exciting at the same time. Whatever it was, images from the past hour kept lingering in her thoughts. The damp heat when their naked bodies first touched. The probing fingers and tongues. The scents and almost animal like sounds that filled the room. The familiar after-taste.

"Shoot!" Sue said, as if just emerging from a deep hypnotic trance. "Where the heck am I?" She suddenly realized she had long ago passed by the entrance to Dan's apartment complex.

The money they had found earlier today further added to the mysteries surrounding her ex-husband's life, and now death. They were confident the answer to the mystery was somewhere in the boxes, now piled on the dining room table in the apartment. But after hours of pouring through the records, any clues there still eluded them.

By mid-afternoon, they both decided to call it quits for the day and stick to their earlier agreed upon plan of sex and a late dinner. Before leaving the apartment, though, they carefully double checked the contents of each and every box to make sure there wasn't more hidden cash. They found none.

Following their afternoon tryst, Jim, still recovering from the previous day's graduation day celebration with the guys, opted for a power nap before dinner. Too wound up to sleep, Sue had decided to return to the apartment to install timers on several lamps, to give the place a lived-in look. The last thing they needed was the added attention of a burglary.

As Sue stepped from her car into the hot humid air, she was glad she had stayed with her first choice of outfits for the evening dinner rendezvous with Jim. The black hip hugger Capris showed off her tanned, flat tummy. Her sheer tank top was just translucent enough for the dark centers of her breasts, which were still perky from the cool air of the car, to be noticed. And the three inch cork sandals, with straps that crisscrossed her slim ankles, complimented her long legs, yet were still comfortable enough for a hopefully late night of dancing.

She felt good about being able to get away with wearing clothes designed for someone thirty years younger.

"Mrs. Lockwood?"

Sue heard a voice off in the distance as she was just about to unlock the door to the apartment. She turned and saw a stocky, elderly man, dressed in a khaki shirt and blue Dockers, walking briskly across the parking lot toward her.

"Hello Mr. Nass. How are you today?" Sue said, with an obvious nervous crackle in her voice.

Nass was impressed that she had remembered his name, even

though it was only yesterday morning that he had given her the key to Lockwood's apartment. He hadn't noticed Sue eyeing the patch over his left shirt pocket that read Fred Nass, Baldwin Estates Facilities Manager.

"I'm fine, thank you. Although, it's a little too hot for my liking," Nass responded, as he reached for a handkerchief from his pants pocket and wiped the beads of sweat from his forehead.

"I like it hot myself," Sue said, trying to calm herself, but then suddenly realizing it was probably the wrong thing to say to the elderly man.

Nass stared at her with a look that a father might give a teenage daughter over her choice of clothes for her evening date.

"I was just about to call you. I noticed that Dr. Lockwood's mailbox was full and I wasn't sure if you knew where the key to it was," Nass finally blurted out.

"Oh, thanks. I think the key is hanging right here," Sue said, as she turned, unlocked and opened the door to the apartment, then reached for the key labeled 'mail,' that was hanging on the key rack next to the door. She quickly stepped back outside and showed Nass the key.

"That's it. The mailboxes for this building are located in the center court entrance," Nass said, pointing to his right. "They're on the wall just across from the storage room."

"Thanks. I'll go down there right now before I forget."

Sue quickly pulled the apartment door shut, made sure it was locked, and headed in the direction Nass had pointed to.

After taking several steps, something Nass had just said made her stop. Her mind flashed back to the image of the key rack she had glanced at only seconds ago, and the words 'storage room' suddenly appeared before her eyes.

She quickly turned and shouted to Nass who was now halfway across the parking lot. "Mr. Nass. Do you know if Dr. Lockwood had anything in the storage room?"

22

"Oh my God," Sue said to herself, as she gazed into the hot, oven-like atmosphere, of the dimly lit storage room. As her eyes adjusted, she began to focus on the individual items in the room. The wicker bassinet, crib toys, the Cabbage Patch Doll named Cindabella, the pink Barbie Corvette, stuffed animals, the colorful plastic hamster house. Boxes all clearly labeled. Baby clothes. Kindergarten papers. Pictures.

She felt faint as she turned off the light, stepped back, and closed the heavy metal door to the room. She started to reach for the key that she had left in the lock, but instead braced herself against the door handle. Her legs felt like rubber as she struggled to remain standing. She took a deep breath, turned and leaned against the door. It felt hot against her bare shoulder blades.

"I hate you for doing this to me," Sue said, almost struggling to get the words out. Suddenly she could feel beads of sweat forming, first on her face, then chest, then arms. "I gotta get out of this heat."

A minute later she was opening the door to Dan's apartment.

She walked in and barely made it to the dining room table, leaning on it with one hand and grasping a chair with the other. She collapsed in the chair as her legs failed her.

She folded her arms, placed them on the table, then leaned over and let her forehead rest on them. With her eyes closed, she sat there motionless.

Minutes later she opened her eyes and sat up, as if awakening from a restful nap. The cool apartment air had worked its magic on her. She took a deep breath to further calm herself.

"I'm not going to let you control me," she said, as she turned and spoke into the open area of the apartment. "I'm sorry that you are dead, but that's not my fault either! Just leave me alone!"

Sue sat there, her eyes fixed on the far wall. She tried, but couldn't recall one thing from her ten years of counseling that would help snap her back into reality.

Subconsciously, her hand started to sort through the pile of mail she had placed on the table following her first visit to the center court area. Most of it was junk mail. She smiled to herself knowing it would be years before the senders realized Dan was dead, and even then, some would still continue to send mail to the current occupant. There were several bills and she felt relieved knowing there was money available to pay them. But it was the last item in the pile that caught her attention. It was a white business envelope, hand addressed, with a Canadian stamp and return address label from Mr. K. C. Drummins.

Where have I seen that name before, she thought, looking at the return address label.

Then she heard it, faintly at first, and finally loud enough to make out the words of the song. She got up from the table and walked the few steps toward the living room. There, in the leather recliner, sat the ghostly image of Dan, holding a blanket swaddled baby in his arms, his voice now clearly audible.

Sue stepped forward into the middle of the living room, then suddenly froze in place as the singing stopped. Dan slowly raised his head until his lifeless eyes met Sue's. The smile on his face slowly disappeared, as his lips tightened, and his jaw began to shake. Sue thought she saw a red glow, deep in each of his eye balls.

He nonchalantly stood up, almost floating out of the chair, as his eyes remained locked on Sue's. After a slight hesitation, he took a step towards her, then stopped when she calmly spoke out.

"I am not going to let you control me!"

She refocused her eyes to his lips as she saw them move. She strained to hear what he was trying to say, as the words went from a whisper to a clearly legible voice.

". . . my little girl. Look what you did to my little girl. Look what you did . . ."

Suddenly the image of Dan disappeared, but not before it thrust the baby into the air. Sue's hands instinctively reached out to catch the bundle coming at her. But as the blanket slowly unraveled, she finally caught a glimpse of the skeletal remains wrapped within.

As she stepped back, the heel of her cork sandal caught on the rug, and as if in slow motion, she fell backwards. She closed her eyes and felt her head, then right shoulder, hit the bookcase behind her. A second after she hit the floor, something landed in her lap.

She screamed and frantically waved her arms to brush off whatever it was that had fallen on her. As her eyes opened, she saw that it was only a book, a volume from the Encyclopedia Britannica that they had bought years ago. It had fallen off the shelf onto her lap. She glanced around the room and saw nothing of the images that were there just moments ago.

"I am not going to let you control me," she repeated, as she moved her right shoulder in a circular motion to make sure it wasn't injured from the fall.

As she got up on to her knees, the book slid off her lap and landed in an open position on the floor in front of her. She reached down to touch what she thought her eyes were seeing. There, hidden within the book, whose pages had been carved out to form a rectangular box, was a black and maroon colored journal.

23

"Where have you been? What the hell is all that stuff?" Jim asked, as he reached out and offered to take the obviously heavy load of books that Sue was holding in her out-stretched arms.

"No, that's okay. Let me just set them on the coffee table . . . man, those things are heavy," Sue gasped, as she bent down on one knee and put the pile of books on the table, being careful not to let them topple over. As she stood up, she looked down at her white top to make sure she hadn't gotten it dirty.

"By the way . . . you look great." Jim stepped forward, put his arms around Sue's waist, slid his hands up under the loose top onto the bare skin of her back and pulled her close to him. After a moment, he leaned over Sue's shoulder to get a better look at the stack of books on the table. "So, what is all this stuff?"

Sue turned away from him and looked at the pile. "These are Dan's journals. I remember when his counselor convinced him to start writing his thoughts down at the end of each day, as a kind of self-therapy. I knew he had started doing it, but I didn't think he had gotten so prolific about it. As far as I can tell, they go back at least five years."

"I didn't remember seeing these when we were at the apartment earlier today."

"You didn't. I just found them tonight. They were hidden."

"Hidden. Where? I thought you went over every inch of that place?"

"I did. But it never dawned on me to look here." Sue handed Jim volume eleven of the encyclopedia from Dan's book shelf.

I don't get it?" Jim looked at the book, then at Sue.

"Open it."

"Holy shit!" Jim's jaw dropped and his eyes widened as he traced his fingers around the hollowed out portion of the book. "Man . . . what the hell did he write that he thought he had to keep hidden like this?"

"Maybe the secret to all that money we found!"

"Ahhhhh . . . good point!"

"So, what-da-ya say we spend the day tomorrow reading through all these?"

"Tomorrow . . . tomorrow. I have some good news and some bad news about tomorrow. What do you want to hear first, the good or the . . . "

"The good," Sue interrupted. She always wanted to hear the good news first.

"Well," Jim continued. "Remember the mandatory Outcome Based Lesson Plan training that I'm scheduled to take the week after the fourth?"

"How could I forget. You've been complaining about it for a month. 'It's screwing up my whole summer!'"

"I don't think those are the exact words I used." Sue rarely, if

112

ever, used profanity, and Jim always tried to edge her on to say something out of character, then watch her blush.

"I told you to take those classes earlier this year, when they offered them in the evenings, but no, you kept putting it off, hoping they'd forget about it. So I take it, the good news is, you've somehow weaseled your way out of it?"

"Well, not exactly . . . the good news is, the class is not going to be conducted the week after the fourth."

"Lucky you."

"The bad news is, the class starts tomorrow morning, eight sharp. Lasts all day. Same thing on Thursday and a half a day on Friday morning. Then Monday, through noon on Wednesday, next week. That way, we're done before the Fourth of July weekend."

"So I guess what you're saying is, I have to read all this stuff by myself."

"Sorry . . . he's your ex. Plus, what if he wrote some deep dark secret about you that you don't want me to know about . . . on second thought, let me see those." Jim started to push Sue out of the way, reaching for the pile of books.

"Funny. All right, I'll do it myself. But could you do me a favor and just look at this one." Sue leaned over and picked up the encyclopedia, volume thirteen, M, and handed it to Jim.

"You mean right now?"

"Yea. Right now. It won't take long."

"I thought we were going out to dinner," Jim whined as he opened the cover to the large book, then turned over a few pages. "By the time we get to the restaurant, they won't be . . . serving . . . " He looked up at Sue. "How much?"

"One hundred thousand!"

24

"Eleven o'clock . . . I still have an hour to see if I can pick up some more spending money," Roger said to himself, as he walked away from the blackjack table and glanced over to see what he might try next.

Since walking onto the casino floor of the Taj Mahal thirty minutes ago, Roger was up well over a thousand dollars, all from the blackjack table he was reluctantly leaving. Being a frequent visitor to the casinos at Atlantic City, he knew when it was time to push away from the table. Though the cards at the table had been kind to him, he knew the longer term odds were in the favor of the house. One of his secrets to winning, or at least not losing too much, was to know when to walk away, as painful as that may be at times, like right now.

Earlier in the day, Roger had concluded that it was time to either shit or get off the pot, a favorite expression of his commanding officer when he was stationed in Brussels. With Lockwood obviously dead, he saw his dream potentially slipping away. He realized that he could no longer just sit back and wait for Lockwood to make the next move. There would be no more discussions about the terrorist plot. No more clues as to how much cash there really was. No more cash in the mail. Roger had to act, and quickly. He knew he needed to get to Lockwood's secret before anyone else did.

Although he had worked out a plan, he wasn't exactly sure of his destinations or what he was likely to encounter. The only thing he was certain of, he was prepared for anything. He had bent a lot of rules over the past six weeks and had resolved to bend more, in fact many more, if he needed to. He wasn't aware of how desperate he had become.

He had originally considered flying to Syracuse. Unfortunately the last flight earlier this evening did not leave him with enough time to finish what he needed to do to get ready for his trip. Since the first step of his plan was to search Lockwood's apartment, something he felt more comfortable doing in the darkness, the next window of opportunity for doing so would not come until tomorrow night. With Syracuse less than ten hours by car, that now became the better travel option.

Besides, driving gave him a lot more flexibility. For one, he could now break up the trip and spend the night in Atlantic City. More importantly, driving also meant he could bring along a gun.

Roger eyed a crowded craps table with four younger, perhaps middle thirties, women standing beside it. Given the option, he would have found it difficult to choose just one among them, as each of them was more than acceptable. They were tanned, pretty, and barely covered in low cut, short dresses that showed off their curvy, leggy bodies.

Roger walked up to the table just as the next game was about to begin. He placed five one-hundred-dollar-chips on the pass line. The shooter, a short, balding man, with a paunchy belly, probably younger than his sixty-year old looking face showed, was surrounded by three tall blondes, all vying no doubt, to share in some of the twenty thousand dollars in chips he had in front of him.

As the dice tumbled across the table, the crowd went silent, then erupted, as a three and a four rolled up. Within seconds Roger's stack of chips doubled in size to a thousand dollars. He looked at the shooter, reached down to move his chips, then hesitated, leaving the entire stack on the pass line again. The second seven doubled his winnings to two thousand dollars.

Roger again looked at the shooter, but this time reached down and picked up all of his chips. The woman standing next to him did the same with her twenty dollar chip.

Craps.

A unanimous cry of "NOOOOO!" along with several other vulgar expressions, came from the crowd around the table.

Roger felt a warm, soft hand touching his left hand. He turned. "How did you know?" the woman next to him asked.

He stared into her blue eyes for several seconds, then answered, "I saw it in his eyes."

She blushed as they both remained locked onto each other, neither one daring to blink.

"My name is Roger," he finally spoke up, sensing the staring had gone on long enough.

"Traci, with an I," the woman responded, reaching out her hand, but not taking her eyes off Roger.

Traci introduced Roger to the other three. They were all school

116

teachers, lived within an hour of Atlantic City, and although two were married and two were divorced, Traci being one of the latter, they were on their annual weekend at the casinos, a tradition started in their single days.

After a few minutes, Roger glanced at his watch and indicated that he had another appointment, business of course. Before he left, Traci handed him a business card and told him to look her up the next time he was in town. When he indicated that he might be back after the weekend, Traci smiled and said, "I'll be looking forward to your call."

Roger winked, turned and slowly walked away without saying anything to her. "Don't look back," was all he muttered to himself.

As he left the casino and walked down the hall to the lobby of the Taj Mahal, he again glanced at his watch. It was already 11:55 p.m. He picked up the pace a little. He did not want to be late for his midnight appointment.

25

"Hi babe, I'm home. Hello . . . Sue?"

"I'm up here," Sue yelled from the loft.

"You don't look much different from when I left this morning," Jim said, as he got to the top of the stairs and saw Sue sitting upright, propped against a half dozen pillows at the head of the bed. Her red puffy eyes and blotchy face, devoid of makeup, clearly told him she had been crying. "Have you spent the whole day reading these things?" Jim sat down on the edge of the bed, picked up one of the journals, opened it, and fanned through the pages. "Anything interesting in here?"

Sue placed the journal she was reading, open and faced down, beside her on the bed. She had in fact spent the entire day reading, deciding to start in chronological order with the first journal from five years ago, which Dan started writing the week after she moved out of the house. She was wearing the same shirt, the only thing she had on her body, that she had put on when she got out of bed that morning. It was an oversized yellow, actually pale ale dyed, according to the manufacturer, T-shirt that had a logo of 'Bill's Bait and Beer Shop' printed on the front in bold black letters. The only breaks she had taken were to refill her iced tea glass and to go to the bathroom. She was so intent on getting through the journals, in hope of finding out how her ex-husband came into all that cash, that she hadn't showered or even bothered to eat.

She put her arms up and clasped her hands behind her head. "No, I don't look much different from when you left this morning. Yes, I've spent the entire day reading these. And so far, the only thing I've found out is that my ex-husband hated me a thousand, no make that a million times more than I ever imagined."

"Who'd a thought it, but it sounds like my day of learning how to develop outcome-based lesson plans was a lot better than yours. Come here," Jim patted the mattress next to him. "Lay down and I'll give you a back rub."

"That would be great," Sue said with a sigh. She pushed the journals laying next to her toward the far edge of the king sized bed, turned to her side, then laid on her stomach, arms stretched above her head.

Jim climbed over her, straddled across her legs, and sat lightly on her calves. She lifted her chest off the bed as Jim slid her shirt up over her head. "Ahhhhhhh," was all Sue said, as Jim placed the palms of his hands on the small of her back, just above her butt, and pushed her body down into the bed. She just laid there enjoying Jim's strong hands stroking her body, knowing the sensations she was feeling now would not last long, fifteen minutes at most. That was usually how long it took for a body rubbing to turn into a love making session.

Sue opened her eyes and glanced at the clock. A twelve minute back rub. Not bad. She felt Jim's warm, bare chest on her back, then the full weight of his body, as his hands slid over her breasts. She took a deep breath and closed her eyes. She knew she would not be able to stay still for long.

"I needed that. I missed your body today."

"Believe me, I would have rather been here with you," Jim whispered into Sue's ear.

They were lying on the bed in their favorite position, spooned, with Sue's back against Jim's chest and both of his arms wrapped tightly around her. They were still both damp with sweat from the just ended love making, with the coolness of the air conditioning only now able to remove the body heat they had just finished creating.

"So, how was the training?" Sue finally spoke up.

"It wasn't that bad. Actually, it was pretty interesting. I just wish I'd have listened to you and taken it last fall. Who wants to sit in a classroom when the weather is like this?"

Sue pushed her rear end back against Jim. "When are you going to listen to me!"

"I know, I know! So, what's for dinner?"

"Don't try and change the subject," Sue answered, pushing against Jim again.

"Keep doing that and we'll have to discuss something else that's about to come up."

"Okay, okay." Sue pushed away from Jim, turned and gave him a kiss. "How about we shower and head over to the Blue Water Grill for a nice leisurely dinner . . . on me of course."

"You bet it's on you. Wait a minute. You didn't find . . . "

"No. No more stacks of hundreds . . . No! No fifties or twenties either."

"By the way, did you call the lawyer?"

Yesterday evening's discovery by Sue of the money in the encyclopedia volume brought the total cash found in her ex's apartment to $172,000. At dinner last night they both decided it was prudent to call Steve Haggas for advice.

"Yes, I did it first thing this morning so I wouldn't forget. He said what we pretty much concluded at dinner last night. Until we suspect something suspicious about the money, it becomes part of the estate. I told him as of now we have no idea where the money came from. He also suggested we call the FBI."

"Did you?"

"Yes. The agent I spoke with on Saturday, Nelson, was out of town. I left word with his assistant that we had found the cash. She said she would let him know and he would probably call me on it."

"Good. So, did you learn anything from all your reading today?" Jim said, as he looked at the pile of books on the far edge of the bed.

"I'll tell you over dinner, after a few drinks." Sue got up and walked toward the bathroom, before Jim could see the tears forming in her eyes. She closed the door behind her, which told Jim that the "how about we shower" meant separately.

Sue stood under the spray of the shower, hoping the splashing water was loud enough to cover up the sound of her muted crying. Although it wasn't going to be easy, Sue knew it was time to share with Jim the whole story of her past life.

26

"Six-thirty . . . that's why I'm hungry, and thirsty."

Roger was already behind schedule for the trip to Syracuse he had planned out the day before. He had originally expected to be there by now, spending a few hours casing out Lockwood's apartment prior to his planned nighttime entry. Instead, he was still about an hour and a half south of Syracuse, on Interstate 81 north, passing through Binghamton, New York.

Nothing to worry about. It won't be dark until nine forty-five, Roger reasoned. He remembered last Saturday had been the longest day of the year.

So far, the drive from Atlantic City had gone smoothly. As he had anticipated, the traffic had been light on this Wednesday afternoon. He had, however, left the Taj Mahal later than he had originally planned. At check-in yesterday, he had indicated he would be staying until the following Tuesday, and maybe longer. Although he knew he would be in Syracuse on the following night, his booked room at the Taj Mahal was an alibi, in the event he needed it.

He also took the hotel up on its special offer to test drive a new Cadillac during his stay. The 'Get a car for a dollar a day during your stay' promotion provided him with unlimited use of a brand new, four hundred horse power, manual six-speed, Cadillac CTS roadster, without having to officially rent it. Therefore, there would be no credit card receipt showing he had a rental car, and more importantly, his Corvette would never leave the hotel parking garage. Another alibi.

To make it look as though he had stayed in his room, he waited until it had been made up earlier this morning. Then before leaving, he messed up the bed, unwrapped some soap, ran the shower, wet two towels and tossed them on the bathroom floor, left a half empty diet Pepsi can on the desk, and placed a few tissues and some paper in the waste basket. He even opened two Trojans, leaving one in the top of the waste basket in the bathroom and one on the floor next to the bed.

But there had also been another reason for his late exit. That was Myra. Or at least that is what she had told him to call her.

Roger had been in the mood for something different, and different is what he got from Myra. Upon his arrival yesterday, he had called the escort service, the same one that he had used many times during his past trips to Atlantic City. He had requested a dominatrix and after describing his desires to the woman on the other end of the line, he was assured that Myra would fulfill his fantasy. She had. The two hour appointment that started promptly at midnight had extended to three, at which point he finally admitted he could take no more from her. Before she left, he booked another session with her for the following Monday evening, confident he would not only be back from his trip north, but flush with new found cash. He was so confident of his pending success and the need to celebrate, he booked her for the entire night.

Roger reached over to the blue and white cooler, one just big enough to hold a six-pack and some ice, that was on the passenger side floor. He removed the cover and carefully started pulling out one of the six plastic bottles by the blue top that was protruding through the ice. He stopped when the contents of the bottle was clearly visible. "Definitely plain diet," he muttered to himself, as he continued to remove the bottle from the cooler and placed it in the center console cup holder.

Before he had left the hotel room earlier today, he had pre-mixed three of the diet Pepsis with Jack Daniel's, just in case he had a craving for a drink on the six hour drive. He had become adept at being able to identify the pre-mixed cocktail by the slightly lighter color the Tennessee sour mash whiskey gave the normally caramel colored tint of the diet Pepsi. It was something only an experienced, well trained eye would pick up, so his secret was usually safe.

"I can drink later tonight," Roger said aloud, as he took a swig of the ice-cold soda from the bottle. Although he craved a real drink, he knew in a few hours he would need to be in full control of all of his faculties, not just for breaking into Lockwood's apartment, but more importantly, for the hours he guessed he was going to need to carefully search it.

It might calm my nerves a little, Roger thought, watching the diet Pepsi bottle shaking slightly, as he held it in his hand. He raised the bottle to his mouth and with two big gulps, finished it off. He put the cap back on the bottle and placed it on the seat next to him so he would remember to toss it at the next rest stop.

"No, I gotta be on my toes tonight," he said, contemplating the pros and cons of a drink. He looked at his watch. It was only seven o'clock. His plan was to wait until midnight before making his forced entry into the apartment. "It might help me get in a good power nap." After a few minutes, Roger reached over, removed the top to the cooler, and this time, without looking, randomly pulled out a bottle. He had decided to leave the choice to chance.

27

"Can I take your plate Mr. Calihan?" the waitress said, as she approached the table.

"You sure can Erin . . . that was excellent by the way," Jim responded, as he sat back in his chair to get a better view of Erin leaning over the table. Erin had been a student of Jim's several years ago and was now home from college for the summer. Although Jim guessed she was twenty, she could easily pass for someone much older. Women are maturing much faster, Jim thought to himself as he watched her.

"Are you finished Mrs. Lockwood?" Erin said, purposefully emphasizing the word 'Mrs.', as if implying some hidden meaning.

Sue looked down at her plate. Although she had eaten most of the shrimp and broccoli, she had hardly touched any of the linguine and alfredo sauce.

"Was everything okay?" Erin spoke up again, after several seconds of watching Sue stare at the plate, sensing something might be wrong, and not wanting to jeopardize a good tip.

Sue finally spoke up. "I guess I wasn't that hungry after all. You can take the plate." Sue looked up at Jim as Erin leaned over the table for the plate. "I'll take another drink when you get a chance," Sue said to Erin, as she lifted the plate.

"Erin, could you get one for me too please," Jim spoke up. As Erin walked away from the table, Jim's eyes moved to Sue's. "Didn't you like your dinner?"

"Don't try and change the subject."

"What?"

"You two have been flirting all night."

"What are you talking about?"

"She's doted on you since we sat down and you've been loving it. So why is it that older men turn to mush when a younger woman pays a little attention to them?"

"Sue, I really don't know what you're . . . "

"Jim," Sue interrupted, "you light up when she comes over to the table. You sit up straight in your chair. You even pull your gut in."

"Sorry the drinks took so long . . . the bartender is new and he's a little backed up." Erin placed the drinks in front of each of them, then hurried away.

Jim sat up and smiled when he heard Erin's voice, then looked at Sue looking at him. They both started laughing at the same time, grabbed the drinks, reached across the table and clanged the glasses together. "Touché," was all Jim said.

"Do you know how much I love you!" Jim said, as he put his drink down and reached across the table for Sue's hand.

"Yea, yea, yea. I've heard that before." Sue leaned over the table closer to Jim. "You can fantasize all you want, but deep down inside, you know she couldn't hold a candle to me in bed.

Not that I'm bragging. But you know I'm right, don't you?"

"Is this a trick question?"

"Can I get you guys anything else?"

"I don't think so Erin," Sue answered, staring at Jim. Jim didn't dare not stare back at her. "We'll be out at the bar. Could you bring us our bill and change." Sue held out a hundred dollar bill.

The bar area was crowded, but that was not unusual for the Blue Water Grill on a warm summer Wednesday night. Located in the center of the small village of Baldwinsville, the newly opened grill, housed in a building that a few years before was on the verge of washing into the Seneca river below, had become a local hot spot for DINK's, the double income, no kids crowd, that lived in the surrounding upscale communities.

"There's one," Jim said, as he pointed to the small round standup table, with two stools, in the very corner of the room. Surrounded by windows on two sides, and overlooking the river, it actually provided a relatively secluded place for a couple to carry on a conversation.

"Erin knew she blew her tip when she saw I was paying. Did you see the look on her face. Let that be a lesson to both of you. Experience over age." Sue clanked her glass against Jim's.

They both stared out the window at the river below, each waiting for the other to speak.

"Whatever it is you wanna talk to me about must be pretty serious, because you've been beating around the bush all night. What is it, Sue?"

After another long pause, Sue looked into Jim's eyes and finally spoke up. "I need to share some things with you about my past. Things that very few people know about." Sue picked up the small

128

navy blue paper napkin that had been under her drink and used it to wipe a tear that had formed in the corner of her right eye. She then looked up at Jim and took a deep breath. "I'm sorry."

28

"Son of a bitch. How many times do I have to tell you not to put shit on my chair!" Nick grabbed the sealed manila envelope and threw it on his desk. He spun the large black leather chair around, fell into it, took a huge breath of air into his chest, and let it out slowly through the slit between his lips. He then slid open the bottom right hand drawer of the credenza, pulled out a glass and his special bottle of Royal Crown Limited Reserve, and placed them both on the credenza.

He lifted the globe shaped, dark green bottle, held it up to the window, and slowly rocked it back and forth until he could see the liquid inside sloshing around. He thought he had just opened the bottle last week. Or was it the week before? He filled the glass and took a long sip, swallowing the entire mouthful of expensive liquor. He sat very still, enjoying the warming sensation, as it traveled toward his stomach.

He leaned back in his chair and rested the glass, surrounded by both of his large, thick fingered hands, on his belly. The sun had dipped behind the warehouse and a shadow covered the dozen black delivery trucks parked in a perfect row at the far end of the lot. As he sat there staring at his empire, he again wondered how he had made such a stupid mistake.

When he took over the wine, beer and liquor distributorship after his father's untimely death, he vowed on his father's grave to turn the small-time family business into an empire. Now, thirty years later, he had done just that. Although most of what he had was built by lying, cheating, and stealing, from anyone and everyone that got in his way, what he had accomplished was impressive.

"I'll only do it for a few years," he remembered saying to himself when he decided to invest in a small time, but highly profitable, drug distribution ring. Within six months he had doubled his initial five hundred thousand dollar investment. So he decided to go for broke on a few more big scores, then get out. He'd take his money and move far away from central New York, as if distancing himself from the blood he had spilled there would be repentance enough to erase his lifetime of past sins.

"How could I have been so stupid!" He gulped the rest of the liquor from his glass and refilled it. Pushing with his feet, he rotated the big chair until he was facing his desk.

"One fuck'n afternoon and look at the mess," he said, as he stared at the desk. When he had left earlier this morning for an afternoon of golf and dinner with one of his biggest customers, a small bribe to pay for the business he received from him, his desk was completely cleared off. Now, it was littered with piles of papers, mostly invoices needing his signature.

"This can all fuck'n wait until tomorrow." As he raised his glass to his lips, his eyes were drawn to the manila envelope that had been on his chair. He immediately recognized the 'Uncle Nick' written in large thick red letters on the center of the envelope as Reannon's.

He put the glass on his desk and reached for the envelope. As he turned it over he noticed the piece of wide clear plastic tape, the kind used for shipping large packages, that sealed the flap. He opened the center drawer of his desk, picked up the onyx handled silver letter opener and slit open the envelope. He looked inside and saw the familiar yellow folder. As he pulled the folder out of the envelope, he immediately noticed the five-by-seven piece of pink stationary paper clipped to the folder.

Uncle Nick,

You had already left for the day. I wanted to let you know that one of the calls did not work right today. It was number 147. I tried it twice, per the instructions, and both times the only response I got was a ten-second-long tone.

Sorry. Maybe I can help you to get it to work right in the morning.

Reannon

Nick read the note again, then opened the folder and shuffled through the papers until he found line 147. He then spun his chair around, unlocked the middle drawer of the credenza and pulled out a red folder that was buried under hundreds of old Christmas cards he had kept from over the years. He opened the folder and searched through the pages until he found number 147. A smile spread over his face.

132

He carefully dialed the number.

"Hello."

"Mike, this is Nick."

"Nick, I've been waiting for your call."

29

Roger slowly pulled into the apartment complex parking lot. The only open spot was located two rows back from the building in front of him, in the very center of the parking lot. He felt as if he had disappeared as soon as he came to a stop.

It had taken him several minutes of wandering through the parking lots before he was able to locate building fifteen. He turned off the ignition and glanced at his watch. It was only 8:58 p.m. "Still too light out," he said, as he looked out across the parking lot. He thought it would be better if he waited until it was darker out, but not too dark, before he scoped out the entrance to the apartment.

Within five minutes, the temperature inside the car had risen to eighty-five degrees and beads of sweat were forming on Roger's forehead. "Screw it . . . it's dark enough," he said, as he opened the car door and got out. He stood next to the car, and, although dressed in a tank top, shorts and sneakers, he still felt dizzy from the heat. "Not much cooler out here."

He walked down the long walkway and into the large covered alcove of the building. As he passed by the first door on the right, he saw the large wood stained number 2 hanging on it. He slowed and leaned over to get a closer look at the small name plate just below the number. Lockwood. He felt his heart thump as he read the name. He continued walking through the open part of the building into the center courtyard area. He bent down to untie, then retie, his right sneaker. He stood up, turned around, and walked back toward the alcove he had just passed through. This time he glanced around before stopping in front of Lockwood's door. It had both a lock and a dead bolt, industrial grade. To make matters worse, the door and jamb were both made of heavy gauge metal. He was not going to be able to jimmy this one open with a screwdriver, as he had originally contemplated.

"Son of a bitch." When he heard his voice echo back from the open area of the alcove, he quickly looked around to see if anyone was around to hear him.

He walked toward the entrance to the alcove and stopped. Glancing to his left, he saw the light gray concrete patio in front of the sliding glass door, the one he knew was Lockwood's. Looking around and seeing no one, he walked the few steps through the grass and onto the patio, again kneeling down to tie his sneaker. He glanced to his left, inspecting the sliding glass door.

"Perfect," he whispered to himself.

Although the builder had provided more than ample security for the main entrance to the apartment, he had, as usual, cut corners on the sliding glass door. This door had become the most popular entry point for burglars in suburban America. The largest opening in the exterior of the home, it was difficult to secure with locking mechanisms that also need to be designed to facilitate ease of opening. To make matters worse, the fixed part of the slider was usually installed on the outside and secured in place with fasteners on the top and bottom of the door. Unfortunately, the fasteners were, in most cases, easily removed with a common screwdriver. Once removed, the fixed door usually just slid open. That was especially true with metal sliders, such as the one on Lockwood's apartment.

Roger bent down to get a closer look at the bottom fastener. Suddenly, as if reacting on instinct, he jumped up and started to run into the parking lot, zigzagging between the parked cars. He stopped behind one of the cars, bent down, then raised his head slowly and looked in the direction of the apartment. The light that had startled him now lit up the entire opening of the sliding glass door to Lockwood's apartment.

30

"Kelly would have been twenty-six today," Sue finally managed to get the words out, after staring out the window for the past few minutes at the yacht that was tied to the docks on the other side of the river.

"Sue, you don't need to do this."

"Yes . . . yes I do," Sue interrupted. "Please."

Although Sue and Jim had been living together for two years, there were certain aspects of their respective pasts that they rarely spoke about. But for them, that seemed only natural. After all, they hadn't met until they were in their late forties, and each had a lifetime of memories that excluded the other, some of which they were each trying to forget. It was one thing for a young couple to talk about their past high school romances, and quite another when the topic involved a spouse of twenty years.

Kelly was one of those memories that had surfaced only a few times in their short relationship.

"Any kids?" Jim had innocently asked Sue, on their second

date, as they were walking into one of the crowded bars on Marshall Street near Syracuse University.

"I did, but she passed away several years ago," was Sue's response.

"I'm sorry," were the only words Jim could think of at the time. What else do you say in response to something like that?

Neither spoke another word for several minutes, and the topic rarely came up again.

"She also died ten years ago today." Sue finally turned her head and looked into Jim's eyes.

Jim took a deep breath as his body visibly shook at hearing the words Sue had just spoken. He reached across the table and clutched Sue's hands. "I . . . I don't know what to say."

"It was a Saturday morning," Sue continued, speaking in a low monotone voice, void of any emotion. "We were getting ready for her sixteenth birthday party."

"Sue . . . is that all you need?" Dan yelled through the screen door, as he stood on the stoop in the garage. "Sue!"

"Wait a minute, I'm thinking," Sue said, as she turned and looked at Dan through the screen.

"I don't see how you could possibly need anything else. You've got enough food here to feed a small army. It's only a birthday party with a bunch of teenagers."

"I know, I know, but give me a second. There was something else I wanted you to get." Sue knew her husband was right. She was probably going a little overboard for the party, but after all, it was their daughter's sixteenth birthday today.

It would also be their first official pool party. For years, they had toyed with the idea of getting a pool. Last year's hot summer, and their daughter's begging, convinced them to finally do it. Although they had contracted to have the pool installed last September, it wasn't until a few weeks ago that the landscaping— deck, concrete patio, bushes, and sod—had transformed the muddy mess that had surrounded the pool for the past eight months.

"You can't do landscaping in the winter in central New York," was the constant reply they got every time they called on the status of getting the job completed. That and, "you're next on the list."

Miraculously, by the first week in June, everything seemed to fall into place. Even the weather cooperated with a stretch of sunny days that quickly warmed the pool water to a swimable temperature. That's when Kelly asked if she could have a coed birthday sleepover pool party.

"Of course you can, pumpkin," was Dan's immediate response. "This year your birthday falls on the first Saturday of summer vacation. It'll be a great way to kick off the summer."

Sue knew better. Being a high school teacher, June, with the end of the year catch-up, final exams, and students anxiously counting down the final days of the school year, was always the worst month for her to try to plan anything outside the classroom. That's exactly why she was standing there now, staring at her husband, one hour before the party was supposed to start, wondering what it was she was forgetting.

"Gas," she suddenly blurted out.

"What?"

"Gas. You need to fill the gas grill tank." Sue had thought about the tank needing filling during the previous evening, as she sat around the pool with several fellow teachers, following their end of the school year happy hour celebration. "It would be just our luck that the tank would run out in the middle of cooking the burgs and dogs. Then we'd have an angry mob of teens on our hands."

"Good point." Dan disappeared from the doorway and returned a minute later with the heavy tank. "Okay. Gas grill tank. I'm outta here. See you in a little while." Dan walked out of the garage toward his car.

"Kelly . . . Kelly. Could you please come down here," Sue yelled down the hall to the upstairs bedroom.

"What Mom," Kelly's voice squeaked, as she slid across the smooth tile floor of the kitchen, stopping just behind her mother. "Wow, got enough food!"

Sue turned around and looked at Kelly. "You and your father are like two peas in a pod. Would you rather have too much food, or run out halfway through your party?"

"Mom, you're so smart," Kelly said, as she reached up and put her arms around Sue. She hugged her tightly. "Thank you for doing all this for me. It's going to be the best birthday party ever. I love you."

"I love you too honey. Happy birthday. Now, are you almost ready? The party starts in an hour."

"I just need to take a shower and wash my hair."

"Before you do that, do me a big favor and straighten out the furniture around the pool. Also, pick up anything that we might have left there last night."

"You guys were getting a little rowdy last night, weren't you?" Kelly asked. "You all act so different when you are out of the classroom, almost like real people!"

"Well, thanks a lot," Sue shot back.

"Woops . . . I think I'll just go and clean up the mess you made last night," Kelly yelled, as she ran out the family room sliding glass door, onto the new concrete patio.

Startled, Sue looked up at the clock hanging on the kitchen wall as she turned to see who was knocking on the garage screen door.

"Hi Mrs. Lockwood," the girl said, as she opened the door and stepped into the kitchen. "Is Kelly here? She said I could come over early."

"Oh, hi Mandy. How are you?"

"Great, now that school is out," she blurted out, then bit her tongue, as she remembered Mrs. Lockwood was a teacher at her school.

"That makes two of us," Sue said winking. They both burst out laughing.

"Kelly is upstairs, either in her room, or in the shower."

"Thanks." Without asking, Mandy headed down the hall and up the stairs to Kelly's room.

"Mrs. Lockwood . . . Kelly's not up there," Mandy said.

"Well, maybe she's out by the pool."

Seconds later, Sue heard Mandy scream and immediately wondered what Kelly had done to scare her best friend. Hearing the second scream, this one even louder than the first, she yelled, "Girls, you're going to scare the neighbors!"

"MRS. LOCKWOOD . . . HURRY!"

Sue ran toward the family room and out the sliding glass door as Mandy, standing next to the pool, turned and collapsed onto the concrete patio, just inches from the edge of the pool.

Sue rushed to her. "Mandy, what's wrong?" She tried to push her onto her back. "Mandy . . . are you okay?"

Sue looked up at Jim. "Then something caught my eye. Between Mandy and the edge of the pool, as if painted on the concrete, was a dark red stain. I turned my head and looked at the water in the pool. It looked pink, like someone had thrown a cherry Popsicle in it. I slowly crawled over Mandy and looked over the edge of the pool. There she was. Just laying there, motionless, on the bottom. Her eyes and mouth were open. Her arms were out to her side. Her long blonde hair was the only thing that was moving.

The police said she must have slipped and hit her head on the concrete before falling into the pool. There was water in her lungs, so she was probably knocked unconscious."

They sat there, looking at each other. Jim started to speak, but Sue interrupted before he could make a sound.

"The police kept asking me over and over if I heard anything. 'Didn't you hear a splashing sound?' they kept asking. Jim, I didn't. I didn't hear anything."

"Honey, I believe you. It was an accident. A terrible accident. There was nothing you could have done."

After a long silence, Sue took a deep breath. "That's what everyone said." She again looked up at Jim. "Everyone except for Dan."

"Sue, it was an accident."

They both sat there looking down at the small table, neither knowing what to say next or even wanting to. Several minutes went by. Jim started to reach for Sue's hand, which was the prompting she needed to begin talking again.

"A child's death makes no sense. It's unnatural . . . it's wrong.

You expect to die before your child does. That's the normal order of things. A parent is supposed to be responsible for her child's life. To protect them. To keep them safe. You're not supposed to bury your own child."

After a long pause, Sue finally looked up at Jim. His head was lowered. "I couldn't keep my daughter alive. That was the most important thing I was supposed to do as a mother, and I failed at it. Now I must live every day, for the rest of my life, without her. Most of the pain has gone away . . . but the feeling of loss lasts forever."

Jim finally raised his head. Sue could see the light reflecting off the tears that had formed along his lower eye lid. She reached and held his hands.

"At first I thought Dan and I were going to get through it, even though I quickly learned that the odds were against us. Did you know that most marriages split up when a child dies . . . and if it was the only child, the odds are even greater. You don't realize how much your relationship revolves around your child, until they are gone."

Sue took a sip from her drink, then reached again for Jim's hands.

"It was as if we were suddenly strangers again. Each day we seemed to drift further and further apart, neither one of us knowing how to, and I'm not sure if we even wanted to, try to make it work. It was never going to be like it was anyway. And every marriage counselor we went to, and there were several, all seemed to agree that we would be better off apart."

Their eyes remained focused on each other. Sue started to rub Jim's hand. She sat up straighter and now spoke more confidently. "I will never get over Kelly's death, but . . . life does go on. I knew I had to make a choice between living . . . or just existing. Then, after five very long years of just existing, I finally made the choice to live. I moved out and decided to try to start my life over again. But it wasn't until today . . . until reading Dan's journals, that I realized how much he blamed me for Kelly's death. He didn't want to be married to me. He didn't want to touch me. He couldn't even stand looking at me. Yet he couldn't tell me. If I had known that then, I would have moved out sooner. After all, the death of our marriage was a small step compared to the death of our daughter."

There was a long pause before Sue spoke up again.

"Thank you for listening to me. I needed to let you know about that part of my past life."

"You know I'm always here for you," Jim finally spoke up, in a very raspy voice. He got up and walked over to Sue, put his arms around her, then kissed her gently on the lips. "Would you like another drink, or are you ready to go home?"

"Actually, I'd like another drink."

"Okay."

As he picked up the glasses and started to walk toward the bar, Sue whispered, "there's something else I need to tell you."

31

Roger reached over and grabbed the flimsy plastic cup from the night stand next to the bed. Several drops of cold water that had formed on the outside of the cup dripped onto his bare chest and mixed with the sweat from his damp body. He tilted the cup to his lips and slowly poured the cold Dewar's, now watered down by the melted ice, into his mouth. He then rested the cup on his chest, rubbing its cool wet bottom over his skin.

As he lay on the bed, his head propped up on three pillows, he glanced to the far side of the room at the air conditioning unit on the wall just below the window. The loud humming noise and the curtains above it blowing from side to side told him the unit was running, but the air in the room still felt as hot and stale smelling as it did when he walked in an hour ago.

The Brookside Motel, aptly named for the creek, actually it was more like a rock filled drainage swale, that ran alongside, was located about twenty miles north of Syracuse in a sparsely populated area between the small towns of Phoenix and Mexico.

Although clean, the rooms had seen better days. But the motel was isolated, with parking in the rear, where a car could go unnoticed, even during the daylight hours. At 11:00 p.m., his was still the only car parked in the gravel lot. He doubted there would be many more this late on a Wednesday night. When Roger asked if he could pay in cash, he knew he had found the right place when the clerk asked if he wanted the room by the hour or for the entire night.

He lifted the cup from his chest, emptied the remaining liquid into his mouth along with an ice cube, and propped himself up on the edge of the bed. As he sat there, he bit down on the ice cube, then again, and again, chewing it like a piece of noisy gum. As soon as he swallowed the slushy mixture, he tipped the glass to his mouth and sucked in the remaining ice. He got up, walked to the small round wooden table that was in the corner, dipped the cup into the plastic bucket, now only half filled with ice, then poured in more of the scotch.

Roger stood, glass in hand, and stared at himself in the cheap plastic mirror that hung above the old wooden dresser. He knew he had no one to blame but himself for letting what he had planned for the evening slip away. It wasn't until he had checked into the motel room earlier that he realized the light in the apartment was probably one set to go on automatically at dusk. It was also probably set to turn off somewhere around midnight, which would still make it possible for him to gain entry through the sliding glass door. Unfortunately, with the drinks he had consumed during the drive up earlier today, and the several he had downed at the town bar down the road, where he stopped to ask for directions to the motel, he knew he was in no shape to retrace his steps and make the forced entry tonight. Besides, he was also exhausted from his late night with Myra.

Roger turned and looked around the room. "What a dump," he said aloud. He then laughed to himself when he realized he still had his suite at the Taj Mahal.

Although he had screwed up this evening, he already had a new plan for tomorrow. He held his drink up and toasted.

32

"No . . . you've talked enough for tonight. Now it's my turn,"
Jim interrupted Sue, as she started to speak even before he had a
chance to put the round of drinks on the table.

"But Jim."

"No . . . it's my turn. You take a rest. Let me say what I have to
say and then you can go again. It's only eleven fifteen and you're
not doing anything tomorrow. You can sleep in."

Sue sat at the table, silent, with her head down. She had learned
over the past two years that when Jim had something on his mind,
it was better to let him go, otherwise he wouldn't absorb anything
you had to say.

"Sue, the first time I laid eyes on you, I was hooked. Something
about you . . . I still can't put my finger on it. Then, when we really got to know each other, I mean intimately . . . well, that was it.
Although, I gotta say, you had me a little worried there when you
played so hard to get in the beginning. I couldn't believe how
much you teased me and egged me on."

"It was worth it in the end, wasn't it?" Sue finally spoke up, after sipping provocatively from her glass.

"Well . . . yeah!"

"Then, what's your point?" It was an expression Sue often used when she was in a cocky, confident about herself, mood.

"The point is . . . well, the point is, the past two years living with you have been great. The best of my life. I think about you all the time. When I'm away from you, I yearn for you. When I'm with you, I can't keep my hands off of you."

"And what, you don't think I feel the same way?"

"No . . . I do. That's not it." Jim looked at Sue for a few seconds, then took a drink from his glass.

"We're both fifty years old. We've both got twenty plus years worth of memories of a past life, spent with someone else, that had both great and not so great times associated with it. But the past is the past. We can be happy about it. We can be sad. We can regret it. We can be sorry. We can try to forget it. But the one thing we can't do is change it."

"Are you supposed to be trying to cheer me up?"

"Actually, yes . . . and I'm getting there." Jim gulped down another mouthful of his drink. "Thank you for sharing some of your past life with me tonight. I know it was hard for you to talk about it. It's impossible for me to know the pain that you've gone through. I couldn't even imagine what it would be like if I lost . . . if I lost Trip. And even if I could imagine it, well, it still wouldn't be the same because imagining it still doesn't make it real.

"We are never going to be able to share everything with each other about our past lives. Memories are going to come up each and every day for the rest of our lives. Some we will want to share with each other, but most we probably will want to just forget. The point is . . . I don't think it matters. I know you pretty well, Sue Lockwood. Sure, I'd like to know more about your past, and I'd like you to know more about my past. But that will come with time. I'm sure of it. I guess what I'm trying to say is, I know enough about you to start asking myself . . . well . . . where is our relationship going? I mean, where do you see us a year from now? Three years? Ten years? Hell, thirty years?"

"James Calihan," Sue sat up straight, then leaned over the table and whispered to Jim, "are you proposing?"

"No . . . is that what it sounded like I was doing? No, no, no."

"Well, I would hope not!"

"What? What-da-ya mean?"

"First of all, I'm not asking you to propose, but, hypothetically."

"Yes, hypothetically," Jim interrupted.

"Hypothetically, if you were to propose, knowing what I know about you, you wouldn't do it in a bar. No, not you. It would most likely be in some gorgeously romantic place, with everything, including the sun, moon, and stars all aligned perfectly."

After a long pause, Jim finally spoke up. "Well yeah, of course . . . what's your point!"

"Exactly." They both laughed.

"I guess we know a lot more about each other than I thought. But you still didn't answer my question!"

"What?"

"Where do you see us a year from now . . . where do you see our relationship going?" Jim was acting noticeably more serious.

There was a long pause in the conversation. Jim wanted to know what Sue's thoughts and feelings were on this issue. He knew the silence would eventually become too unbearable. Someone would have to speak up, and he was determined that it wouldn't be him.

"To be honest, I don't really know where we will be next week, let alone next year. I just don't know . . . right now, especially with all that has happened in the past week, I'm . . . I'm quite frankly having a difficult time getting through today."

Sue sipped her drink. Jim could tell she wanted to say more, so he waited patiently.

"My daughter died ten years ago . . . and my life was changed forever. Then, five years ago, I found myself divorced and going through another life changing event." She looked up at Jim. "Two years ago . . . I met you. Another, I hope, no wait, I know, life changing event. But this time, a beautiful one. Then . . . just when things seem to be falling into place for me, for us, my past comes back to haunt me.

"I haven't seen the man in years. He's dead for God sake. Yet, look at me." Sue held her hands out. They were shaking. "I'm a wreck. Reading those journals, it's like traveling back in time . . . and experiencing the pain of it all over again. I don't know if I can do it all over again."

"Honey, no one says you have to read those things. Tell ya what. Next week, when I'm done with my training, I'll go through them. If I can't find the answer to where the money came from, we'll call the FBI again. Lay all the facts out to them and see what advice they have. Okay?"

Sue just sat there, staring at her drink. Jim wondered if she even heard what he had just said.

"Does that sound like a plan to you . . . Sue?" Jim reached over and touched Sue's hand. She jumped, then looked up at Jim with a blank stare on her face.

"Does that sound good to you?" Jim said again.

"Jim," Sue took a deep breath, "there is something else I need to tell you about my past."

"Why won't you answer any of my questions tonight!"

Sue just looked at Jim.

"Okay . . . let me try again. Stop reading those damned journals. I'll go through them next week. Then we'll figure out where to go from there. Is that okay with you?"

After a long pause, all the while their eyes locked on each other, Sue finally responded, "No."

"No . . . why not? Sue, don't you see what these things are doing to you"

"Yes . . . yes I do. But maybe this is something I need to . . . I need to read the words that he wrote. Know what he was thinking. Maybe I can find the answers to questions I still have. Answers that will help my pain."

They both sat there in silence.

"I have to do this, Jim. I'm not going to spend the rest of my life wondering about the words in the journals, no matter how painful they may be to me."

Sue finished the rest of her now watered down drink.

"Would you like another?"

"In a minute. I need to tell you . . . "

"Sue, did you hear what I said earlier? It doesn't matter to me what you did in the past. Nothing you could have done will change how I feel about you now."

"Remember."

"Sue!"

"Remember last Friday. That woman Nikki. At the bar. When I bought my townhouse, I rented a room to her."

"Yeah, so what!"

"No, I don't think you understand . . . we ended up living together for a while."

33

Sue jumped when she heard the low pitched chime of the doorbell. She glanced at her watch, instinctively got up from the dining room table, and walked to the door. The doorbell chimed again. Reaching for the door handle, she saw it turn slightly, first counterclockwise, then clockwise. She froze.

Leaning forward, she placed her eye against the peep hole in the door. She jumped to the side when she saw another eye staring back at her. She looked again. This time there was a man dressed in a dark suit, white shirt, and solid blue tie, standing in front of the door. His jet black hair was combed straight back, held in place with an over abundance of styling gel. The thick rimmed glasses he was wearing were slightly tinted, hiding the true color of his eyes. He was holding a briefcase in his left hand. As he leaned forward, she quickly moved to the side. The doorbell chimed again.

She reached up, unlocked the two dead bolts, turned the door knob, and pulled the door toward her.

"Good morning. Is Dr. Lockwood in?"

"No he isn't . . . he."

"Do you know when you might expect him back?"

Sue hesitated at first, not knowing if she should confide any-thing to a total stranger, then, upon deciding to answer, did not know what to say.

Before she could speak, the man stepped forward and extended his right hand. "How rude of me. My name is Richard Williams . . . Dr. Richard Williams. Dr. Lockwood has been doing some consulting work for us. I happened to be in town, and I thought I'd stop by to see what kind of progress he was making. I'm sorry I didn't catch your name."

"Susan Lockwood," Sue naturally responded, then suddenly realized she was shaking hands with the stranger in front of her.

"Mrs. Lockwood?" the man responded with a curious look on his face. "I'm sorry . . . I thought Dan, I mean Dr. Lockwood, was divorced."

"He was. We are. I mean he is divorced." Sue's apprehension suddenly disappeared when she realized whoever this person was, he had obviously been close enough with her ex-husband to know something about his personal life.

"Well . . . is, a, when Dr. Lockwood gets back, could you please tell him Dr. Williams stopped by and that I will call him in the morning." The man was already turning away to leave even before he finished his sentence. He turned his head back toward Sue. "It was nice to meet you."

"No, wait!" Sue finally blurted out, still in shock over meeting someone from Dan's recent past.

The man stopped and turned around. Though he had a surprised, questioning look on his face, he was smiling to himself, confident Sue was not going to let him just walk away.

When Roger had blown his opportunity to break into the apartment the night before, he realized it had been a week since the plane crash. Surely by now, someone had gained access to Lockwood's apartment. Too anxious to wait until evening before attempting another break in, he decided to use the daylight hours to try to determine if anyone had been in the apartment and, although he thought it remote, if someone else was living there. The latter would certainly complicate any future attempts by him to gain access.

Earlier this morning, Roger had called Fred Nass, the Facilities Manager for Lockwood's apartment complex. With Jack Nelson's detailed interview notes, documented in the FBI report compiled after the crash, it was not difficult for Roger to masquerade as Nelson's assistant. He purported to be following up to see if Nass had contacted Mrs. Lockwood. Initially, Nass thought it odd that the FBI would follow up on such a minor issue, but finally concluded that in this post-911 environment, no government agency would want to be accused of not dotting all the I's and crossing all the T's, especially when it came to a potential terrorist issue.

Nass told Roger everything he wanted to know and more. He had contacted Lockwood's ex-wife, she had been to the apartment several times this week and, in fact, he had met her. Nass even volunteered that Mrs. Lockwood had put timers on the lights to make it look like the place was still occupied.

"Son of a bitch," were the first words out of Roger's mouth when he hung up with Nass. "She knows. She fuck'n knows!"

came next.

Roger quickly concluded he needed to meet with Susan Lockwood. Somehow he had to find out what she knew about the terrorist plot, and, more importantly, did she know about the money, the latter being the more important issue.

His plan was bold and risky. In fact, it bordered on being foolish. But Roger reasoned the more preposterous the plan, the more likely it was to succeed. He would go to Sue Lockwood's house, introduce himself as an agent working for the Department of Homeland Security and interview her, much the same as Jack Nelson had done. This follow-up interview, he would tell her, was part of a project to improve the fact gathering following an incident such as this. He had a copy of Nelson's report, with everything she had told him. How more convincing could he be? From that interview, somehow, he would find out what she knew about her ex-husband's activities.

Anticipating that his visit to Syracuse might eventually entail a face-to-face meeting, he had come prepared with an alias of his own. The reflection that stared back at him from the mirror this morning would be remembered, first and foremost, as a middle aged geek.

His plan vaporized before his very eyes though, when, upon pulling up to the Cadys Arbor address, he saw a woman backing out of the driveway in a silver Blazer. Noting a cul-de-sac ahead, he decided to loop around and follow the Blazer. Though unfamiliar with the area, within minutes, he determined that the car was headed in the direction of Lockwood's apartment.

He needed a new plan.

"You knew Dan?" Sue blurted out excitingly.

"Knew? What do you mean knew?" Roger responded, playing his part like a veteran Hollywood actor.

"Dan was killed in the plane that crashed in Syracuse last week."

"Oh my God. You're kidding. I'm sorry . . . that explains it then."

"Explains what?"

"Well, for the past week, I've been trying to contact Dr. Lockwood by e-mail. That's usually the best way to get in touch with him. He rarely takes more than a day to get back to me. Anyway, I hadn't heard from him, and since I was in Syracuse today, I thought I'd just pay him a visit." Roger put his briefcase down, and even though he rarely perspired, grabbed a handkerchief from his pocket, removed his glasses, and pretended to wipe his forehead. "I'm sorry, could I trouble you for a glass of water." God I'm good, Roger thought to himself, as he followed Sue into the apartment.

Once inside, Roger asked to use the bathroom, which provided him the perfect opportunity to look over the apartment. He could immediately tell that it had been thoroughly searched. Nothing was where you would normally expect it to be. Books were stacked on the floor, clothes were lying on the bed, papers were piled on the dining room table. He wondered what Susan Lockwood had found.

"I had always thought Dr. Lockwood was a little eccentric, but, is this the way he lived?" Roger said, as he stood in the living room and gazed at the clutter.

Sue quickly turned around. She had been standing in the kitchen with her back to the living room and had not heard him come out of the bathroom.

"No, no," Sue finally spoke up. Over the past few days, in her

158

attempt to both try to uncover the source of the money and gather those items she intended to take with her, she had made a complete mess of the apartment. "I've been going through the apartment to . . . " Sue hesitated, but immediately regrouped. "Even though we were divorced, Dan still left me everything in his will. I've been trying to figure out what things I want to keep. You know . . . sentimental things." She pointed to the corner of the living room. "As you can see, it's not much."

"Well, I don't want to take up any more of your time," Roger said teasingly, again knowing Sue would not let him leave so easily.

"No, wait," Sue anxiously jumped in. "Can I ask what it was Dan was working on for you?"

Roger went on to explain the project Dan was working on for the Department of Homeland Security, making it up as he went along. He told her the project was called Papertrail. Its primary purpose was to field test the prototype surveillance software being developed for the Patriot Act. For security reasons, he wasn't able to go into a lot of detail about it, although he did say Dan was one of several hundred independent contractors scattered across the country to help with the effort. He used a lot of computer jargon, hoping that it would deter further questions from her. It did, except for one.

"Can I ask you how much compensation Dan had received?"

Although showing no outward emotion, Roger's blood pressure shot up when he heard these words. The bitch obviously knows something about the cash, he thought.

"Actually, the contractors have only been on board for about three months, and you know how slow the government is in paying their bills. We just got all the paperwork straightened out, so the first checks won't go out until the end of the month. It's for the first two months of part-time effort, so it's a ten thousand dollar check. We are anticipating a twelve to eighteen month time frame to complete the current project scope. But there could be some more follow-on work." Roger knew he was making up more than he was going to be able to remember, but he doubted he would need to repeat it to anyone again.

"Obviously, the government will pay Dan, or his estate, for all services he provided up until the time of his death." Although Roger had only met Sue fifteen minutes ago, he could tell she had a disappointed look about her. "This was only a part-time effort on Dr. Lockwood's part. He wasn't going to get rich off of it. Sorry . . . you look disappointed."

"No, it's just that." Sue hesitated, then looked up at Roger. "I'm glad Dan was doing something useful with his life."

Roger knew Sue was hiding something. Something to do with the money, no doubt.

"Well, I really do have to be going," Roger said, as he picked up his briefcase. "Most of the work Dan was doing was by remote computer access, but I don't suppose you came across any paper files he might have kept on the project. I really should take those with me."

For some reason, those words sent a chill through Sue's body. Except for the remaining journals she had planned to read later this afternoon, she had been through every square foot of the apartment and had not recalled any paperwork associated with a project called Papertrail. Of that she was certain.

Sensing Sue's uneasiness, Roger started for the door. "Well, if you should come across anything, please give me a call." He handed her an official looking business card, one he had printed himself, with a telephone number that led to a spare DOD phone line, one with a voice mail for a non-existent Dr. Williams. "Also, what's the best way to get a hold of you should I need to?"

Sue went into the kitchen and wrote down her name, address, phone number, and email address for him.

On a hunch, Roger asked one more question as he walked out the door. "If I need to get a hold of you over the weekend, is this where you will be?" holding up the piece of paper.

As he left the alcove of the apartment, Roger smiled to himself. He removed his heavy glasses, which were already starting to give him a headache, and reached in his right coat pocket for his sun glasses. Before putting them on, he glanced to his left at the sliding glass door.

34

"That'll get him hot." Sue heard the voice whispering from behind her, as she held up the hanger with the three tiny triangular pieces of black, silky fabric and string dangling from it. She hesitantly turned, hoping whoever it was spying on her was a total stranger. She didn't want to have to explain why she was in a store like this.

Fantasy Fashions was a small boutique that specialized in intimate clothing for the discriminating woman. Except for the men that swarmed the place during holidays, like Christmas and Valentines Day, most of the customers were suburban housewives looking for a special outfit to help spice up a boring love life. From leather to lace, wigs to spiked platform shoes, if you couldn't find it here, they probably didn't make it. And if you did find it, it was usually something you didn't want a friend, no matter how close, to know you owned.

The store also specialized in bathing suits. Sexy ones. The kind whose price went up as the amount of cloth needed to make them went down.

"Hi." Sue's face lit up, relieved to see who it was standing behind her.

"I go from not seeing you for years at a time, to twice in one week. Maybe it's an omen," Nikki said, as she reached out and hugged Sue.

"So . . . you think this'll do the trick?" Sue held up the hanger again.

"It is a bathing suit, right?" Nikki reached up and held one of the tiny black triangles between her fingers. "Come on. Lets go try it on. Then I can give you an honest opinion."

Both women walked to the rear of the store and into a small room, covered totally with mirrors on three walls. Nikki closed the door then sank into the thickly cushioned, high backed, black velvet chair. As she removed the flimsy cloth from the hanger, Sue turned away and lifted her white tank top over her head. Nikki looked up at Sue and held out the bikini top.

"Here." Sue reached behind and Nikki placed the top in her hand. "I hope you're not mad at me for the other day."

"No . . . why would I be mad at you," Sue responded, as she tied the string around her chest, inches below her breasts.

"Well . . . first of all, most women would be a little upset if they were asked by another woman to go to bed with them. And secondly, in the past you never would have turned your back to me to try on a bathing suit."

Sue froze, then slowly turned around and faced Nikki, as if under some spell to do so, and stood with her arms to her side. She could feel Nikki's hot stare roaming over her body. She reached up to adjust the strings again. "You're right . . . I shouldn't have turned away. I'm sorry if I hurt your feelings. And as far as the other day, regardless of what we shared in the past, I know it was the alcohol and emotions talking . . . right?" Nikki forced a reluctant nod. "I'm just glad you were there for me, and . . . I hope you're not mad at me for letting it go as far as it did before I said stop."

"No, of course not." Again, Nikki forced out her response, only because she knew it was what Sue wanted to hear.

"How does this look?" Sue turned around, her head moving from mirror to mirror, eyeing herself at the varying angles.

"Like I said . . . that'll get him hot."

"I agree," Sue said, as she gave herself one more look-over in the mirror. She then turned to Nikki. "Are you hungry? I'm starving. How about lunch?" Sue reached behind her neck, untied the string and let the black triangles drop, exposing her breasts.

"Sounds good." Nikki's eyes again drifted down Sue's body.

"Great. I can tell you about my latest discoveries."

"I just saw you three days ago. What more could have happened to you?"

"Three days . . . seems like its been weeks."

"You seem like you're in a better mood than you were on Monday."

"I am. I took your advice and I told Jim everything."

"Everything?"

"Well . . . I didn't go into details about, you know, us. But I did tell him."

"And how did he take it?"

"He's fine."

Those were not the words Nikki had hoped for.

As she followed Sue to the restaurant, Nikki was glad they had driven separately. It gave her a chance to vent the rage boiling up inside of her. Monday's failed seduction had left her angry and jealous. She initially viewed today's encounter as a second chance, but now realized that it too, like Monday's, would not go where she wanted it to. As Sue turned into the crowded restaurant parking lot, Nikki almost didn't follow. Almost.

Nikki listened politely as Sue summarized the events of the past three days. Her caring and concerned demeanor secretly applauded every rotten experience Sue had encountered. As Sue discussed the morning's adventures, Nikki, who never balanced a checkbook without a calculator, was busy trying to mentally add up the cash figures whispered over lunch.

"This was great. Thanks again for being here," Sue said, as she reached across the table for Nikki's hand.

"Anytime, Sue. I told you. I'll always be here for you."

As Sue disappeared to the ladies room, Nikki sat, eyes locked on the seat across from her. Then she saw the black purse. It took her all of ten seconds to decide to reach over, grab the purse and place it on the table in front of her. She lifted the soft leather flap and slipped her hand into the front pocket until her fingers found what she was looking for. It took a minute for her to finally feel her heart rate start to slow.

35

"Come with me and sit down," were the first words Jim heard when he walked in the door.

"What . . . no kiss?" he responded, as Sue grabbed his hand and led him to the couch in the living room.

Before they sat down, she turned and gave Jim a quick peck on the lips.

"Big deal. Can I at least get something to . . . " Before he could finish, Sue pointed to the tall glass on the coffee table in front of him.

"Now that's more like my little woman." He brought the glass to his lips, and just before he took a sip, he asked, "is it a Nice-Tea?'"

A Nice-Tea was Jim's favorite summer drink, as well it should be, since he came up with the sweet tasting mixture. Similar to a Long Island Iced Tea, it had the same liquors, rum, gin, tequila, and vodka, but instead of coke, there was a concoction of fresh brewed tea, the contents from half a squeezed lemon, a lemon slice, and three heaping teaspoons of sugar, all mixed in a tall glass filled with ice.

"Nice."

"Perfect," Jim said, after he took a long sip from the glass. "So, what's up?"

Sue sat there staring at him.

"No, please. No more true confessions. I love you, but last night's conversation had enough emotional content to last me for weeks. You women forget that men can't take as much emotion as you can. We're not built like you are."

"And, I'm glad of that!"

Without missing a beat, Jim continued. "Plus, we didn't get much sleep and I've just sat through eight hours of classroom training, trying hard not to stare out the window and daydream about being at the lake on this almost, and I say almost because I couldn't experience it first hand, perfect summer day."

The previous night's discussions had been liberating for Sue. By the end of the evening she felt as if a heavy burden had been lifted from her shoulders. For a long time she had wanted to confide her innermost secrets to Jim, but each time she tried, the ensuing pain would overtake her. She knew though, that unless she was completely open with him about her past, it would become more and more difficult to move into a future together. The events of the past week had been the catalyst she needed to get beyond the pain. To finally clear the air. She had felt more at peace with herself than she had in months and even more committed than ever to her relationship with Jim.

Although it had been important for Sue to finally get her past out in the open, she understood the potential impacts it could have on her relationship with Jim, especially her last confession about Nikki. She knew he had more to ask her about it, and eventually she would confide it all to him, but, for now, she wanted to make sure her emotional upswing was not at Jim's expense.

Once home, she had made it very clear by her actions, how she felt about him as her partner and lover. It was well after two before they had fallen asleep in each other's arms, physically and emotionally exhausted, but very content.

As Jim took another sip of his drink, he finally noticed that the coffee table and a good portion of the couch and floor on the other side of Sue was covered with papers, shoe boxes, and journals. He looked up at Sue who was still sitting there silent.

"You found out where the money came from . . . was it legal? Are you just gonna sit there with that shit-eating-grin on your face, or are you gonna tell me what you found?"

"Dan was working for the government."

"What!"

Sue told Jim about the visit she had from Dr. Williams earlier in the day. She repeated every detail of the morning's encounter, as if it had been permanently etched in her brain.

"But Sue, if all that is true, it still doesn't explain the money."

"I know."

"And how come we didn't find one piece of paper that even hinted that he had a job, let alone one working for the government. As a minimum, there'd be a signed contract or a purchase order. You know the government . . . paper, paper, paper."

"I know, I know. The only explanation I can think of is, Dan must have had a portable PC and had it with him on the plane. Dr. Williams mentioned this morning that the work Dan was doing was all on the computer. He even said he doubted that there was any paper, but if I did find any, that I was to let him know."

"What about the journals. Did you find anything about it in what you read today?"

"Well, not exactly."

"I'm listening."

"There's a reference to something Dan is working on that shows up in his journals in April of this year. That would be consistent with what Williams told me about the project starting three months ago. There is no mention of it being a government project, or getting paid to do consulting, or anything like that."

"Maybe because it was classified, he wasn't allowed to write about it."

"Could be, but unless he's using some kind of code, the plan he writes about in the journal doesn't seem to have anything to do with homeland security. Almost daily, from April on, he makes reference to the plan. The plan is on schedule. Everything is going according to the plan. I don't get the feeling it's a government project he's talking about."

"What then?"

"I don't know, but I came across something else that was strange. Look at this." Sue picked up one of the journals that was lying open and faced down on the coffee table. "He made an entry that he was going away for a few days to Lake George. The next entry is dated three days later. But look." She bent the book wide open. "Pages have been torn out of the book. Whatever happened, he later decided he didn't want anyone to read about it."

"Strange," Jim said, as he looked closely at the torn edge of the pages. "What was the date of that entry?"

"August ninth, from two years ago."

Jim looked up at Sue. "Just after that . . . "

"He started paying cash for everything," Sue interrupted. "That's not all. Up until this point, all of his journal entries revolve around things in his life. The death of Kelly, how much he missed her, how much he despised me, the divorce, how he couldn't get up in front of a classroom any more. He would write at least a half a dozen pages, sometimes much more, every day, without fail. Then, after the August trip to Lake George, his daily entries were only a page or two. He even skips some days. And most of what he wrote was about the weather for the day and how much he missed Kelly. It was as if something else was now on his mind."

"Maybe that's when he finally hit the brick wall and totally lost it."

"You could be right, but . . . I think there was something else."

"I'm still listening."

"I think . . . I think he was keeping track of whatever else he was doing someplace else."

"You mean in another journal or something?" Jim saw Sue shaking her head up and down. "Come on. I mean, I think you've done a great job trying to unravel what is going on here, but I also think you're getting a little carried away with this Sue. Where are these missing journals?"

There was a long pause during which neither of them spoke or even dared to look at the other.

"You never asked me why I went over to Dan's apartment earlier today."

Jim looked at her inquisitively. "Okay, you've got my attention again, Sherlock. You were going to lay around all day again today and finish reading these things," he said, pointing to one of the journals on the table. "So, what happened?"

"I started reading right after you left this morning. Does the name K. C. Drummins sound familiar to you?"

"No . . . should it?"

"Remember Dan's canceled checks."

All of a sudden Jim's eyes grew wide. "The thousand dollar check. Who is he?"

Sue told him how she had come across the name in one of the journals. It was an innocent enough entry—Called Drummins again today, everything is finalized.—written on April 24th. She almost went right by it. Then, she remembered the envelope Dan had received from Canada with the return address of K. C. Drummins. With everything else that happened last evening, she had forgotten about the letter.

"I showered and raced over to the apartment. I was certain this had something to do with the money. I sat down at the dining room table and stared at the letter, almost afraid to open it. As I picked it up from the table, I noticed my hands were shaking. Then . . . the doorbell rang. You should've seen me jump. It was the Williams guy.

"After he left, I almost forgot about the letter again." Sue sat there, reflecting upon the discussion with Williams earlier in the day.

"Well . . . what was in the letter?"

Sue reached for the envelope on the table and removed the letter. "For the past two years Dan has been renting a cottage on Loon Island in the Canadian waters of the Thousand Islands, from K. C. Drummins. The letter indicates receipt of the thousand dollar check, with the remaining payments to be made the same as last year."

"By cash," they both said aloud.

Sue again reached down to the coffee table, picked something up in her hand, and held it in her closed fist. "This now makes sense to me." She held her fist out, palm down, and Jim placed his open hand below it. "I found it on the key rack in the apartment," she said, as she opened her hand, letting the object fall into Jim's.

Jim picked the key chain up with his other hand and held it in front of him. The large silver ring had three different shaped keys and a tag that had 'LIC' written on it.

"LIC?"

"Loon Island Cottage," Sue whispered.

36

"I think I'd like to order an appetizer too."

"Okay, what can I get ya?"

"How about . . . a half pound of drunken spicy shameless shrimp."

"You got it."

Jim stared at the waitress as she walked away.

"She'd kill you," Sue whispered to him as she leaned over the small table.

"No kidding."

"No . . . I mean she'd KILL you."

"I know! I agree. That's exactly what I was thinking as I watched her walk away."

The Dinosaur Bar-B-Q Restaurant was opened years ago by a couple of hard-core Harley bikers. Located in downtown Syracuse, the Cajun style barbecue food and atmosphere catered to the biker crowd. On a summer night, such as this, there were always dozens of bikes, lined up like dominos, in front of the place. If one of them ever fell, they'd all topple over.

The reputation for great food and the unique atmosphere of the place quickly spread, which eventually attracted a more diverse clientele. Now, it wasn't uncommon to see leather-clad bikers vying for a spot at the bar with suited businessmen, college kids and aging baby boomers standing around, drinks in hand, waiting for a table, and a young family, kids taking in the sights, seated at a booth eating dinner.

The atmosphere was rough, and that included the bartenders and waitresses. You wouldn't want to mess with one of these tight-jeaned, tank-topped, tattooed-bodied biker babes. They'd kill you.

But that was all part of the ambiance, and why the place was always crowded.

Jim and Sue had waited an hour before being seated at one of the small, square, well used, wooden tables that lined the isle directly in front of the bar. Although they were both famished, dinner was not their primary motive for being there on this partic-ular night. At 10:00 p.m., The Joe Whiting Band was scheduled to play. Whiting, a local musician, had played his unique combina-tion of oldies, jazz and blues sounds throughout central New York for over thirty years. For Sue and Jim, it was the band they had lis-tened and danced to on their first date, over two years ago.

"Thank you for being there last night for me."

"I have to tell you, Sue, you look like a totally different person tonight. I guess there is something to be said about confessions and cleansing the soul."

"I feel like a different person. I feel, I don't know, free."

"Well, whatever it is, it's becoming on you."

"Here ya go," the waitress said, as she placed their drinks and the plate of shrimp, covered with garlic Cajun sauce, the kind that makes your mouth water even before you taste it, on the table. "Enjoy."

"So, do you think we will be able to find Loon Island with the boat?" Sue said, after washing down her first spicy hot shrimp with the ice cold Absolut and orange.

"It's gotta be on the chart, and I have all the charts for the St. Lawrence River at the boat. It shouldn't be that difficult."

"When do you think we can go?" Sue finally got up the nerve to ask, her voice sounding anxious.

Jim looked up at her as he devoured another shrimp. He licked the sauce off his fingers, then grabbed his napkin. "Are you thinking you want to go there this weekend?"

"Well?"

Jim sat there, his mind obviously racing.

"With my classes on Friday and Monday, we only have the weekend. If the lake and weather cooperated, which it is supposed to, we could easily make it there in a day. But, we'd almost have to turn right around and come back." Jim took a sip from his glass. "Sue, I'm just as anxious as you are to find out what's at that cottage, but it's probably going to have to wait until after the fourth. We were planning to be up in the Kingston area then anyway."

"I suppose you're right. It's just that . . . I don't know. I'm beginning to feel uncomfortable about this whole thing. I mean, trying to handle this all ourselves."

"What do you mean?"

"Well . . . Dan's death, the money, the journals, the cottage, the FBI, now the Department of Homeland Security."

"Sue, it's your call, but I've been giving this a lot of thought, and I have a suggestion. Maybe you should call the FBI again. I

175

mean, if you feel that uncomfortable. Give them everything you've found. The money, the journals, everything. Let them try to sort it out."

Sue looked at Jim. "Wow, talk about great minds. Ever since that guy left the apartment this morning and I found out about the cottage, I started to think the same thing. I sincerely doubt it, but what if Dan was involved in some kind of trouble. The last thing I want is to be dragged into it. I just wish I could get to that cottage, find a logical explanation for the money, go to Steve Haggas, have him wave his magic legal wand and be done with it all. Dragging it on another week kinda bums me out."

"I know it does. It does me too. I'd still like to be able to get away on the boat for at least four to five weeks this summer. We had planned a trip up the Rideau Canal again this year, remember? If you don't get this straightened out by the fourth, we might not be able to do that."

"I thought about that today too, and I'm not going to let my ex-husband ruin our summer. He's dead. Whatever issues there are that need to be closed out, as far as I'm concerned, can wait until the fall. I plan to call Steve Haggas on Monday and tell him that."

"Sue . . . I know you better than that. You just said you were bummed to be dragging it out another week. There is no way you are going to let this hang out there until the fall. You'd be antsy all summer. Am I right?"

"Well, maybe."

"Well maybe nothing. You know I'm right. Maybe there's a way we can get this cleared up in a week or so and still have most of the summer to ourselves."

"Actually, I'm working on a plan to do just that."

"Sorry that took so long. Lets see, you had the Pig salad and you had the Cajun chicken salad. Can I get you another refill?"

"I'm ready."

"Me too."

"You got it."

37

"It's like we're on a . . . a deserted island somewhere in the Caribbean. I've lived in central New York all my life and never knew this place existed. What did you call it again?"

"The Bahamas-of-the-North."

As they walked along the beach, the soft, dry, white sand, still hot from the day's sun, filled in the spaces between their toes. Every few minutes, they would veer off to the left to let the bottoms of their feet cool in the wave-wetted sand.

"Stop . . . listen."

The only sound that could be heard was the gurgling of a small wave that appeared from nowhere in the now calm lake, as it gently rolled up onto the sandy beach. They stood there, looking into each other's eyes. Slowly their bodies drifted toward one another, and they embraced in a soft sensuous kiss. Suddenly, they both jumped as the tranquil moment was broken by two seagulls, less than a hundred feet down the beach, squawking over a newly found dead fish.

"It's everything you said it would be. No wonder you like it here so much. Thank you for bringing me." They hugged again.

"The sun is getting lower in the sky, so we better head back to the boat. On evenings like this, Dad likes to time dinner around watching the sun set."

"Now I know where you get your charm from."

Trip put his arm on Brandi's shoulder and they started walking out into the lake toward the Obsession, which was anchored in four feet of water near a sandbar, about a hundred yards from shore.

As planned, they had pulled away from the harbor slip just before five. The weather forecast called for more of what they had been experiencing over the past week—bright, sunny, cloudless skies, higher than normal daytime temperatures, well into the upper eighties, even near the lake, and light and variable winds. That later item was what Jim had been most hoping for.

The Bahamas-of-the-North, so nicknamed by Jim years ago, was a twenty mile stretch of sand dune laden beach, along the eastern shore of Lake Ontario. Jim called it one of the best kept secrets on the lake. Although dotted with private camps and home to Southwick Beach State Park, there were vast portions of the shoreline that were forever destined to be undeveloped. It was along those areas where Jim preferred to moor the Obsession. There were certain coves where, once anchored, you felt as if you were hundreds of miles from everywhere.

The only potential spoiler to this paradise was the wind and resulting waves. Winds from the west, blowing along the entire two hundred mile length of the lake, ended up crashing along this shore line. That wave action over the eons had been responsible for creating the miles of fine sand beaches. But a sudden surge of eight-to ten-foot white-capped waves would not only ruin a peaceful night's sleep, but worse, could easily break loose the most securely anchored boat and heave it onto the beach.

Although Jim had feared that the unusually warm weather of the past week and the Lake Ontario water, still cool from the winter melt-off, would combine to create a fury of wind driven waves, by late afternoon, what minor daytime waves there were had dissipated, and the lake was now dead-calm. The marine weather forecast called for it to stay that way through the weekend.

It had taken less than two hours to make the thirty-mile journey from Henderson Harbor to the small, dune lined, half moon shaped bay they were anchored in, which was halfway between Stony Point and Drowned Island. With calm weather and clear skies, the cruise had been relaxing and uneventful. Trip, who normally shared the captain seat with Jim, decided to pilot the entire way, with Brandi by his side. This gave Sue and Jim the opportunity to relax on the aft deck lounge chair. The warm sun, swirling air, and low muffled rumble of the twin diesels, along with the emotional events of the past week, quickly lulled both into a much needed respite.

"Why is there smoke coming from the back of your boat?"

Trip looked up, but had to squint his eyes, as the sun, both hovering above the boat and reflecting off the water in front of him, was too strong even for his polarized Oakley Halfwires. Blinking several times, he finally was able to make out the rear deck of the boat and the trail of smoke that rose straight up, disappearing high into the sky.

"That's my Dad cooking on the grill. My guess is there's a batch of barbecue shrimp ready to come off and lobster shish kebabs ready to take their place. Hungry is something you won't experience on the Obsession."

"Hi guys . . . how was your walk?" Jim yelled, leaning over the side of the boat, as Brandi and Trip climbed up the ladder onto the teak swim platform and stood next to the Sea Doo that was resting there. "Here, catch," he continued, as he dropped two colorful beach towels down to them.

"Thanks Dad . . . it was great. The sand was hot, the water was cool, and not a soul in sight."

"What did you think Brandi?"

"I think Bahamas-of-the-North says it all."

Brandi and Trip dried themselves off, then climbed up the steep steps along the aft of the boat to the deck area where Jim was cooking. "The shrimp is almost done. Why don't you guys go down and get something to drink, then we can start on these."

"Anybody want more salt potatoes or corn on the cob?"

"Are you kidding . . . I couldn't eat another bite."

"Dad . . . you outdid yourself again."

"Brandi?"

"No thank you Mr. Cal . . . I mean Jim." Upon meeting only hours ago, Jim had insisted on her calling both him and Sue by their first names.

In no time the dinner dishes were cleared, the table was stowed, and the four of them were seated on the aft deck, with two conversations going simultaneously, guy to guy, and gal to gal.

Suddenly Trip spoke up. "Wait . . . quiet. Listen. Do you hear it? Sssssssss."

Jim, whose back was to the west, quickly turned to catch the bottom edge of the sun as it touched the far end of the lake. For as long as Trip could remember, sunsets were something his father never seemed to get tired of. "If more people took the time to watch the sunset, the world would be a better place," his Dad would say. Trip shared many sunsets with his father, and as promised no two had ever been the same.

For the next several minutes, not a sound was made, as the four of them took in the sight of the giant orange ball that disappeared into the water. As the last orange speck flickered out, Jim turned, reached for his drink, and toasted, "It doesn't get any better than this."

38

"Isn't this the beach where you learned to ride the stand-up jet ski?"

"I was just think'n the same thing."

"You were a terror on that thing."

"What was I, four years old?"

"Three."

"How could you have even let me do such a thing?"

"What? There was no one around. You were riding up and down the beach in knee deep water, twenty feet from shore, and I was standing right there watching you."

"That was a fun little machine."

"Nothing compared to the Sea Doo. I saw you doing donuts with Brandi on the back. She must have been scared stiff. I'm surprised she didn't fly off the back."

"That's the point . . . who do you think she had to hold onto that much tighter!"

"Never thought of that."

"Are we gonna stay here again tonight?"

"I don't know. What do you guys wanna do?"

"Dad, anything you wanna do is great with us."

"I was thinking about spending the night at Sandy Pond. Maybe get a little fishing in after dinner. I know Sue is up for that. How do you think Brandi would feel about it?"

"Actually, I mentioned that it was something we might do. As it turns out, she fished a lot when she was a kid. So on the way up yesterday we stopped in Port Ontario and she got a fishing license."

"Women that like to fish . . . what more could a man ask for?" Jim leaned over in his chair and gave a high five to Trip.

The four of them had spent the previous evening on the aft deck of the Obsession playing Yahtzee until well past midnight. It was a cloudless, moonless night, and with no lights from suburbia reflecting off the atmosphere, the black sky was awash in stars. While Sue and Jim retired for the evening, Brandi and Trip opted for a midnight swim.

They had slept in this morning and, after a light breakfast, decided to launch the Sea Doo and get some waterskiing and knee-boarding in before lunch. With all four of them sore in muscles not used in normal daily activities, it was now time to relax.

The two men had been sitting on the beach for the past hour, half reading and half catching up on each other's lives. Most of the time was spent by Jim, updating Trip on Sue's week, dealing with her ex-husband's issues. The will, the FBI, the journals, her daughter's death, the guy from Homeland Security, and the cottage in Canada. He also hinted at finding some cash, without disclosing the amount. Trip knew better than to ask, but his curiosity was piqued none the less.

184

The women had somehow sensed the need for the men to have their bonding time and went off to do their own thing. Sue left first, to catch some rays on the sun pad that was mounted on the long hood of the boat. Brandi had been walking along the beach collecting shells and small pieces of drift wood. Warmed from the mid-day heat, she decided to drop her collection off at the boat and take a swim.

After a long silence, Trip spoke up. "Dad, about the cottage up in Canada. I was talking with Sue yesterday morning and . . . " But before he could finish, he saw his father lean forward in his chair and put his hand above his eyes to block out the sun.

"What the hell is she doing . . . NOOOOO!" Jim yelled. "IT'S TOO SHALLOW!" But it was too late. Sue had already dived off the hood of the boat, which was over eight feet above the surface of the lake, into less than four feet of water. Fearing the worst, Jim jumped up and ran towards the boat, closely followed by Trip.

Sue had been lying face down on the sun pad, her skin baking in the hot afternoon sun. Still trying to catch up on much needed rest, she dozed in and out of a light sleep. Then the dream started. She felt herself moving in slow motion toward the pool, then leaning over the edge. But, before she could see what was in the water, she would suddenly awaken, heart pounding, realize she'd been dreaming, then doze off and start the cycle over again.

As she lay there with her head to the side and eyes half open, she subconsciously focused on something floating in the water, about a hundred feet from the boat. Her eyes closed and the dream started. This time, as she leaned over the pool, she instead saw the object floating in the water. She lifted her head. Still in a half dream-like state, she stared out into the lake. Whatever it was, it just floated there, as if held in place by the water around it.

No matter how hard she tried, her brain was unable to comprehend what her eyes were seeing. Then, as if suddenly awakening, she saw what it was. A body. A person. A girl. Lying face down in the water with arms and legs stretched out. Long blond hair floated around her head on the surface of the water. It's a dream she thought. She blinked. The girl would not go away.

I'm dreaming, she thought. "I'm dream . . . " She stopped when she heard her own voice. She sat up, her eyes glued on the girl, still motionless. She tried to stand up. Although she felt as if she was using every ounce of her strength to do so, she seemed to be moving in slow motion. Finally standing, she could feel her heart pounding in her chest. Her head was floating. Though her eyes were open, her vision slowly faded to complete darkness, then light reappeared again. The girl was still there.

"Oh my God," she said, each word louder than the one before it. "BRANDI!" she screamed, just before stepping to the edge of the boat and diving into the water.

As she started to swim towards Brandi, she again felt as if she were moving in slow motion, with each stroke taking longer and longer to complete. She tried to remember how long she had been staring at the floating, motionless body. Why hadn't she recognized what it was sooner? Was she already too late?

She felt every beat of her heart. She gasped for more air. She tried to look straight ahead, to see if Brandi was still there. How much farther did she have to go? Then, everything faded to black again.

"Sue, are you okay?" She finally heard a voice, as if just awakening from a deep sleep.

"Sue." A hand touched her on the shoulder. She turned to see Brandi kneeling next to her. A dive mask was glued to her forehead. A snorkel was hanging from the strap.

Sue finally realized she was sitting on the sandy bottom of the lake, in water barely deep enough to cover her bikini top.

"Are you okay?" Jim shouted, out of breath, as he ran up to Sue, water splashing on her, first from him, then from Trip. He knelt down next to her. "Did you hurt yourself diving off the boat? Did you forget how shallow it was?" He put his hands on either side of Sue's head and looked closely at her face. "It doesn't look like you scraped your face . . . did you hit bottom?"

"No, I'm fine," Sue finally spoke up. "It got so hot laying in the sun. I saw Brandi out here. I . . . I didn't know you were snorkeling. The water looked so refreshing, so I dove in. It was a shallow dive. Then I guess I must have fainted. Too much waterskiing or something. I'm okay now." As she tried to stand up, her legs buckled beneath her and Jim caught her before she fell back into the water.

"Are you sure you're okay?"

"I'm fine," Sue shot back, picking up the pace a little as they walked in the cool wet sand, being careful to avoid the pile of sharp Zebra mussel shells that had washed up on the beach.

Zebra mussels were unintentionally imported from Europe to the Great Lakes in the ballasts of ocean going freighters about twenty years ago. With no natural enemy, they had flourished in the nutrient rich waters. The black and white striped, clam shaped, shelled creatures, no bigger than a thumb nail, washed up onto the sand beaches in piles sometimes a foot high. Although one time called an environmental calamity, the little creatures that can filter up to a half gallon of water a day had also been responsible for cleaning up the lakes, turning the water, when the sun was at a certain angle, to a Caribbean blue-green color.

Jim reached up, grabbed Sue's arm, and pulled her to a stop. He stepped in front of her, cupped her face in his hands, tilted her head back, then gently touched his lips to hers.

Sue stretched her arms around Jim's body, pulled her head away, turned it to the side and tightened her grip around him, squeezing the air from his chest. "Hold me."

Sue was the first to loosen her arms, lean back, and look up at Jim with her watery eyes. "You know me so well, don't you James Calihan."

"Well . . . I may not know everything about you Sue Lockwood, but I do know when something is bothering you."

"I . . . I thought."

"You thought she was drowning, didn't you?"

"Do you think I'm going crazy?"

"Going? I thought you were crazy the first time I met you. That's one of the qualities I like about you. Actually, the real question should be are you getting crazier than you already are. The answer to that is . . . no.

"Sue . . . you've been on an emotional roller-coaster ride over the past week. Frankly, under the circumstances, I think you're holding up quite well. The important thing I want you to know is, I'm here for you." They wrapped their arms around each other again. "Just give it a little time . . . time has a way of making things better. Things are going to get better, you'll see."

39

"What a way to start off the summer." Jim leaned his head back on the warm cushioned seat and extended his left arm out the side of the speeding boat, catching the cool wind and spray in his open hand. Sue was sprawled out on the rest of the seat, eyes closed, head resting on Jim's thigh.

"They make a great couple, don't they," Jim whispered in a low voice, as he watched Trip sitting upright in the captain's chair, Brandi leaning against him, her long red finger nails slowly rubbing the base of his neck.

Sue turned her head to the side, then back to Jim and whispered, "They remind me a lot of us. Remember the first time you brought me on the boat?"

"Do I!" Jim started to squirm. "We spent the whole weekend down below."

"We did not . . . well, not the whole weekend."

"Oh wait, you're right. We did it up here a few times too. And on the hood. And in the water."

"And don't forget the beach."

"How could I?"

After Sue's fainting spell yesterday, they had decided to lift anchor and make the fifteen-mile trip south to Sandy Pond. Sandy Pond, which was only pond sized in comparison to Lake Ontario, was lined with several thousand cottages, and accessible from the great lake through a narrow, sand dune lined channel, just deep enough to handle the three and a half foot draft of the Obsession. The thin, deserted, sand peninsulas, on either side of the channel, that divided the two lakes, provided a barrier for any waves that formed on the larger lake, and made for a perfect anchorage in any weather.

But the weather had not been the reason for their move to the pond. It was the fishing. Jim had been taught by his father, at an early age, how to fish, and that passion and skill was in turn passed down to Trip. Shortly after they had started dating, Sue decided to tag along with them on one of their weekend fishing trips. Toying with one of the spare fishing poles on the boat, Sue ended up catching the biggest fish that weekend. She, too, was hooked.

Sandy Pond, noted for its great northern pike and large mouth bass, did not disappoint them. They fished for almost two hours, from just after dinner, until they were finally driven below by the hungry, biting mosquitoes. They each caught several fish, with Brandi landing the biggest, a twenty-seven inch northern. She was now hooked too.

The boat traffic earlier this morning, something expected on such a picture perfect, warm, sunny, summer Sunday on Sandy Pond, made their decision to leave the pond and head out into the quiet, calm, open waters of Lake Ontario an easy one. Ten miles out from shore, they killed the engines and drifted for the rest of the afternoon in the blue-green, three hundred-foot deep water. Besides their own voices, the only other sounds they heard were an occasional whine of a boat motor, far off in the distance, water splashing from their swimming and diving, and the sea gulls flying high overhead.

"One last thing before we go," Trip spoke up, as the four of them stood on the swim platform, the afternoon sun drying the water from their bodies, following the last swim of the day.

"I'm almost all dried off," Jim said, as he looked at Trip looking at him.

"Not here. It's too deep," Sue chimed in.

"How can a lake be too deep for swimming?"

"That's not swimming."

"What is it then?"

"What are you guys talking about?" Brandi finally spoke up.

"They both dive off the boat and see how far they can swim under water. Whoever swims the farthest, wins."

"What's so bad about that?"

"Okay guys. Go ahead. Show her."

Jim and Trip both stood on each end of the swim platform, taking in several deep breaths, one after the other.

"Ready?" Sue spoke up. They both nodded, stood on the very edge of the platform, toes curved around the side and crouched, ready to dive. "One . . . two . . . three . . . GO!"

You could hear them both gulp in a huge chest full of air just before they hit the water, then silence, as they slowly disappeared below the surface. Sue glanced at the second hand on her watch.

"Where are they?" Brandi was the first to break the silence

after what seemed like an eternity.

Sue glanced at her watch. "Its only been forty-five seconds."

"How long has it been now?"

"One minute."

"Sue . . . "

Suddenly, within seconds of each other, several hundred feet from the boat and slightly to the left, two heads popped out of the water. The yelling, between loud, throaty inhaling, was barely audible at the boat.

"Are they okay?"

"Now you see why I don't like this game. They're fine. They're arguing over who won. They both must be having a bad day though. They were only under water for a minute and twenty seconds."

Sue woke up as she heard Brandi and Trip talking about the abandoned light house on Stony Point. She turned and looked at Jim. He too had fallen asleep. She nudged him.

"What, where are we?" he said, as he awoke with a startle.

"We're just going by Stony Point now."

"Wow, I must have really conked off. Was I snoring?"

"Yup," Trip and Brandi both yelled back in unison.

Sue sat up and cuddled next to Jim. "Are you sure you want to go through with this?"

"Sue, look. I told you last night. I think it's a great idea. The sooner you can close out all this crap your ex-husband left you, the sooner you can get your life back to normal." He looked into her eyes. "I've seen what the past week has done to you. I don't mean this in a bad way, so don't take it wrong, but I'm worried about you. I'm worried about what the hell else you're going to find out there. I'm not sure if you, I mean we, can take another week of . . . I don't think you should wait until after the fourth. Get it done now. This week."

Instead of pulling into their slip, they tied the Obsession up to the fuel dock, located just around the corner. "Hi Kerry," Jim said to the man walking out of the office door. "We need fuel and a pump out."

"Perfect timing. I was just about to close up for the day," Kerry said, as he handed Jim the nozzle from the diesel pump.

Brandi and Trip carried the suitcases and a bag of dirty laundry, mostly beach towels, to the car. As they started walking back to the boat, Brandi stepped in front of Trip, wrapped her arms around his neck as she stretched up on her tip toes, and gave him a long, passionate kiss.

"What was that for?"

"I just wanted to let you know that I had a great time this weekend. The last three weeks."

"Actually three weeks and two days, but who's counting?"

"The last three weeks and two days have been . . . well, lets just say, you've swept me off my feet." She reached up and kissed him again, this time even longer and more probing than the first. It would have lasted longer, were it not for the whistles they heard from two young boys who were watching from across the parking lot.

"Wow . . . I guess I should have taken you fishing sooner."

The four of them were sitting on the aft deck of the boat when Kerry walked over and handed the credit card, a pen, and receipt to Jim. He signed the receipt and handed the white copy and pen back to Kerry.

"Thanks, and have a great trip to Kingston."

"How long does it take to get to Kingston?" Brandi asked.

"On an evening as calm as this, it should take less than three hours," Jim piped up.

"It's a little over forty miles, depending if you follow the buoys or take a few shortcuts," Trip added.

"Well, we probably should get going. It's almost five-thirty," Sue said, as she got up and gathered the empty glasses from the table. "Do you want something to drink for the trip to Kingston, and do you guys want something for the car ride home?"

"I'll take a diet."

"Make it two."

"Brandi?"

"I'll take a water, thanks."

As Sue went below, Jim started the engines, then he, Brandi, and Trip stepped onto the dock. The guys untied the lines and held onto the boat.

"I'll get those," Brandi said, as she reached out and took the can of diet and plastic water bottle from Sue. "Have a good trip."

"We will . . . and, thank you Brandi."

Jim and Trip momentarily let go of the boat, which didn't move in the still evening air, then hugged each other.

"You have a safe trip."

"You too. Drive carefully."

They both slowly pushed the boat away from the dock, then Trip stepped on board and waved to Brandi and Jim. Seconds later he was in the captain's chair and the boat slowly moved forward, water gurgling behind it.

As the boat disappeared from view, Jim turned to Brandi. "So, where in Liverpool do you live?"

40

It was just after 7:30 p.m. before Jim pulled into the driveway at Cadys Arbor. He thought the drive home with Brandi had gone well. It was a perfect evening to cruise with the top down. Warm, but not that sticky humid kind of warm. Jim had been worried that the noise from the wind, blowing through the open car, would put a damper on their conversation, but there was rarely a lull. The only disappointing part was that Brandi's parents were not at home when he dropped her off. He had been looking forward to meeting them, but after the way he had seen his son act this weekend, he was certain he would be soon.

"They should be in Canadian waters by now," he said aloud, as he pushed the button on the garage door opener that was clipped to the visor of the Firebird. His thoughts immediately went back to yesterday evening when Trip and Sue broached the idea of taking the boat to Loon Island. As they sat in the lazy cool night air at Sandy Pond, it hadn't taken him long to figure out that they had already discussed it between themselves.

"I tried to tell you about it when we were sitting on the beach," Trip explained, "just before Sue took her Olympic dive."

In fact, Sue had talked to Trip about it on Friday morning, when Jim was at his training class. With the excellent weather they had been having over the past few weeks, Trip was actually a few days ahead of his mowing schedule. And the summer help he had hired afforded him the luxury of a few days off. He had briefed Brandi, and any nervousness she initially had about driving back with Jim disappeared within minutes of meeting him on Friday afternoon. Trip and Sue had packed extra clothes, so the only thing left was to convince Jim of the soundness of the idea.

After listening to what they had to say, Jim could find no reason why they shouldn't go, especially if it would help Sue put final closure to that part of her past. And the sooner, the better.

As soon as Jim got to the top of the steep incline of the driveway and could see into the dark shadows of the garage, he sensed something amiss.

"We left the door to the house open?" he uttered aloud, as the car came to a stop halfway into the garage. He sat there for a moment looking at the open door. "Shit . . . somebody broke into the house!"

He put the shifter in park and without turning off the car, got out, raced up the steps, through the door, and headed straight for the dining room table.

"Fuck," he said, as he saw the shoe boxes laying empty on the table.

41

"Where are we?" Sue yelled out the hatchway to the upper deck. She had been down below for the past half hour taking a shower, the first time she had ever done so while the boat was underway.

"We're coming up on Simcoe Island."

"Is that the one with the lighthouse on it?"

"Yup. It's called Nine Mile Point lighthouse. Come up here and take a look. The way the sun is shining on it, it almost looks like it's glowing."

"Wow . . . I've gotta get a picture of that."

"Did you know that this lighthouse and the one on Stony Point are two of only forty-one left on the entire lake. At one time there were close to a hundred."

"Gee . . . I think I have heard that somewhere before."

Trip looked at Sue, puzzled at first, then, with a smile, shook his head. "I forgot, we both have the same teacher."

"We've made great time, haven't we."

"We sure have. We entered Canadian waters just after you went below and we've got about ten more miles, maybe another half hour, before we get to Confederation Basin. We'll be there by eight-thirty at the latest."

"It's been a perfect evening for cruising. Look out there. It's like glass." Sue turned toward the back of the boat. "Look at our wake. It goes forever, then disappears into the horizon."

"Remember the trip we took last fall?"

"Remember! I still have nightmares about it. What was the name of that girl you brought?"

"Trina."

"Ah yes, Trina. I never saw anyone throw up as much as she did that afternoon."

The trip to Kingston on that final weekend in September last year had been a spur of the moment thing. The temperature on that Saturday morning had cooled down to the upper sixties, the winds were less than ten knots, and the waves were two feet, at most. The fish weren't biting and it was too cold to swim, so an overnight trip to Canada seemed like the logical thing to do.

Although a cold front, with strong winds, was approaching from central Canada, it wasn't scheduled to arrive until after the weekend. The waves on Sunday were forecast to be in the two to four foot range, something the Obsession could handle easily. Unfortunately, the cold front advanced quicker than originally predicted, and although by Sunday morning the winds were exceeding thirty knots, coming from the north, it wasn't until they were more than an hour out of Kingston, on the return trip back to Henderson Harbor, that they started to experience first four, then six, then eight foot waves. Traveling with the waves, there were times when the bow of the boat dipped beneath the water, as it first traveled up, over, and then down into the wave trough.

Jim and Trip had traveled in waves like this before and were confident the Obsession could handle them. It was Sue's first experience with eight footers, but she was confident of Jim's ability to get them safely back to the harbor. Trina on the other hand was scared to death, panicked, hysterical, then sick.

"I told her not to eat such a big lunch before we left Kingston that day."

"It took us six hours to get back, didn't it?"

"Six and a half."

"Did you ever see her again?"

"Nope."

As they rounded the tip of Simcoe Island, the city of Kingston, still ten miles away, came into view. It was nicknamed The Limestone City because of its vintage gray limestone buildings, many of which now shimmered in the late afternoon sun. The port city, strategically located at the junction of Lake Ontario and the St. Lawrence River, had several harbors and marinas.

Trip had made the journey from Henderson Harbor to Kingston, Ontario dozens of times in his short lifetime, though never without his father. The course just completed over the open waters of the lake, although dotted with several shallow rocky shoals, some far from shore, was clearly marked with large buoys, primarily to guide the commercial boat traffic entering the lake from the St. Lawrence River. Once they rounded Simcoe Island, and proceeded into the Lower Gap and Middle Ground water ways, the shoals and shallow areas not only became more plentiful, but many were only marked with tall, thin, yellow pencil buoys, which were difficult to see, even in calm water.

Sue could sense Trip's nervousness, so she reached into the compartment in front of her and pulled out the top chart, the one she knew was for this area.

"Dad always stays close to Simcoe Island. It's the deepest part of the channel." Trip glanced at the depth gauge. It showed forty feet. "When we get to Four Mile Point, just ahead on the right," Trip pointed, "we then head straight to Confederation Basin. We still have to look out for Penitentiary and Myles shoals, but they're marked with large green buoys."

Mindful of his course, he continued to pilot the boat parallel to Simcoe, keeping a constant eye on the depth gauge. The depth gauge readout, only seconds before at forty feet, was now down to thirty and dropping. At twenty-five feet, Trip looked up and carefully scanned the water in front of the boat for any buoys, which would have been there to mark any dangerous water. He looked down and the depth gauge now read twenty-one . . . twenty . . . nineteen . . . eighteen. Confused, he pulled back on the throttle levers to slow the boat and again gazed over the water.

"Is that the buoy you're looking for," Sue spoke up, pointing to her left. "See it . . . it's a red one. It's directly across from . . . oh, that's Four Mile Point."

Trip finally caught sight of the buoy, then looked at the depth gauge. Fifteen feet! He pulled back on the throttle levers again and brought the boat to a crawl. He was now unsure of which side of the buoy he should be on. He thought to himself, red-right-return. He had learned it in the Coast Guard boating course he took when he was thirteen. It meant, keep the red buoys to your right when you are returning to port. Returning to port, in this case, would mean from the river to the lake, opposite the direction they were heading. So therefore, he reasoned, the buoy should be on his left. He looked at the depth gauge. It still read fifteen feet.

"The chart shows fifteen feet between the buoy and the point, right?" Trip tried to state a as fact, even though Sue could tell it was more a question.

"Yes . . . then it starts to get deep again, twenty, then fifty . . . no, fifty-six feet."

As they slowly cruised past the red buoy, Trip looked at the depth gauge. Sixteen . . . seventeen . . . eighteen. He pushed the throttle lever forward and the bow of the boat raised out of the water as the boat picked up speed. Twenty feet. Bringing the boat back up to cruising speed, he carefully turned to the left, aiming directly for Confederation Basin, still eight miles ahead.

Of the many harbors in the Kingston area, Confederation Basin was the most popular, primarily because of its location at the heart of downtown. The city run marina, with over four hundred slips, was surrounded by a large, fifteen foot high, stone breakwall, that provided a barrier from winds and waves that can sweep in off the lake.

"I can always tell where we need to go by that round building. What is it called?" Sue spoke up, breaking the silence that had ensued since passing Four Mile Point.

"A Martello Tower."

The large round stone towers, built in the mid-eighteen hundreds as a defense against a feared American invasion, were located at several strategic points in and around the Kingston area. This one happened to be located right in Confederation Basin itself. Trip had been heading directly for it for the past fifteen minutes.

"Confederation Basin, Confederation Basin, Confederation Basin, this is the Obsession calling. Over," Trip spoke loudly and clearly into the hand held microphone.

"Obsession, this is Confederation Basin. Over," came the sound of a young woman's voice over the radio's speaker.

"We are a forty-four foot motor yacht looking for a slip, with power, for the night. Over."

"Do you have a reservation? Over."

"No we do not. Over."

"Stand by, Obsession."

There was a long pause. Trip looked at Sue. "Shoot."

"What."

"I just remembered. Tuesday is July first. That's Canada Day."

"Their Fourth of July?"

"Exactly. I was hoping there'd be plenty of slips because it was a Sunday night. But, maybe not."

"Obsession, Obsession, this is Confederation Basin. Come in please. Over."

"This is the Obsession. Over."

"We do not have any slips available for your size boat. The day docks and the wall along the hotel are full too."

"Shit," Trip whispered, as if they could hear him.

"But, there is space available along the wall to the west of the day docks. Unfortunately there is no power. Are you familiar with that area? Over."

"Yes I am. Over"

"You may tie up anywhere on an open space along that wall. Over."

"It's eight-thirty, it's Canada Day weekend, we're here for one night and outta here in the morning."

"The wall sounds good to me."

"We stayed there once before. At least it will be quiet."

"Confederation Basin, this is the Obsession. Over."

"Go ahead Obsession. Over."

"We will tie up along the wall. Over."

"Roger. Please check in with us at the light house when you arrive. This is Confederation Basin standing by on channel sixty-eight."

42

"You're right. It looks like he came in through the sliding glass door." The State Trooper, standing well over six feet and pushing two hundred pounds of what looked to be mostly muscle, was holding two small metal plates, with screws sticking out of them. "We see this all the time. It's a very common entry point for burglars."

Jim held his hand out and the Trooper dropped the pieces into it.

"An entry like this is usually done by an amateur, mostly teenagers. They break-in, look for cash lying around, then party for a while. Eat your food. Drink your beer. Even have sex in your bed. They usually trash the place a little." The Trooper took a few steps and looked around. "I don't see that here though. Except for the mess in the dining room, everything seems to be in order, both here and upstairs. That would usually indicate that whoever broke in, knew what they were looking for, found it, then left.

"Have you been able to determine if anything is missing?"

"I made a quick run through the house and I haven't found

anything missing yet."

"What about this stuff on the table."

"That, I'm not entirely sure of." Jim was trying to act calm, but he sensed a nervous tone in his voice. The Trooper looked up at him. "This stuff belongs to the woman who lives with me. It's her ex-husband's. He just died. Last week. In the plane that crashed in Syracuse."

"I'm sorry to hear that," the Trooper said, as he stepped toward the table, eyeing a little closer the papers scattered about. "Did you say ex-husband?"

"Yes, but he left her as the sole beneficiary and executor of his will. It's been driving her crazy."

"Anything you know of here that would have been of interest to a burglar?" The Trooper had now picked up some of the papers.

"I don't know. There was some cash." The Trooper looked up at Jim as he heard the word cash. "But I'm not sure exactly how much." Jim chose his words carefully.

The Trooper looked back at the table. After a long pause he asked, "Were we talking hundreds, thousands, tens of thousands?"

"It was tens of thousands," Jim answered quickly, hopefully to show that he was not trying to hide anything. The Trooper looked back at Jim. "But to be honest, I've been tied up in a training class this past week and she's been trying to sort this all out by herself. So I'm not sure what she's found."

"Your girlfriend's name," he lifted his clip board, ready to write.

"Susan Lockwood, that's spelled L O C K W O O D."

"And the ex-husband's name?"

"Dan, uh, Daniel Lockwood. Dr. Lockwood."

"Can you tell me where Mrs. Lockwood is now?"

"She's up at the lake. Lake Ontario. Henderson Harbor. With my son. We have a boat up there. Although, now she should be in Kingston, Ontario. I've been trying to get in touch with her, but the cell phone coverage up there stinks. Hopefully, she'll call me tonight."

"Well, I don't think we can go much further with this tonight without Mrs. Lockwood's help. Once she has had a chance to look things over, have her give me a call." He handed Jim a business card. "My number is on here. We can meet then to complete my report."

The Trooper started walking toward the front door, then turned to Jim. "It's possible some kids broke in, found the cash right off the bat, then took off. Call me right away if you find anything else missing." Then he walked out the door.

Jim stood there, shaking, as he heard the Trooper's car backing out of the driveway, exhaust pipe scraping on the road at the end of the steep driveway.

"What the hell am I shaking for?" he whispered, looking at his hands. "We haven't done anything illegal."

Jim justified in his own mind their innocence. Sue was the executor of the will and the sole beneficiary of her ex-husband's assets. Nothing illegal there. In fact she was abiding by a legal document, the will. They had found some cash. They had reported it to the lawyer. And FBI. Although questioning where it came from, there was no evidence to support anything illegal. No laws had been broken. So why was he shaking. Almost two hundred thousand dollars, that's why, he thought.

"The wireless customer you have called is not available. Please try again later."

"Where the hell are they," Jim yelled, as he listened to the recording.

Jim had been trying to call both Sue's and Trip's cell phones since he had arrived home. He knew his initial calls, those made before eight-thirty, were fruitless, since they would still be on route to Kingston, and even if their cell phones had been on, their rings would not likely be heard over the rumble of the diesels. But it was now ten-thirty, and still no answer.

Jim walked into the dining room and started to straighten out the papers that were scattered about the table and floor. He had just completed a second walk through of the entire townhouse and could find nothing missing.

Maybe the Trooper was right. Maybe it was a bunch of kids and when they came upon the cash, they split. With finding that much cash, why stick around and risk being caught.

He lifted the encyclopedia and opened it. The hollowed out interior, made to hold neatly stacked bills, was empty. He looked at the book. "With two shoe boxes full of cash, lots of cash, why would anyone have bothered to pick this up and look in here?" he mumbled.

Suddenly, two thoughts simultaneously popped into his head. The first was, that the thieves hadn't looked in the book and Sue had taken his advice last Friday morning, that it wasn't a smart idea to leave the money laying around on the dining room table, and hid it elsewhere. His second thought, the more disturbing of the two, was someone, somehow, knew exactly where to look. He felt a chill.

As he lifted the second encyclopedia volume, the one hollowed out to conceal the journal, his eyes focused on what had been hidden beneath it.

"What the hell is that?"

He poked at it with the tip of his index finger. Then, with his thumb and index finger, he picked up what appeared to be a piece of crumpled up plastic. It stuck to the wooden table. As he pulled harder, he could see it stretch, until suddenly, it broke free of the table and snapped against his hand.

He held his hand up closer to his face, shook it, then stared at the object, as it dangled from his fingers.

"A teenager wouldn't bother to wear rubber gloves."

43

"So . . . how do you like it?"

Trip just sat there, slowly chewing, his mouth filling with juices.

"This is great," he finally spoke up, still savoring the aftertaste in his mouth. "The meat is so tender, it's like biting into a tab of butter. Then the juices just pour out. Coffee-bean-encrusted filet mignon. I'll have to remember that."

Trip had been in the mood for a nice thick juicy New York strip, medium rare, smothered in onions and mushrooms. He knew when he got to the top of the stairs and saw the small but sophisticated dining area, that he was probably not going to get his wish. He also knew why Sue had told him to wear something nice.

Clark's on King was a small but elegant restaurant, with big windows that overlooked the street below, just two blocks from Confederation Basin. The crowded streets, on the short walk from the boat, had Sue convinced they would not be eating at her favorite Kingston restaurant that evening. As fate would have it, a couple had phoned in and canceled a table for two, just minutes before. Ironically, without the navigational delay at Four Mile Point, they would have instead walked into a booked restaurant.

"I don't think you'll find that anywhere but here. The chef adds his own twist to everything served."

"Well, whatever, it's excellent. Now I see why you wanted to come here. I'm going to have to bring Brandi here. She'd love it."

"For having just met three weeks ago, you two seem to be hitting it off quite well."

Trip looked up at Sue.

"What, you didn't think we noticed?"

"Noticed what?"

"Come on Trip. You two couldn't take your eyes off each other the entire weekend."

"Was it that obvious?"

"Yes . . . but, it was very nice. There is obviously some great chemistry going on there. I'm happy for you. So is your Dad. And, he's very proud of how much of a gentleman you were this weekend. You gave up your room to Brandi. You slept in the bunks. You waited on her hand and foot.

"We both know how bummed out you've been over Joyce. And it's good to see you back to your old self.

"You've grown up a lot in the last year."

There was little said between them while they ate their meals, until Trip spoke up. "Sue . . . can I ask you something?" Sue looked up. "You and Dad have been living together for what, two years now." Sue shook her head as she sipped her coffee. "Do you think you'll ever be getting married?"

"I'm assuming you mean to your father?"

"Come on, I'm trying to be serious here."

"Where did this come from?"

"Sue . . . don't you be naive with me. What about the way you and Dad act around each other. Sometimes you're worse than two teenagers. It's not hard for anyone to tell how you feel about one another. Brandi even noticed, and she just met you. I would think by now you'd know if you wanted to continue to just play house, or move in forever."

There was a long silence before Sue finally spoke up. "I would like nothing more than to be married to your father. But to be honest with you, I think he's afraid to make the relationship a permanent one. At least right now anyway. Actually, I think he's more afraid that it won't be permanent . . . forever, if you know what I mean. He was obviously very hurt in the past and . . . "

"Sue, that was ten years ago. Thanks to you, he has finally gotten over that. My God, my Mom certainly has. She's been married for five years now."

"Well maybe, but . . . "

"Maybe, but, nothing. You two aren't getting any younger." Sue tilted her head down and looked at him with her eyebrows raised. "You know what I mean. If you two are as happy as you appear to be, why not do it? Take a shot at living happily ever after."

"Well . . . you never know. Maybe we will. Right now though, with my ex-husband haunting me, that's the last thing on my mind. Not to change the subject, but have you figured out a game plan for tomorrow yet?"

"I know roughly where Loon Island is. Unfortunately, the charts Dad has onboard aren't detailed enough to tell me how to get through what appear to be some rocky shoals around the island.

The boat supply store, the one overlooking the basin, opens at eight tomorrow. I should be able to get a more detailed chart there."

"What time do we have to be out of here tomorrow, eleven?"

"Actually, more like ten. That's why they wanted us to check in with them when we got here earlier. Apparently there is a big yacht coming in tomorrow morning and they need to tie up right where we are. Since it was so late and we were leaving in the morning, we didn't need to register or pay to stay there tonight."

"That was nice of them, but it sounds like they did it just so we would leave on time."

Sue glanced at her watch, then around the restaurant, which was almost empty. "It's almost midnight and I forgot to call Jim."

"Oh, don't worry. If he was worried about us, he'd a called us. You can call him in the morning."

Sue reached into her purse for her cell phone. "Oh darn!"

"What's wrong?"

"Battery's dead."

"Oh boy, so is mine."

"That's what we get for keeping them on all weekend without being connected to shore power. We'll have to call him in the morning from the pay-phone in the marina."

As they left the restaurant, they headed down Clarence Street toward Confederation Basin. When they got to Ontario Street, one block before the Basin, Trip stopped and reached for Sue's hand. "Are you in the mood for the White Mountain?"

The White Mountain, located one block to the right on Ontario, just past a half dozen bars and restaurants, served the best ice-cream and frozen yogurt in all of Canada. Every voyage to Kingston that Trip could remember always included at least one

212

visit to the Mountain.

"I'm game, if they're still open."

As they walked by The Cocamo Bar and Grill, Sue stopped to look inside when she heard the words to Brown Eyed Girl coming from the open front door.

"I understand you are quite a dancer."

Sue felt her face go hot, then realized what kind of dancing he meant. "Your father and I have been known to tear up a few dance floors."

As they walked a few more steps, the lack of a line of people, normally extending out the door and onto the sidewalk, told them before they even got there that the ice cream store was closed.

"Well, what now?"

They continued walking down Ontario in the direction of the Obsession.

"Are you in the mood for some dancing?"

"No . . . I don't think so. It's a little late." They continued walking. "Unless, you could, well . . . teach me how to dance?"

44

"Mr. Calihan, Jack Nelson with the FBI." The agent held up a small black leather billfold showing his badge and identification.

"Jim Calihan."

The two men shook hands and Jim led him into the living room, where they both sat down on the couch.

"Thanks for stopping by first thing this morning and I'm sorry I called you so late last night."

"No problem . . . actually, I live a few miles from here, so it was easier for me to stop in on my way into the office. Now, you said you had some additional information that you wanted to share with me regarding Daniel Lockwood." Jack opened the leather notebook he was holding and placed it on his lap.

"Yes, I do . . . but I really don't know where to start."

"Well, why don't you let me review what I have in my report." Jack looked down and shuffled through the papers he had in the folder on his lap. "There really isn't much. Dr. Lockwood bought a round trip ticket on Wednesday, June 18, in Albany, New York, less than twenty-four hours before the flight. He had a return ticket for that evening. The only thing out of the ordinary was a mix up on the spelling of his first name. We do not know why he was flying to Washington, but, we have no reason to believe he had anything to do with the crash.

"In fact, last Friday, I was in Washington and I had a chance to review the latest FAA report on the crash investigation. They have concluded that a mechanical failure, something to do with . . ." Jack pulled out a piece of paper from the pile that had several sentences highlighted in yellow. "It's kind of technical, so it's better if I read it. Here it is. Stress corrosion cracking in one of the structural supports in the wing, which may have been caused by de-icing chemicals." Jack looked up from his notes. "That's what they are now saying is the cause of the crash. An FAA bulletin may be out this week requesting inspections on these types of planes, especially those flying in and out of LaGuardia this past winter. Although that part of the investigation is not one hundred percent complete yet, they have categorically ruled out any kind of foul play.

"What I'm trying to say is, I know Mrs. Lockwood was concerned with, well, she had expressed some concern to me about the emotional state of her ex-husband. I can assure you that there is nothing to indicate that Dr. Lockwood had anything to do with the crash. Basically, he was in the wrong place at the wrong time."

Jim wasn't sure if the agent was trying to comfort him or end the meeting as quickly as possible and leave, as if he had something else more important to work on.

"My house was broken into over the weekend."

"I'm sorry to hear that, but it's really something you should be reporting to the local authorities." Jack closed the leather folder and left it on his lap. "Have you reported it to the police?" Jim shook his head up and down.

"We found a considerable amount of cash in Dan Lockwood's apartment." Jack looked up at Jim. "In going through his financial records, we have not been able to explain where it came from. Sue left you a message about it last week."

"I was in Washington last week, and I haven't been back in the office yet. When you say considerable?"

"In excess of $150,000." Jack stared at Jim with a look you might expect from a well trained FBI agent, cold and reserved on the outside, but bursting with fervent emotions on the inside. "We haven't found anything to suggest anything illegal either," Jim added.

"Are you telling me that someone broke into your house and walked away with $150,000 in cash?"

"To be honest, I'm not sure." They both sat there in silence, each waiting for the other to speak. "My . . . " Jim was always at a loss as to what to call Sue, since at fifty, girlfriend did not sound appropriate, and lady-friend made him sound too old. "Sue was trying to figure out where the money came from. I've been tied up in a training class this past week. I'm not sure what she did with the money on Friday. She may have hidden it . . . she may have left it all on the dining room table. We went away for the week-end. I have a boat up in Henderson Harbor that we stay on. Sue is still up there, and I haven't been able to get in touch with her. So I'm really not sure what, if anything, was taken."

Jack sat there, his eyes focused across the room. "I can understand your concerns, but I'm still not sure this is a matter for the

FBI. There is certainly nothing here to suggest any tie in to the crash, and until you find evidence of a Federal crime . . . "

"Dan Lockwood's apartment was also broken into over the weekend," Jim interrupted.

45

"You're up early . . . is that coffee for me?" Sue walked by Trip and down the steps to the galley, her mouth watering with each breath she inhaled of the coffee flavored air.

"Yup," Trip said without looking up, as he sat on the cushioned bench seat, huddled over the table. The dining area of the boat reminded Sue of a booth in a restaurant, except this one was made of hand worked teak, covered with layers of clear polyurethane. The bench seat bottoms and backs were made of soft, cream dyed leather, and were so thick you felt as if you were floating when you sat in them, which, technically, you were.

Sue poured herself some coffee, walked back up the steps, and sat across from Trip. "Did you already go to the store?" Sue glanced at her watch. "Oh, it's not as early as I thought. I was up at seven, but must have dozed off again. I guess all that dancing tired me out last night."

Sue was looking at Trip and from the way he was concentrating on what he was doing, wasn't sure if he even heard what she was saying. He could be so much like Jim, she thought to herself, as a smile came over her. "So, did they have the chart you needed?"

"Actually, they did," Trip answered immediately, surprising Sue. "Here's where we need to go, Loon Island." Trip pointed to an island on the chart, circled in pencil. Trailing from it was a line, also drawn in pencil, that zigzagged through the narrow water-ways of the St. Lawrence River, between what appeared to be hundreds of islands, and eventually off the chart.

"You already have the course plotted out?"

Trip looked at Sue, surprised that she had figured out what he had been doing all morning. "I just remembered, Dad told me that you were one heck of a navigator . . . is it true?"

"Well, I don't want to brag, but I have taken the Coast Guard Power Squadron Course." Sue sat up and flung her hair back with her right hand.

"I forgot you took that. Great! You're gonna need it."

"Why?" Sue's face went from cocky to worried.

Trip pointed to the circled island on the chart. "Look at where Loon Island is. To get there, we need to navigate in between these rocky shoals." They both leaned over the chart to get a better view, their heads almost touching.

Sue looked at the chart confused. "Does that say one-half foot?" She pointed to an area on the chart, just adjacent to the circle, where the zigzagged line went through.

"It sure does."

She gazed up at Trip.

"No . . . I'm kidding. It's a Canadian chart. It's in fathoms. So it's about three to four feet."

Sue recalled the first time she was on the Obsession and Jim lectured her about never going into less than four feet of water with the boat, unless you were drifting and absolutely certain the bottom was sand. The Bahamas-of-the-North was the only place she ever saw Jim do so.

"Isn't that a little shallow to be . . . "

"Yes it is," Trip interrupted. "Dad doesn't go in less than four feet of water when he's under power, especially over a rocky bottom like the St. Lawrence."

"So, what are we going to do?"

"Well, let me tell you something about the Obsession." Trip leaned back in the cushioned bench with his arms stretched out and laying on the top of the seat back. "You know Dad and I rebuilt this boat. We just about took the whole thing apart and put it all back together." Sue still sat forward with her elbows on the table, holding her coffee cup in her hands. "I can still remember the day we first saw her. I was thirteen. We had just finished restoring the Firebird. It had taken us a whole year, but I have to admit it was a lot of fun. We were out for a drive in the fall, up near Alex Bay, when we came across this boat, sitting in a back lot, with a for sale sign on it. 'Just for the fun of it,' I remember Dad saying. We stopped and looked at it. At first I thought he was kidding. I mean you could see sun-light shining through parts of the hull. But you know Dad. Once his mind starts working, look out."

"I know exactly what you mean."

"We worked on her for almost two years. Every weekend. Every vacation. That whole next summer. While my friends were off doing things teens going through puberty do, I worked on the Obsession. I know every inch of this boat, inside and out. Dad and I worked side by side. He took the time to explain why he was doing everything that he did. He let me work on things all by myself. He even let me screw up a few times. Nothing big though.

"I can remember the first night we slept on her, when we launched her, the first time I drove her, the first time Dad let me invite my friends up for a weekend sleepover.

"I can also remember the way we measured how much draft she needed. She had only been in the water for a week, but we wanted to get an accurate measurement and set the alarm on the depth gauge. So I put on my scuba tank and went under the rear of the boat near the props. Dad put a stick down along the back of the boat and I lined it up with the bottom of the props. But to be safe, I added a few inches on. Well, Dad wanted to be safe too, so he added a few inches on his end. A boat, whose design had a draft of a little over three feet, suddenly needed a safe clearance of four."

Sue sat there laughing. "You two are so much alike it isn't funny."

"There are worse people I could take after."

"Your father is so proud of you Trip," she said in a more serious tone. "You are the number one priority in his life."

"But, I don't need to be anymore."

"Well, you probably always will be."

After a long silence, they both jumped when they heard someone knocking on the outside of the boat. Trip slid out of the seat, walked to the rear of the cabin, up the stairs to the open hatchway, and disappeared.

"We need to be outta here in thirty minutes. The eighty-five foot Guitar Man is on its way in."

"Well, you can tell the eighty-five foot Guitar Man that the five-foot-five Sue still needs to take a shower."

46

"How do you know it was broken in to," Jack asked Jim, his face looking, and voice sounding, less like an FBI agent's.

"Last night, after the State Police left here, I walked through the entire house. Nothing, I mean nothing, was out of place. Except for going through the papers on the dining room table, whoever broke in was either lucky that they found whatever cash was on the table, right off the bat, and high tailed it out of here, satisfied with what they got, or they knew exactly what they were looking for."

"If I was a common house burglar and happened upon thousands of dollars, I'd be outta here so fast . . . "

"It wasn't a common house burglar," Jim interrupted.

Jack was beginning to learn that Jim had given this a lot of thought and it was probably best if he just sat and listened carefully, especially since he wasn't taking any notes and didn't want to get Jim nervous by doing so now.

"He was someone who knew enough to use these," Jim picked

up the rubber glove from the coffee table, "and he knew enough to look in here." Jim handed Nelson the encyclopedia. "Open it. Sue found money hidden in it in Dan Lockwood's apartment. It was empty when I got here on Sunday evening."

"Do you know if there was any money in it when you went away on Friday?" Jack interrupted, realizing mid-sentence he had promised himself to remain silent.

"I don't know . . . only Sue would. Anyway, when I found the glove and the empty book, I'm not sure why, maybe it was Dan's apartment keys that caught my eye on the table, I don't know, but I decided to check out his apartment. When I got there, I found these on the patio," Jim reached for the small metal plates and screws on the table and handed them to Nelson. "They're from the sliding glass door. The burglar there broke into his apartment the same way as the burglar here broke into mine." Jim pointed to the other clips on the table. "I wasn't in the mood to spend a lot of time there and with the way Sue had been going through the place, I wouldn't know if anything had been disturbed anyway.

I got back here about eleven and that's when I called you."

The two of them sat there silent, Jim waiting for words of wisdom from the all-knowing FBI agent, and Jack trying to digest what Jim had hours to think about.

"It seems to me, we need to talk to your . . . to Mrs. Lockwood. She might be able to shed some additional light on things, based upon what she found going through Dr. Lockwood's things. Something that would help make more sense of this. I believe you said she was up on your boat with your son."

"Yes."

"Where exactly?"

"That's the problem, I don't know. I can't find her."

"Excuse me."

"When I left them yesterday evening, they were on their way to Kingston."

"The Kingston in Ontario, Canada?"

"Yes. They should have gotten there well before dark. I've tried their cell phones with no luck. I called the marina they were going to stay at last night. They have no record of them checking in. I called our marina in Henderson Harbor this morning, thinking they may have developed a problem and returned last night. The boat isn't there either."

"Could they have changed their plans?"

"They could have. With the weather being so nice, there are a few places, Big Sandy Bay on Wolf Island for example, where they might have decided to stay instead. The cell phone coverage there is poor at best, which would explain them not calling me to let me know of their change in plans."

"If they did do that, when would you expect them to arrive in Kingston?"

"I wouldn't. Kingston was not their final destination. They were only spending the night there. This morning they were heading down the St. Lawrence River to Loon Island, one of the Thousand Islands, about thirty miles from Kingston. Sue found out her ex-husband was renting a cottage there. She was going there to see if she could find out where the money came from."

By now, Jack had opened his leather notebook and was busy writing, starting with "over $150,000 in cash found in Lockwood's apartment." He made Jim repeat everything he had just told him.

When he was done writing, Jack went back and reread all that he had written, four pages of notes in all. He asked Jim a few clarifying questions, then sat there silent for a few minutes. He finally looked up at Jim. "I'm sure there is some logical explanation to all of this . . . right now, I can't think of what it might be. I need some more time to think about it.

"Meanwhile, I suggest you continue to try to get a hold of Mrs. Lockwood. Let me know as soon as you do. If you don't reach her by late this afternoon, say five, that will mean that she has officially been missing for twenty-four hours and we can get law enforcement to respond."

They both got up and headed for the door. "If there is anything else you can think of in the meantime that might be helpful, don't hesitate to call me."

When Jim heard those words, don't hesitate to call me, it sparked something in his head. "Wait," he said suddenly, "there is something else. Dan Lockwood was doing some consulting work for the Department of Homeland Security." When the agent stopped and turned around, the look on his face told Jim he wasn't leaving yet.

47

"What number buoy should we be coming up to next?"

They left Kingston in a rush. As they pulled out of the basin, Guitar Man was a few miles to the west, cruising toward them from the open waters of Lake Ontario. Its pure white silhouette dwarfed every other boat on the lake that morning.

The zigzagging course Trip had plotted to Loon Island kept them on the Canadian side of the St. Lawrence. The river, at some points miles wide, at others, where islands intersected its path, less than a few hundred feet, was the border between the United States and Canada. The actual border wove up the middle of the river and between the Thousand Islands, which actually numbered over eighteen hundred islands. Legally, each time you ventured across the border and anchored or set foot on land, you were required to report to Customs in the country just entered. Since they had reported into Canadian Customs when arriving in Kingston yesterday evening, they could cruise the Canadian waters unrestricted.

Trip's course from Kingston initially took them along the northern path of the river known as the Bateau Channel, which ran between mainland Canada and Howe Island. It was not only the course he was most familiar with, it was also the most scenic. The narrow river, at some points less than two football fields wide, and steep banks, offered a great view of the surrounding countryside.

They were about twenty miles from Kingston, near the end of the relatively straight channel. "That should be J-17," Sue said as she glanced up from the chart, and eyed the green buoy, just off to the right. She looked back down at the chart. "Those two points of land, Bishop's Point on the left, and Gillespie's Point on the right, are about a mile away. There's a cable ferry crossing there too. The next buoy beyond that is J-16, a red one. Then we bear to the left."

She unfolded the chart which showed the penciled line continuing on a route zigzagging through a number of islands, along a narrow channel, marked by dozens of buoys. She also noticed that if they instead went to the right at buoy J-16, they could head for the open waters of the Canadian Middle Channel, circle around the islands, and eventually end up on the same course farther down river, but without having to navigate the narrow, shallower part of the river. Although she had confidence in Trip, she now wished she had waited to make the journey the following week, when Jim was available.

"It's the same route we always take."

Sue jumped at the sound of Trip's voice.

"When we go to Gananoque . . . see." Trip pointed to the chart. Printed in large black letters, just at the end of the torturous path through the buoys, was the city's name. "It's not as bad as it looks and a lot quicker than going around all those islands. Admiralty

Islands, right?"

Sue looked at the chart. It did say Admiralty Islands.

"From there we head through the Gananoque Narrows. Loon Island is less than five miles down river. We should be there by early afternoon."

As the city of Gananoque came into view, Sue's anxiousness subsided and suddenly she felt lonely. The few times she had been there were with Jim. She now recalled how romantic each of the visits had been. She longed for him more than ever.

"That should be it," Trip said, as he looked through the binoculars at the small tree covered island, straight in front of them, but still far off in the distance.

"Which one?" Sue asked, with an obvious anxious tone in her voice, as she looked up from the chart she had been studying on her lap, and saw almost a dozen separate land masses in front of her.

"The smallest one . . . directly in front of us. The one with the pines. It looks like it has a green colored cottage on it. Here." He handed her the binoculars. "Do you see it?"

"No . . . wait, yes. I see it. Are you sure that's it?"

"I'm almost positive that's the one. See that red buoy over there on the point of that first island." Sue turned in the direction he was pointing. "Can you make out the number?"

"HV-8."

"Great. That's Ivy Island." He pointed to the chart. "We need to pass by these three smaller islands, then turn here. That's when it's going to get a little tricky." He pointed to the chart again. "Getting through these rocks. But we'll take it slow. It's dead calm out, so we won't have to worry about the wind at all."

As they got closer to Loon Island, Trip brought the Obsession to a crawl, the engines idling as slow as they would go. The island that had looked like a speck only minutes ago was well over a hundred feet wide, but still small compared to those surrounding it. A small, one story, green shingled cottage, with an enclosed porch that went along its entire length, came into view between the large pine trees surrounding it, as they wove their way between two larger islands, to either side of the boat.

"Can you tell how big that dock is?" Trip asked Sue, who was perusing the island with the binoculars.

"On the right side?"

"Yes. It's a dock, isn't it?"

"I see it now. It's hard to tell from this angle, but it looks big enough for us to tie up."

BEEP, BEEP, BEEP, BEEP.

Suddenly the shallow water alarm on the depth gauge sounded. Trip calmly pushed the silence button.

"It's set for five feet. We are still at four and a half," he tried to reassure Sue, who had jumped at the sound of the beeping.

Trip shifted the engines into neutral, and the boat slowly drifted to a stop. He looked over the side of the boat toward the island that was less than a hundred feet directly to the right. "See those rocks." Sue stood up, leaned toward him, and stared in the direction he was pointing. At first she saw nothing. Then every few seconds she noticed the water would move such that it would momentarily expose the rounded top of a huge boulder. It was halfway between them and the shore of the island.

"Shouldn't we be more to the left?" Sue whispered.

"Not really." Trip pointed to a spot just ahead on the left side of the boat.

"Is that another one?" Sue again whispered as she noticed a ripple in the water, this one more visible than the first.

"Yup." Trip shifted both engines into forward, then back to neutral. The boat momentarily surged ahead, then kept drifting forward, inching closer to the island in front of them.

Sue moved to the left side of the boat. "Are you sure we can make it in there?" She looked at Trip.

"It's too late to change our minds now. Anyway, that should be the last of the rocks."

BEEP, BEEP, BEEP, BEEP.

"Sorry." Trip pushed the reset button again. "It resets itself every two minutes. We're still in four feet of water."

The dock was now less than a football field length away. Trip again shifted the boat into forward, then immediately back to neutral. He repeated the process several times as the boat slowly made its way to the dock.

As they pulled along side, Sue descended to the swim platform, jumped onto the dock with the aft line in her hand, then looped it onto one of the dock cleats. "Okay, she's tied up back here," she yelled.

Trip walked around to the bow of the boat and tossed a line to Sue who secured it to the cleat at that end of the dock.

Just as she looked up at him, he said, "I sure hope this is the right island."

48

"Thanks. No, I'll get back to you." Jack hung up his cell phone, then turned and looked at Jim.

"We were able to verify with Canadian Customs that your son and Mrs. Lockwood did enter Canadian waters last evening."

"Thank God!"

"They called into customs at 8:46 p.m. from Confederation Basin in Kingston. However, there is no record of them registering there for the night. Customs just completed a walk-through of the docks and your boat was not there. They also indicated that the marina was full last night, so maybe they had to stay somewhere else."

"The marina was full on a Sunday night?"

"It's Canada Day weekend."

"Shit . . . I forgot about that. July first."

"The more disturbing news is," Jack looked up from his notes, "there is no one by the name of Dr. Williams working at the Department of Homeland Security at the Pentagon. And unless he is working for a subcontractor, there is no record of Dr. Lockwood ever doing any consulting work for the Government."

Jack glanced at his watch. It was now 11:00 a.m.

49

"Nick?"

"Yea."

"It's me . . . can ya talk?"

"Hold on." Nick got up from his chair, walked over to the door to his office, gently closed it, then walked back to his chair.

"Where are you?"

"I'm go'in fish'n"

"Any problems?"

"None, except da fuck'n guide tell'n me we ain't gonna catch no goddamn fish where I want um ta take me. Shithead."

"How long before you get to the island?"

"One, maybe two hours."

"Good. Let's hope you make out better than you did over the weekend."

"I told ya. Somebody fuck'n got ta doze places before me. I know it."

"Well, let's hope they don't beat you to this place."

"I'll tell ya somedin. If dey do and dare still dare when I get dare, dey won't be leave'n da place alive."

"Call me as soon as you get back. I'll be here till late."

"I'll do dat."

50

"This is one heck of a secluded hiding place, if one were to need a place to hide," Trip said, as he walked into the door of the cottage from the enclosed porch. "Wow, it's like a flashback to the seventies."

"More like the fifties."

"It smells like something from the fifties. You need to air this place out." It was obvious that earlier in the day, the morning sun had warmed the cottage interior, driving out more of the winter mustiness into the closed room. "You could hide anything here and no one would ever find it."

"That's what I'm hoping. I mean that you can, and we will," Sue responded, as she stood in the middle of the room.

"The only other thing on this island is a small dock, over on that side." Trip pointed to his right. "Maybe twenty feet long. There are some old wooden chairs, so it probably catches the afternoon sun. You can't see it from this side of the island because of the pine trees. Did you see how big they are? Must be pretty old. Any discoveries in here yet?"

"I just took a quick tour. There are five rooms. This is the main room of the cottage. It's the biggest."

"Looks well lived in. I don't think you could put another knick-knack or picture in this room. Look at this stuff." He picked up an old brass compass from the small table under the window. "I wonder how much this is worth?"

"I'm sure none of this stuff is Dan's. I imagine this place comes fully furnished. Even if you rented it for the summer, you wouldn't want to lug all of this stuff on and off the island. It looks like a lifetime of nautical collectibles."

"It's still some pretty neat stuff."

"Here's the kitchen and eating area. It looks like it's all circa nineteen sixties stuff. Not even a microwave." Sue opened the refrigerator. "It's been recently stocked, though. The expiration date on this orange juice is July fifteenth, so someone has been here in the past few weeks or so." She closed the refrigerator door. "Over here is the bathroom and these are the two bedrooms. That's it."

"Well, while you are snooping through all of this stuff, I think I'll take the Sea Doo out and see if there is an easier way to get out of here."

Sue looked up at Trip. "Why, don't you think we can get back out the way we came in?"

"No . . . we shouldn't have a problem. It's just that if there is an easier way, I'd rather not have to deal with those rocks again."

A few minutes later, Sue heard the Sea Doo start, and then speed away, as the buzzing sound of its engine faded in the distance. She suddenly felt very alone. "I should feel alone," she mumbled. She was on an island in the middle of the St. Lawrence

River, miles from anyone, as far as she knew. Jim was a hundred miles away. If anything happened to Trip, she'd be there until someone came looking for her.

Even though it was in the low eighties, she felt a chill as she looked around the room and wondered when Dan had last been there, and more importantly, for what reason. She looked in the corner and stared at the over-stuffed recliner. At least it's not leather, she thought.

For the next hour, she searched the entire cottage for—she wasn't quite sure what. The smaller of the two bedrooms, the one she guessed at one time had been a little boy's, had, except for the items that seemed to belong there forever, nothing out of the ordi-nary. The larger bedroom was obviously where Dan slept. It too was over-furnished with nautical paraphernalia, and except for clothing in the dresser and closet, the first thing she recognized as Dan's, it was similar to the first.

Although she didn't expect to find whatever it was she was looking for in the bathroom or kitchen, she still searched every drawer and cupboard.

Finally, she stood in the middle of the main room and slowly turned around, rotating in a full circle. She had purposefully left that room for last, mainly because she did not know where to begin to look.

"Where would I hide . . . what?" she said aloud, as she slowly turned in a circle, eyes surveying the room like radar on a ship. Not knowing what it was she was looking for made finding it that much more difficult she thought.

"Where would I hide . . . it?" she said, as she walked over to one of the small tables against the wall and picked up a light green tinted glass jar filled with sea shells. She stared at the jar wondering if there might be something hidden among the shells. She shook the jar, then put it back on the table.

"Where would I hide it?" she said again, then, suddenly froze. "No . . . not where would I hide it? Where would DAN hide it?" This time she almost shouted it out, as if she knew what it was she was looking for.

Sue walked back to the center of the room and slowly turned around again. This time, before she even turned halfway around, she stopped. It was so obvious, she couldn't believe she hadn't seen it before. There, against the far wall, was a floor to ceiling bookcase, about six feet wide, with eight shelves in all. To someone not knowing what they were looking for, nothing would seem out of the ordinary. But Sue noticed it right away. Every shelf was completely filled with books, most of them, like everything else in the cottage, old and faded from the years of exposure to the light. Yet scattered among the books, one or two to a shelf, were books noticeably thicker and with covers shinier than the rest.

She walked over to the shelf and pulled out the book on the third shelf from the top, which was almost at eye level. Although she stared at the cover for a few seconds, without reading the title, she opened it. Her heart thumped harder when she saw the neatly banded hundred dollar bills hidden in the hollowed out interior of the book. She closed the book, held it in her arm, then reached for another on the shelf above it, this time noticing the title, The Reckoning by David Halberstam. She placed it on top of the other book and opened it.

"My God!"

She placed the books on the floor and retrieved the remaining ones from the shelf, twelve in all, and laid those on the floor. She then sat down, legs crossed, opened each book, one by one, and began to count the money.

Suddenly she heard the door to the porch open, then the screen door to the cottage squeak, as it opened. Without turning around, she held up a stack of hundreds, banded together with a two thousand dollar money strap, in her right hand, and a journal in her left. "Look what I found." Expecting, but not hearing any kind of reply, she then turned and looked toward the door. A surprised look came over her face as she felt her heart thump.

"What are you doing here?" she gasped.

51

Sue was first to hear the Sea Doo pull up to the dock. Though it seemed longer, a minute later, the porch door creaked open, then the screen door to the cottage.

"Well, the only way we're gonna get outta here is the same way we came in. You wouldn't believe the rocks around this place. And the weeds. I had to get into the water twice and unclog the jet pump intake."

Sue sat on the floor at the far end of the room, with her back toward Trip. She didn't move.

"Hey . . . did you hear me?" he spoke up again, seeing that Sue was obviously concentrating on something. Trip then took the large beach towel he was holding and dried the water that was dripping down his leg from his wet bathing suit.

"Sue." He walked over to her and put his hand on her shoulder. "You okay?" When she turned her head, he saw the tears dripping down her almost milk white face. He also noticed her shaking body. "What's wrong?"

"Don't fuck'n move." A voice suddenly filled the silence of the room, startling Trip, who instinctively turned in the direction of it.

"I said don't move!" The voice was now louder and more ominous sounding. This time Trip obeyed the command.

"No, please don't," Sue screamed out, as she too turned and looked across the room.

"What the hell is going on?"

"Shut up, both of you. And you, get down on the fuck'n floor."

Trip, knowing he should be doing as instructed, couldn't. It was like he was frozen. He stood there, his eyes locked on the eyes locked on his. Neither one blinked.

"I said get down on the fuck'n floor . . . NOW!"

Sue reached up, grasped Trip's hand and tugged. As if in slow motion, Trip bent his knees and sat down on the floor next to Sue, all the while his eyes not moving. He hadn't needed Sue's coaxing, though. The gun pointed at him was reason enough.

52

"I'm not sure if we have the jurisdictional authority to do that."

"Well I certainly do." Jim noticed that his voice was louder. "A friend of mine lives in a cottage on Mink Island during the summer. It's just north of Alex Bay. I could be on his boat and to Loon Island, well before nightfall." Jim looked down at his watch.

"Mr. Calihan, as a private citizen, you certainly have the right to do that. To be honest with you, if I were in your shoes, I probably would do the same. But you need to look at this from the Bureau's perspective. Although you haven't spoken to them, all indications are that they are heading where you thought they were going. And, it's been less than twenty-four hours since you last saw them. Until we straighten out who this person is from the Department of Homeland Security . . . after all, you weren't even certain of his name, isn't that correct?" Jim nodded in agreement. "Until that's done, we have no reason to believe that they are in any danger. I know it's frustrating, but I'm sure they will eventually call you."

Jim instinctively reached for his cell phone when he heard the ring, then stopped when he realized it wasn't his.

"Excuse me," Jack said, as he reached for his phone and walked into the kitchen. "Nelson."

"I'm sorry Mr. Calihan, but the Department of Homeland Security has just raised the Terrorist Alert to orange and I have to get back to the office for a briefing. I recommend you sit tight for a few more hours. Let me do some more digging. And call me if you hear from Mrs. Lockwood or your son. If you don't hear anything from them by five, call me anyway, and I will get the wheels in motion for a search."

It was almost noon. Jim knew what Jack Nelson had just told him was what any reasonable person would conclude about the events of the past eighteen hours. But still, his gut, which had an uncanny way of being right most of the time, told him that something didn't feel right. The death of Sue's ex-husband, the will, the money, the person from Homeland Security, and now the break-ins, all in the span of a week, seemed too planned. Almost scripted.

He looked at his watch again. If he left now, he could be at Mink Island by three. Although he didn't have a chart in front of him, he knew Loon Island was near Gananoque and probably less than two hours by water from Mink Island. If everything fell into place, he could be there by five, six at the latest.

"Hello."

"Dennis?"

"Hey, Jim, how the hell are you. Don't worry, I'm all set for next week. I assume you and Sue are still coming up to do some diving. I've mapped out some new places."

"Yeah, that's still on, but I have a favor to ask you. A big favor."

53

"Meeting over already?"

"Yes," Jack glanced at his watch, "same old thing. Increased chatter on the Internet, but nothing concrete to react to. I guess it's better to be safe than sorry when it comes to terrorism, but I'm really not sure what raising the threat level means to the average citizen. Anyway, what's up?"

"Remember the issue you asked me to look into this morning?" There was a long pause. "The one about the guy who supposedly worked for the Department of Homeland Security?"

"Yes, yes, yes," Jack finally got his mind refocused on the morning's activities, "Dr. Williams. You said there was no record of him working for them."

"Right."

"And Dr. Lockwood, the person on Flight 2145 who supposedly consulted for Homeland Security. There was nothing there on him either."

"Right again."

Dyan, a tall, thin, twentysomething, dressed in a conservative black pantsuit with a plain white blouse, followed Jack into his office and stood in front of his desk, as Jack homed in on the dozen pink While-You-Were-Out message slips, arranged neatly next to his phone. She stood quietly, her large glasses perched on her nose, waiting for Jack to finish fingering each slip. Although Dyan had only worked with Jack for the past few months, she learned quickly that unless you had his full attention, you ended up repeating yourself, especially if something you said suddenly interested him.

When Jack finally turned around, he was startled to see Dyan still standing there. "I'm sorry."

"That's okay . . . hectic day, huh."

"Why are Mondays always like this?" he said, as he sat down.

"Plus, you were out of town most of last week, right?" Jack looked up at her, wondering how she knew that. Dyan looked at him, hoping he wasn't thinking she was keeping track of him. She also hoped he hadn't noticed her blushing, as she felt a rush of warmth slowly flow through her body.

"So, have you found something?" he finally spoke up.

"I think I might have," she responded, trying to pull herself back into her official FBI persona.

Jack leaned forward, clasped his hands together, then put them down on the desk in front of him.

"On a hunch." Upon hearing those three simple words, Jack knew he was in for something good. Although he had only been working in the Syracuse office a few months, he had already worked on several cases with the very young, very innocent look-ing analyst. Each time, she had impressed him with her abilities to think outside the box and come up with unique ways of looking at evidence. He also liked the way she appeared to have, to use an old high school term, a crush on him. "I did a little research on the files that have been collected on the 2145 crash. I took a look at the FINGERPRINT data."

"Fingerprint?" Jack interrupted.

"Okay, FINGERPRINT is a computer code that keeps track of who accesses a database. In other words, any time you touch a piece of data, the program remembers you did. It keeps a running track. It takes your fingerprint, so to speak. FINGERPRINT was originally developed by the IRS to keep track of which files their employees were looking at."

"You mean to see if they were looking up their neighbor's tax returns."

"Or to see if the guy that they had met the night before could really afford the Corvette he was driving."

"Better yet."

"The program is a standard part of almost every government database, although most people don't know it. Anyway, I looked at the files compiled as part of the 2145 investigation. Although hundreds of people have accessed the various files—FAA's, the airline, ours—there was one name that had more hits against the databases than any other. In fact, he started looking at the files that first Sunday after the crash."

"Sunday? What department is he with?"

"Ever heard of DARPA?"

"Sounds familiar."

"It's the Defense Advanced Research Projects Agency. It's part of the Department of Defense. They've been in the news recently.

They were the ones who came up with the idea to create a huge database on each of us to help fight terror. Got shot down though, big brother syndrome.

"Anyway, there's a guy, Roger Stone, who works for DARPA, who's accessed the 2145 data more than anyone, including our file on Dr. Lockwood."

"So, have you talked to him yet."

"I tried calling him this morning. He's on vacation until the middle of the month."

"So, I guess you're telling me we won't be able to talk to him."

"No . . . actually, I know exactly where he is right now. Well, at least I know where his car is. He drives a 2008 Z06 Corvette."

A smile came across Jack's face. A month ago, he had worked on a case involving an interstate chop shop ring that dealt in high performance cars. They were able to find the location of one of the garages used to dismantle the cars when the thieves forgot to dis- arm the car's OnStar system which, among other things, can be used to pinpoint the exact location of a car or truck. That particu- lar car was a 2008 Z06 Corvette.

"You're kidding. So where is the car?"

"At the parking garage of the Taj Mahal in Atlantic City. I called the hotel. Stone checked in last Thursday and he's still registered."

Jack leaned back in his chair and put his hands behind his head. "Get in touch with the hotel's security chief. I'd like to know if Mr. Stone is in his hotel room right now."

54

"Room service." The bellman nervously shouted, as he stood in front of the door of room 924, breaking one of the cardinal rules of the Taj Mahal, knocking on a door with a do-not-disturb sign hanging on it. He glanced to his left. The six-three, short haired giant, dressed smartly in a blue blazer, gray slacks, white shirt, and red tie, peered down at the bellman, signaling with his hand to knock on the door again.

"Room service."

"I didn't order any room service," a voice spoke up from the other side of the door. "And, can't you read the do-not-disturb sign."

The giant reached for the plastic coated sign, pulled it from the door handle, then stuffed it into the outside pocket of his blazer.

"I'm sorry to disturb you sir, but there is no sign on the door and the hotel manager wanted you to have this complimentary bottle of champagne. I could come back sir, if this is not a conven-ient time for you."

Seconds later, the bellman jumped when the dull clank from the dead bolt cranking open broke the silence of the hallway, and the door slowly opened.

"You have got to be kidding." The man stood in the half opened doorway, the bellman initially mistaking his milk white skin against the rest of his darkened body, as a towel. He then swung the door fully open, letting it crash against the door stop. "Your timing is terrible too," he said, as he proudly pointed to the large king sized bed across the dimly lit room. It took a few seconds, but when the bellman's eyes had finally adjusted to the darkness of the room, he could make out the woman, a shapely blond, sprawled out on the bed, her head propped up on her arm, gazing back at him, unconcerned he was now staring at her naked body.

"Put the cart here," the man said, as he turned and walked toward the bed, "and be sure to close the door on your way . . . "

"Roger Stone?" a deep, serious sounding voice interrupted.

The man spun around and saw the large dark silhouette blocking the hall light from the rest of the rectangular opening of the doorway.

55

Jack looked up immediately when he heard the knock at his door, then glanced down at his watch.

"That didn't take long. What did you find?"

"They confirmed it was Roger Stone. Said he's been there since last Thursday. The hotel records show his car hasn't left the parking garage. There was a pile of cash lying on the table in his room. He said he's had a good week and may never leave the casino. Some of the money was banded, thousand dollar straps."

"Is that normal?"

"No. According to the guy I talked to in their security department, no casino would ever hand out cash winnings like that. All of the cash is counted out in front of the customer."

Jack leaned back in his chair. "Let's get them to pull the hotel security tapes."

"There is a video camera on every floor of the hotel," Dyan interrupted. "Seven-day cycle. They are reviewing the tape now for Stone's floor. I've also put a tracer on his credit cards over the past week. Should have that report by the end of the day."

"Great job Dyan. Let me know how you make out." Jack leaned back over his desk, but noticed Dyan was still standing in the doorway of his office. Jack looked up. "Is there something else?"

Without speaking, Dyan stepped inside the office, reached over and closed the door. When she turned to him, her face foretold the seriousness of what she was about to disclose.

"Dr. Lockwood's name has come up in another case I am working on."

"What. What case?"

"We've had a two year undercover operation on a local businessman. Wire taps mostly. Drugs, money laundering, tax evasion, maybe even murder. While I was waiting for the people from the Taj Mahal to get back to me, I was reviewing the transcripts of some phone conversations from this past week. Dr. Lockwood's name was mentioned, along with the money his ex-wife found. I'm not sure, but I think it might have had something to do with the break-in over the weekend."

"Wait a minute. You're moving too fast for me. Why do you think it has something to do with the break-in?"

"I think the guy we are tapping hired someone to check out the doctor's and his ex-wife's houses. He's even checking out some island."

"What did you say?"

"There's an island." Dyan flipped through the bound notebook she always carried with her. "Loon Island. It's located in the river. That's all he said. He wants that place checked out too."

Neither one said a word. Although Dyan had more to share, she could tell Jack's mind was racing. She knew not to interrupt him.

"How did this person find out about the doctor's money?"

There was a long pause before Dyan leaned over the desk and whispered, "I think we have a mole in our office."

56

"What the fuck was that all about?"

Up until an hour ago, the events over the past six days had gone almost exactly as Roger had planned. After he had paid a visit to Lockwood's apartment last Thursday, masquerading as Dr. Richard Williams, his anticipated break-in for that evening was moved to Friday night, when Sue let him know that she would be away for the entire weekend. Sharing information like that with a total stranger was tantamount to handing him a key to the place.

He had spent most of Friday night at Lockwood's apartment. It was obvious to him that Lockwood's ex-wife had thoroughly searched the apartment and removed anything of value. As he sat in the large leather recliner, scanning the room one more time, he began to feel strange. Dizzy. He then realized he hadn't had anything to eat or drink in hours. He reached both hands over the sides of the recliner, his right hand finding the wooden handle used to raise the footrest. He pushed his body back and pulled up on the handle, but the chair remained frozen.

"Fuck'n figures," he said, as he stood up and kicked the side of the chair. Suddenly the footrest sprang up. Roger jumped back, caught his leg on the coffee table, and fell straight back, onto the carpeted floor. As he lay there on his side, something flashed red before his eyes. He got up on both knees and lowered his body until his head was under the footrest. He reached back with his left hand, pinched the cool, smooth fabric, between his fingers, and pulled. As he straightened his body back up, he pulled the red duffel bag out from under the chair and placed it on his lap. His heart was pounding. The sound of air whooshing in and out of his nose broke the silence of the room. He opened his mouth and took a deep breath. He reached for the three-inch piece of nylon cloth tied to the zipper tab and tugged on it, slow enough to hear each tooth snap apart. With the zipper half open, he slipped his fingers between the cold metal teeth, then shoved his hand deeper into the bag until he found what he was searching for. He pulled his hand out. The first thing that caught his eye was the one, zero, zero, on the upper left hand corner of the bill. The second thing he saw was the money strap surrounding the wad of bills. It had four zero's after the one.

Within minutes, Roger was driving slowly, but not so slow as to draw attention, like a drunk might, back to his motel. Once inside the dump he had called home for the past three days, he spilled the contents of the bag onto the bed. It didn't take him long to determine there were over fifty bundles of bills.

"Fuck . . . I did it," he said, as he stared at the half million dollars in cash. He laid back with his head on the pillow, closed his eyes and nodded off to sleep, the first time he had done so in years, sober.

The next day, he debated returning to his Atlantic City digs, but greed got the better of him. He patiently waited for nightfall and his foray into Calihan's and Lockwood's townhouse. Upon entry through the sliding glass door, he immediately noticed the papers strewn about the dining room table and floor. There was something about what he saw that made him uneasy. Within minutes of the entry, he decided to cut his losses and run.

He returned to his hotel by 2:00 a.m. and was back on the road headed for Atlantic City within the hour.

"So what did I do wrong . . . where'd I fuck up?"

No one could have known anything about where he had been in the past few days. Routine hotel security check of guests? Had to be because he hadn't been there in a few days. Room was untouched. Maid must have said something. Had to be that, he reasoned. Just checking up. He took another sip of his drink.

In any event, so as not to raise any suspicions, he decided to stay a few more nights in Atlantic City. Besides, Traci, whom he had called upon his return yesterday, although very inexperienced, had been an excellent student in bed last night. When he had asked her to take him around the world, she agreed, even before knowing what it was she needed to do. By morning, she had found out. Now she was off, with a thousand dollars of his cash, to find a suitable outfit for tonight's class with Myra.

57

She turned her head and brushed her nose against the rough cloth of the over stuffed recliner. The pungent, musty odor was similar to the one that hit her when she walked into the room earlier. The same smell she remembered from long ago. Grandma's living room. The forbidden room, with glass doors, always closed, except on Christmas and Easter.

"Nikki, can we."

"SHUT THE FUCK UP, YOU LITTLE SLUT!" She screamed so loud, the windows rattled.

Her right hand was clenched tightly around the wooden pistol grip of the Smith & Wesson, as it laid in her lap, backing up the power in her voice. She glanced at the two people lying on the carpeted floor just twenty feet away. Then her eyes returned to the pile of money, by her quick count, just over a million dollars, on the floor near her feet.

Her mind started racing again. What the fuck was she gonna do now?

Depressed over her latest failed seduction, one on a list of many that had occurred since she had turned thirty, Sue had been the last person Nikki wanted to run into at Fantasy Fashions last week. Her depression combined with wanton jealousy when she heard of the fortunes Sue was finding, fortunes she should be sharing. Fortunes she was determined to make hers.

Friday night's foray into Sue's townhouse, the front door entry made easy by the keys she had lifted from Sue's purse at Thursday's chance luncheon encounter, spare keys she knew Sue carried and would never notice missing, was better than she could have imagined. It was just the pick-me-up she needed. As Sue had confided during their luncheon, she found the cash stuffed in hollowed out books and old shoe boxes, in plain view, on the dining room table. Over a hundred thousand dollars. More money than she had ever seen. Although a tidy sum, Sue had led her to believe there was more, much more. She spent a considerable amount of time reviewing the paperwork that was neatly arranged on the dining room table. But, it wasn't the bank statements, tax returns, and other documents with numbers that she was searching for. Those bored her. She wanted information on the island hideaway. Knowing Sue would not be going there for another week, she was determined to get there before her.

As it turned out, finding the location of the island proved to be much simpler than getting there. Renting a boat, difficult in itself, becomes infinitely more so if you are a woman, especially one dressed in a bikini top and shorts, not your normal fishing attire. The test drive, one where she confidently maneuvered the twenty-seven foot Baja cigarette boat around the crowded marina, a skill she had picked up, among others, in her younger days whoring for the summer with an older, but very wealthy divorcee, was not what convinced the old man to finally rent her the boat. It was the five thousand dollars, cash, US, she waved at him that finally did the trick. She was hoping that it would, since her final ace in the hole of oral sex would have probably given him a heart attack.

Though she was ready for almost anything upon arriving on the island, the last person she expected to see was Sue. She had told her at their luncheon last Thursday that she was going away for the weekend, but would be back on Sunday night. Any trip to the mysterious island would have to wait until after the fourth. Obviously plans had changed. Now Nikki needed to change hers.

Sitting in the old chair, she knew her options were few. She glanced at the two people lying on the floor, then at the pile of cash. Could she negotiate a deal? A fifty-fifty split? Everyone return to their previous lives, like nothing had happened, except for being richer?

The musty odor of the room returned. She snapped back into reality.

"Get up, both of you."

"What are you."

"SHUT UP!" She pointed the gun straight at Sue's face. "Do exactly as I say and you will live. Step even one inch out of line and I won't hesitate to kill you both. I don't want to hear a fuck'n word out of either of you."

58

"Nelson."

"Agent Nelson?"

"Yes it is."

"Agent Nelson, this is Ensign Bristol of the United States Coast Guard in Alexandria Bay, New York. I'm sorry sir, but your voice keeps fading in and out."

"Can you hear me better now?" Jack had removed his cell phone from its hands free cradle and held it to his ear. He knew he was breaking the New York State law regarding the use of cell phones while driving, but the hands free devices provided by the FBI were obviously from the lowest bidder, since their performance, even when in the close proximity to a cell tower, was marginal at best. Add to that the road noise from a Ford Taurus traveling close to a hundred miles an hour up Interstate 81, and the hands free device was useless.

"I can hear you much better now sir. We were told to contact you. Our Coast Guard boat, the Natali I, is docked at the Municipal

Dock at the end of St. James Street in Alexandria Bay. Are you familiar with the town?"

"Yes, I know exactly where the dock is."

Being a northern New York native, Jack had actually spent many a summer night in the Bay, especially during his college years. This party town came alive during its brief season from mid-May through Labor Day, and you could always score points with your date by including a romantic nighttime stroll on the Municipal Dock. Though he hadn't been there in over ten years, he doubted the town had changed much. In fact, it hadn't changed at all.

"What is your ETA?"

"I passed through Watertown a few minutes ago. I should be there in about twenty minutes. Lets say four-thirty at the latest."

"Copy that, ETA at sixteen-thirty hours."

"How long do you think it will take us to get to Loon Island?"

"It should take no more than forty-five minutes."

"Great. I will see you at . . . in about a half hour."

Jack glanced at the speedometer. He was still cruising at just under a hundred miles an hour. Even with his head start, there was no way Jim Calihan could make it to the island before him, he thought. He pressed down harder on the accelerator, but his foot did not move. He was traveling as fast as the stock Taurus would go.

59

"I made great time," Jim said aloud, as he turned off Route 12 and onto the narrow winding road leading to Schermerhorn Marina. He had taken the longer, back road route, rather than Interstate 81, hoping his speed would go undetected. The gamble had paid off.

Unfortunately, his longtime friend was not at his Mink Island cottage that day. Jim had hoped he would be, since his knowledge of the river would easily cut in half the time he estimated it was going to take him to get to Loon Island. Luckily though, the twenty-four foot, center console fishing boat his friend used to get to his island retreat was in slip thirty-seven at Schermerhorn's. As promised, the key was in the forward bait well.

Within ten minutes of purchasing the charts he needed from the marina store, Jim was cruising out of the docks, heading across Chippewa Bay toward the St. Lawrence River. As he stood at the wheel, he squinted at the sunlight reflecting off the calm water in front of him. His sunglasses provided little help against the glare.

The wind swept over the top of the bug splattered windshield and blew his hair straight back. He glanced down at his watch. For the first time since arriving home yesterday evening, he breathed a sigh of relief.

Then suddenly, the Honda outboard went silent for a moment, came back to life, then went silent again, this time for good. Jim raised his left hand to brace himself against the windshield as the boat glided to a stop in the middle of the river.

"FUCK!"

60

"Do you smell something?" Trip whispered, hoping Nikki, whose foot steps could be heard on the deck above, wouldn't overhear him.

Trip and Sue had been sitting on the edge of the bed, in the aft state room of the Obsession, where Nikki had put them almost two hours before. They had originally thought that the pounding and scraping they had heard, obviously something being wedged between the thick teak door to the state room and stairway forward, would be the last sound that they would hear from the woman. But after an hour of silence, the sound of the foot steps above told them it wasn't so.

Although Jim's and Trip's renovation of the Obsession had kept the exterior of the motor yacht as original as when she was first built, they had decided from the beginning of the project that they would modernize the interior. A microwave oven, coffee maker, and glass topped stove were added to the galley. The salon featured a mini-bar and full entertainment center, including a TV,

VCR, DVD player and surround sound stereo system. The front state room, the master in the original boat, with its less than comfortable V-birth in the very bow of the boat, had a large hatch that opened to the cool night air, and had been claimed by Trip, early on in the renovation project, as his room. The aft area, originally two small state rooms, became the new large master state room.

The original design also included a small six-by-twelve inch rectangular porthole in each state room, along the port and starboard sides of the boat. In an emergency, where the main doors to the rooms were not useable, any occupants would be trapped below, as the existing porthole was too small for anyone but a baby to squeeze through. To alleviate this risk in the newly designed master state room, Jim had designed an escape hatch into the aft transom of the motor yacht, which, from the outside of the boat, was almost invisible to the naked eye. Yet once opened, it was large enough to enable an adult to crawl out onto the swim platform.

Trip and Sue had been waiting for the opportunity to use this escape route when they spotted Nikki through the side porthole, heading for the boat, carrying an old rusty bucket. They felt the boat list as she boarded, then heard the dull banging sound of the bucket hitting against the stern, followed by the words, "son of a fuck'n bitch."

The footsteps went silent. "I think she went below," Trip whispered into his hands, which were cupped around Sue's left ear. She nodded in agreement. They sat motionless, trying to figure out what the woman was doing. They both jumped when they heard the sound of the first foot hit the deck above. Seconds later the boat rocked again, then they could see Nikki running toward the cottage.

"Let's wait a few minutes, then we'll try and make a run for it," Trip whispered. Sue again nodded in agreement.

As they stood there staring out the porthole, Trip took a long slow deep breath, and exhaled. Then he dropped to his knees, bent over, touched his nose to the carpet and breathed again. He crawled to the door of the state room, wedged his nose as far as he could into the space between the door and the floor, and took another deep breath.

"FUCK!" Trip yelled out, as he bolted up and stared at Sue, who was now looking at him instead of out the porthole.

"What's wrong?"

"I smell gasoline."

Sue took a deep breath, then another. "I don't smell anything." She was again whispering.

"Get down on the floor."

Gasoline vapors, heavier than air, tended to make their way to the lowest parts of a boat. That was why Federal Regulations required all enclosed engine compartments on a boat, usually the source of any gasoline leaks, to be equipped with blowers to exhaust any accumulated gasoline fumes.

"I smell it now. Is there a leak?"

Trip looked at her, his face an ashen color. "Can't be. This boat runs on diesel. The bitch had gas in that bucket. We gotta get outta here now."

Trip crawled to the head of the bed and, with a wave of his arm, cleared the shelf that was along the back wall, just above the pillows. There in plain view were four latches. He turned the two on his left counter clockwise one half turn. The two on his right he turned clockwise. Then he pushed. The hatch would not budge.

When the latches were closed, they tightly compressed the rubber seal around the hatch to assure water from the outside would never leak into the boat. The hatch had not been opened since the Obsession was launched eight years ago, and the seal, now hardened, acted like dried putty, gluing the hatch in place.

Trip got up on his knees and lunged his right shoulder against the hatch. "Shit." The door didn't budge. He double checked the position of the latches to make sure they were all in the open position.

"I can really smell the gas now," Sue whispered as she kept watch near the porthole.

Trip rammed against the center of the hatch again, this time even harder than before. "Ugh . . . damn it." The pain shot through his entire body as the bone of his shoulder slammed against the hard wooden hatch.

Sue looked at Trip, then turned her head back to the porthole. "SHE'S COMING BACK!," she screamed, as she saw Nikki walking down the cottage porch steps towards the boat.

61

Nikki reassured herself that her plan was foolproof. Her first idea had been to take the old boat out into the river and sink it, with the two hostages aboard. It would be years, if ever, before anyone found it in the two hundred foot deep watery grave. But the difficulty she had getting through the shallow waters surrounding the island with the boat she brought in would be nothing compared to what it would take to get the much larger boat out into the deeper water of the river. She would surely run her aground. That thought, however, then became her new plan of choice. She would run the old boat onto the rocks in front of the island where, assisted by the bucket of gasoline she had managed to dump out of an old lawn mower and spill in the enclosed cabin, it would blow to kingdom come.

She untied the bow line and pushed the boat away from the dock. With the stern line tied securely, the back of the boat was still close enough for her to jump onto the swim platform. She climbed up the stairs and headed for the helm. In seconds, both engines roared to life. As she put the shifters into forward, the boat jerked ahead, then abruptly stopped, held in place by the stern line. She nudged both throttles. The dock began to creak against the strain of the boat pulling on it. She jumped down the ladder onto the swim platform, then ran and leaped the five feet to the dock. She grabbed the long serrated kitchen knife that she had placed on the dock and began cutting the stretched line, like a bow on a violin string. At the end of the third pass, the line snapped and the boat started moving away from the dock. It was headed straight for the island on the other side of the bay, less than half a mile away.

"If she makes it that far," Nikki said in a calm voice, hoping the explosion she was expecting to hear would come well before the boat made it to the island, as it instead crashed onto a rocky shoal.

Nikki stepped back from the dock. She raised her hand to her forehead as the sun reflected off something on the back of the boat. "What the fuck is that?" Suddenly, she saw one, then two people appear from a small opening in the rear of the boat. As they stood up on the back of the swim platform, Nikki pulled out the pistol that had been tucked in the belt of her jeans, and took careful aim. If the boat didn't explode by itself in the next few seconds, she would speed the process by carefully placing a red-hot bullet into the gasoline-vapor-filled-cabin of the motor yacht.

As her finger pressed down on the curved metal trigger, she flinched when she heard the voice to her left.

"Hey . . . HEY!"

Nikki turned. At first she saw no one. Then, a man appeared from the far side of the cottage, walking toward the shore, arms waving, and head pointed in the direction of the yacht, which was still motoring away from the island.

Nikki glanced back toward the boat in time to see the Sea Doo slide off the swim platform and bob up and down in the water. She raised the pistol again and took careful aim.

"SUE, GET ON!" Trip shouted as he jumped on the Sea Doo and fumbled for the key in the storage compartment in front of the seat. Sue jumped and landed knees first on the small rear deck, just as the engine cranked over on its own power.

As Trip squeezed his thumb against the throttle, the deafening blast from the exploding boat blew the Sea Doo sideways across the water until it flipped over, throwing both of them into what was now a fiery inferno of burning diesel fuel.

Nikki quickly shifted her aim to the left, searching for the man she had spotted seconds before, but he was no where to be seen. It wasn't until she lowered her gun that she saw him, lying face down at the edge of the water. She ran towards him, gun ready, then stopped. She smiled as she took aim, then froze when she saw the piece of wood, looking like a thick arrow, sticking out of the man's back.

She lowered the pistol, knowing the projectile from the exploding boat had already done what she was planning to do.

62

"What the hell was that!"

They heard the sound, then felt the shock wave, as it traveled across the water, echoing off the maze of islands surrounding them. It even rocked the twin engine, twenty-five foot, bright orange inflatable, as it motored slowly through the rocky shoals.

Looking up, the fireball and black smoke was clearly visible, rising from the burning boat a mile in front of them.

"GUN IT!" Jack shouted.

The Coast Guard Seaman at the wheel, who looked old enough to vote but not drink, legally anyway, glanced first at Jack, then to the young Ensign standing next to him.

"We've got to get past these rocks first or we'll tear the bottom out of the boat," yelled the second seaman, by his looks, the oldest and most experienced of the three sailors.

"Anybody still alive will drown if we don't get there in a hurry," Jack shouted back.

The Ensign turned and looked at the dirty orange flames now

shooting well above the tree tops on the surrounding islands. The black smoke was already starting to block out the bright sun. "FULL SPEED AHEAD!" he suddenly yelled.

As the boat lunged forward they heard a loud bang when one of the outboard engines popped out of the water after striking the rocky shoal below.

63

"TRIP . . . TRIP!" Though Sue was yelling as loud as she could, the ringing in her ears, along with the crackle of burning fuel and debris still raining down, made her voice sound like a whisper. As she opened her mouth to breathe in enough air to yell out again, it filled with diesel slime, causing her to cough up what little air she had. With her lungs empty, she felt herself slowly sink into the black, oily river.

As she kicked, her feet scraped against something hard. She straightened her legs and her head popped out of the water. Standing on her tiptoes, with her head tilted back, her chin bobbed slowly in and out of the water. After a few deep breaths, she felt a burning sensation in her eyes as they squeezed shut. She reached up and wiped them, which only pushed more of the oily mixture into her sockets. Squinting, she saw Trip less than ten feet away, his head and shoulders sticking out of the water. The Sea Doo was floating upside down next to him.

"TRIP . . . TRIP!" She walked toward him along the rocky river bottom. "TRIP!" She put her hand on his right shoulder.

"Ahhhh!" The scream made Sue jump back. Trip turned his head toward her. "I think I dislocated my right shoulder," He slowly turned to face her. "Are you okay?"

"I think so. My eyes are burning."

"Mine too. It's the diesel fuel."

"What are we gonna do?"

"We need to flip the Sea Doo over. You get on this side, and I'll get on that side. On three, you push up and I'll pull down. It needs to be flipped over this way to make sure the engine doesn't fill up with water."

"Okay."

"One, two, three!" A second later the Sea Doo was floating upright.

"You get on first . . . you're gonna have to drive." Sue pulled down the boarding step, boosted herself up and sat on the seat. It took Trip three agonizing, painful tries before he was onboard and seated behind Sue.

"Head out that way," Trip pointed with his left hand, which had been wrapped around Sue's waist, to an opening of clear water between the burning boat and the island to their right. "Don't worry about the stuff floating in the water. Stay away from the seaweed though."

Sue pushed the start button, and without hesitation, the Sea Doo engine roared to life. She pushed the throttle with her thumb. The watercraft lunged forward. They could feel the heat from the burning Obsession on the left side of their bodies, as they slowly passed by. Sue started to speed up as she got into the open water.

Trip turned to his left when he first heard, then saw, the speeding boat heading towards them. A second later, Sue turned to the left, and without thinking about it, squeezed the throttle lever down to the handle. The Sea Doo instantly jumped forward. The speeding boat passed just feet behind them. Sue let up on the throttle and they both looked to the right at the boat that had just missed hitting them. It slowed down, quickly turned to the left, then headed directly for them again.

"That way," Trip shouted, as he pointed, then quickly wrapped his arm around Sue again. Sue gunned it and headed straight between the two islands less than a mile ahead.

Trip turned his head around. The speed boat was in their wake and gaining on them. He looked over Sue's shoulder at the speedometer. Thirty-five. On a calm day like this, with two people onboard, they should easily be hitting sixty-five. "Squeeze the throttle all the way!"

"I am."

Trip looked at the speedometer again. "There must be grass in the intake."

"What do you want me to do?"

"Just keep heading straight between those two islands and don't let up on the gas."

Trip turned again. The speed boat was getting closer. There was no way they were going to make it to the islands. Not with the intake plugged and the two of them on the Sea Doo.

"No matter what happens, head straight between the two islands. Don't look back. Do you hear me?" He squeezed Sue around the waist. She nodded.

"What are you gonna do?"

Before she could finish her sentence, Trip loosened his arm

from Sue's waist and rolled off the seat into the water.

"NOOOOO!" she screamed, as she felt the Sea Doo wobble when Trip pushed himself off.

Trip rolled across the water several times, then, with a huge splash that sprayed a wave of water twenty feet into the air, he came to an abrupt stop and sank, just before the speeding boat roared overhead.

Nikki thought she heard a noise, like a dull thud, as she purposefully drove over the spot where the man had sunk. She looked back at her wake hoping to catch a glimpse of floating body parts, sliced up by the boat props. She quickly turned forward when the boat rocked to the right, as it glided over the wake of the Sea Doo, now just in front of her.

Sue looked down at the speedometer. She was now moving at close to fifty miles an hour. Within seconds she was in between the two islands. Suddenly, the Sea Doo flew out of the water, as if it had glided over a small ski jump. Starved of water, the jet pump whined as the water craft flew through the air. Sue braced herself for the landing, but her arms gave way when the Sea Doo hit the water. Her chest smashed into the padded handle bar. Within seconds, her arms straightened and her body flew back in the seat, as the jet pump refilled with water and rocketed the water craft forward.

Nikki was still closing in on the Sea Doo in front of her. She was less than twenty feet behind it. It was the only thing that stood between her and the money. Just as the Sea Doo seemed to fly out of the water, she felt the boat tilt first slightly to the left, then hard to the right. A moment later, the boat flew up and out of the water, then exploded in a fireball, falling upside down where it came to a sudden, screeching stop on the shallow rocky bottom.

First Sue felt a blast of heat on her back, then the shock wave, then the ear deafening sound. She slowed, then quickly turned to the right, whipping the rear end of the Sea Doo around. She squeezed the throttle, flew by the flaming wreckage of the boat that moments ago was trying to run her over, and headed into the center of its still visible wake, searching for the man who had saved her life.

64

"What the hell!" The four of them ducked as the sound of the blast, not as loud as the one minutes before, vibrated their ear drums.

"OVER THERE," Jack shouted, as he pointed to the latest smoky fireball rising into the sky, from the otherwise serene river.

"What the fuck is going on!" the Ensign said, as he finally saw the second plume through the smoke still billowing from the burning yacht, now directly in front of them.

The Natali I had hit a rocky shoal as it entered the passageway leading to Loon Island. One of her twin Johnson outboard engines was totally inoperable, its lower unit sheared off and resting somewhere on the rocky river bottom. The second outboard was vibrating so badly, they didn't dare go above half throttle, for fear of it falling completely off the rear transom of the boat. With a top speed normally in excess of fifty knots, the craft now limped along at less than ten.

"I don't see anyone in the water here, sir." The older Seaman had been perched in the bow of the boat during the entire time the craft slowly motored toward the burning wreckage, scanning over the surface of the water with a giant pair of gray binoculars. Although the black smoke had darkened the once clear blue sky above, the intense heat of the burning yacht had kept the smoke rising well above the water, making it easy for him to search for any movement in the still water around the wreckage.

"Roger. Steer to port and head for the second wreckage. Keep it less than half throttle."

"Aye-aye sir."

As they motored by the burning yacht, the four of them stared at the flames that now fully engulfed the entire wooden structure, making it look as though the water itself was on fire. Once past, they refocused on the second wreckage, with the Seaman again scanning the horizon with his binoculars.

"Talk to me sailor," the Ensign finally spoke up.

"It's the yellow speed boat sir, upside down. By its attitude, I'd say it's laying on the bottom, in no more than a foot of water. No sign of the personal watercraft. No sign of any survivors."

After the first explosion, the Seaman thought he had spotted a personal watercraft, with two people onboard, leaving the scene, followed closely by a yellow speed boat, which to him looked as if it was chasing the first.

"Still no sign of anyone in the water, sir." The Seaman then lowered his binoculars and looked into the water directly in front of the bow of the boat. He then turned and eyed the Ensign. "Looks like we are getting into some shallow water sir."

"REVERSE, REVERSE, REVERSE!" the Ensign yelled, as a loud clanging could be heard coming out of the vibrating outboard, and the boat suddenly slowed, came to a dead stop, only for a moment, then started backing up.

As Jack caught his balance, he saw something glowing white far down the river. "What's that?"

The forward Seaman raised his binoculars. "It's a personal water-craft with someone onboard. They might be hurt. They are lying over the handle bar and the craft appears to be idling in circles."

"Ahoy there . . . ma'am, are you all right?" the Ensign yelled, as the inflatable neared the circling watercraft. Seconds later the Sea Doo bumped into the side of the inflatable and the Seaman reached for the handle and pressed the red kill switch, silencing the idling engine.

"Ma'am . . . are you all right?" The Seaman touched the woman's shoulder. She raised her body from the handle bar and gazed at the man.

"She's in shock. Get her onboard." The two Seaman leaned over the side, grabbed the woman under the arms and lifted her limp body into the boat. "Lay her down on the blanket. Get her covered up."

Jack kneeled and then leaned over the woman. "Mrs. Lockwood, it's me, Jack Nelson. From the FBI."

Sue gazed up at him with a blank look on her face.

"Lets head back to Loon Island. From there we'll see if we can get her air lifted to a hospital. Secure that watercraft with a tow line and prepare to get underway."

The vibrating outboard caused Sue to suddenly bolt upright. She almost knocked Jack over, who had been kneeling beside her. Sue tried to stand, then fell back to the blanket.

"TRIP! TRIP! WE CAN'T GO!" she yelled, her hands frantically reaching for anything she could latch onto, including Jack's ear, as she tried to pull herself back up.

"Mrs. Lockwood, please, lie down." Both Jack and the Ensign pushed her back onto the blanket. "Do you remember me? I'm Jack Nelson."

"Yes . . . FBI."

"That's right."

"Please." She began to cry when she realized she didn't have the strength to break Jack's hold of her. "Trip is out there somewhere. Please. You need to find him."

"Is that Jim's son?"

"Yes. Please. Find him."

"Sir, the Natali II is approaching off the port bow."

When they had damaged their outboards on the approach to Loon, the Ensign had placed what had been a very embarrassing call for emergency assistance to their back-up sister ship. With the Natali II on-site, she continued with the search for survivors while the Natali I proceeded to limp back to Loon Island.

"Would you like to try to stand up?" Jack said, as Sue sat next to him, wrapped in a blanket in the chair they had brought from the cottage and placed on the dock.

"Can we take the boat back out and help with the search?" Sue strained to get the words out, as she struggled to stand.

"Let me talk to the Coast Guard." Jack walked to the edge of the dock where the three sailors were inspecting the damaged outboards on the inflatable.

As Sue stood there, she started to feel dizzy and leaned on the chair beside her. As she raised her head, she saw the man laying in the grass along the waters edge. "OH MY GOD!" she yelled out.

All four men turned and looked at her, then in the direction of where she was pointing.

Jack was the first to get there. "What the hell?"

The young Seaman was a second behind. He immediately jumped back, turned to his right, doubled over, gagged once, then with a grunting heave, threw up the half digested pizza he had scarfed down, just hours before.

Somehow, the man was still alive, even though a two foot long, pointed mahogany splinter, that had shot like a spear from the exploding yacht, was sticking out both sides of his body, just below the rib cage. Miraculously, the wooden splinter, shaped like a pool cue, thin at its point and gradually thicker along its length, had missed any vital organs, and as it penetrated his body, had stretched the wound, self sealing any severed blood vessels.

As he heard foot steps behind him, Jack turned to block Sue's view, but he knew he was too late when he heard her scream.

"JIM!"

65

"Nick, it's me."

"Did you find it?"

"No. I couldn't get ta da fuck'n island."

"Why not?"

"Some fuck'n boats crashed into each other, right near da place. Goddamn cops were all over da place. It ain't gonna be safe ta go back dare for a few days."

"Fine. We'll hit that place later on in the week. In the mean-time, I've got someplace else I want you to visit."

66

"Mrs. Calihan, I'm Dr. Harris." The tall, middle aged man, still dressed in his green scrubs, extended his hand to Sue who had been standing in the cold, dimly lit waiting room of the River Hospital in Alexandria Bay, staring out the window at the red, green, and white lights, on the boats speeding along the dark river below.

"It's Mrs. Lockwood . . . we're not married."

"Mrs. Lockwood, your . . . Mr. Calihan is resting in the recovery room. He is in a stable condition. He's not out of the woods yet, but, other than a few scars, he should recover completely. He was very lucky. A fraction of an inch either way and . . . "

Sue dropped onto the large sofa she was standing next to, doubled over and rested her head on her arms which she had crossed over her knees. In this position, she could smell the oily residue that permeated her clothes. Although she wasn't crying, tears dripped from her cheeks onto the skin of her still grime-covered legs.

"Thank you doctor." Sue stood up, wiped the tears from her

283

eyes with her bare hands, then reached out for the doctor's hand. "When will I be able to see him."

"The nurse will come and get you when they've moved him to a room. That should be within the hour. He is heavily sedated though, and he might not be fully awake until the morning."

As the doctor walked out of the room, Sue resumed her gaze out the window. Since leaving the island hours ago, she had prayed for Jim's recovery. It had been the only thing on her mind. Now that that prayer had been answered, she had only minutes to think about how she would tell Jim about his son.

She closed her eyes and instead prayed that when she opened them, she would awaken and realize this had all been a terrible nightmare.

67

Sue awoke when she felt cold fingers trying to squeeze her hand.

Jim had been moved from the recovery room to an unoccupied semi-private room on the third floor of the hospital, as the doctor had predicted. Sue entered the room to find Jim sleeping and decided it was best not to disturb him. She sat next to the bed and within minutes was overtaken by her own exhaustion.

"Hi," he whispered, his voice barely audible. "You're a sight for sore eyes."

Although she still had on the same clothes she had been wearing all day, she had cleaned herself up in the woman's room as best she could. She used a soapy paper towel to wash the oil residue from her arms, legs, and face, and had pinned up her hair, which tended to camouflage the grease soaked strands. Without makeup, the redness in her eyes was clearly visible.

Sue could feel her heart pounding as she stood next to the bed. She leaned over the rail and lightly pressed her mouth to his, then pulled back, when she noticed how hard, dry, and cracked his lips felt.

"Can I have some water?" Sue propped Jim's head up, then held the straw, sticking through the hole in the plastic top on the Styrofoam cup, to his lips. He sucked enough water to wet the inside of his mouth, then used the tip of his now moist tongue to wet his lips.

"Are you okay?" This time Jim's voice was much louder.

Sue stood leaning over the bed rail, her eyes straining to hold back the tears. "I'm fine. How are you feeling?"

"Actually . . . I'm feeling pretty good." Jim was now talking much slower than normal. "Must be the drugs." His voice was getting whispery again.

"More water?"

"Yes . . . please."

Sue again fed him the straw.

"That's better, thanks."

There was a long period of silence where Jim laid motionless with his eyes closed. Sue used the opportunity to wipe the tears away that were slowly dripping down her cheeks.

Jim finally opened his eyes and stared over Sue's shoulder into a distant corner of the room, as if to purposefully avoid eye contact with her. "Trip."

Sue stood there looking at Jim. Her head pounding. Her stomach contracting. Her mouth watering. She felt like throwing up.

"Trip." His voice was now louder, but still he wouldn't look at Sue.

"Jim," Sue choked out the word. She was shaking. Her lips moved, but no words came out. "He is miss . . . "

"Trip," Jim interrupted, this time his voice was loud and clear.

"I'm right here Dad," a low voice echoed through the room.

Sue turned, then started to drop as her knees went limp. Trip reached out with one arm and held her upright. She looked up, giving herself a second or two to make sure she wasn't hallucinating, then lunged forward and wrapped her arms tightly around Trip. She then turned her head to the right. Through her blurry, tear-filled eyes, she saw a glimpse of Jack Nelson as he walked out the door of the room and disappeared into the dimly lit hall.

68

Nick watched the last drop of the Crown Royal as it fell from the neck of the bottle and landed in the glass. He placed the bottle on the desk. He lifted the full glass, being careful not to spill it, then held it high in the air in front of him.

"It was fun while it lasted." The simple toast was appropriate he thought. He filled his mouth, savored the taste for a few seconds, then swallowed.

Hours ago, Nick had received an update from his informant in the Syracuse FBI office, that the money that had rumored to have been found on an island in the St. Lawrence River a few days ago, the same money presumed aboard one of the exploding boats, had been traced to a drug ring operating in Central New York. Although unconfirmed, several million dollars may have been involved.

Nick took another mouthful of the liquor. Several million. That was not what he wanted to hear. Although he had guessed all along that the money that had turned up last week was his, he had hoped that only a portion of it had been destroyed in the fire in the river. The rest, he was certain, had been stolen by a Roger Stone, who his informant in the FBI had told him was under suspicion of doing so.

Nick was so certain of the latter that he dispatched his man to Stone's home in Georgetown to hopefully recover part of his losses. Now with the news that most of the money was gone, he assumed his man would find nothing.

Nick held the glass up one more time, saying nothing, then placed it to his lips and swallowed the last of the liquid. He put the glass down on the desk in front of him and slid his hand to the right until he felt the cold metal against his pinkie. He hesitated, for just a second, then, in one continuous motion, leaving no time to think about it, he picked up the silver snub-nosed thirty-eight, placed the barrel in his mouth, and pulled the trigger.

The deafening blast that filled the room was immediately followed by the ring of his phone. Then a second ring. Then a third. It rang over fifty times before it stopped. Then a minute later, the ringing started again.

"Where da fuck is he. He said he'd fuck'n be dare." He let the phone ring. He'd let it ring for hours if he had to. He needed to tell Nick the good news. He'd found the money, and, coincidentally, Stone would not be needing it any more.

69

"I thought you said he was going to be here at two?" Just then the door bell rang.

"I did."

"Good afternoon Mrs. Lockwood."

"Let me take that for you," Sue said as she took Jack's drenched, dark overcoat and hung it on the empty hook in the entryway.

"Thank you."

"You're welcome. It looks a little wet out there." Sue then took Jack's hand. "And please, after all that we have been through together, call me Sue."

As Jack stood there looking at her, his face slowly warmed with a smile, transforming from its standard, official looking, agent mode. "Okay, Sue. And you can call me," he hesitated for a moment, then realized she was right, they had been through a lot together, "Jack."

"I was just pouring some iced tea. Can I get you a glass?"

"That would be great."

"Lemon and sugar?"

"Just lemon please."

They both walked into the living room, where Jim was sitting in his shorts and a cut off sweatshirt, his feet propped up on the coffee table. When Jim saw them enter, he stood up to greet Jack.

"Please, don't get up on my account."

"I'm fine. The doctor says I'll be back to one hundred percent in another week. Just in time for the new school year to begin." Jim extended his right hand to Jack. "I never did get a chance to thank you," Jim hesitated, finding it difficult to even say the words, "for saving my life."

The two men stood motionless, except for the up and down movement of their hands.

"Shall we sit down?" Sue finally spoke up, sensing they both needed help dealing with whatever emotions each was feeling.

"I wanted to meet with the both of you today to brief you on where we stand with our investigation, which is essentially complete.

"First, Sue, did you know your ex-husband had been diagnosed with pancreatic cancer?"

"Oh my God, no?"

"He had refused treatment and probably had less than six months to live."

Jim reached out for Sue's hand.

After a long silence, Jack proceeded to explain what they had found in their investigation. He told them about the journals they had found in the cottage on Loon Island, journals that told a much different story of Dan's life over the past two years than the ones

Sue had found in his apartment.

"What we've concluded from our investigation is, your ex-husband was planning something that was going to make your life miserable. Something that would all play out after he died."

"After he died?"

"That's right. We will never be one hundred percent sure. His last journal, the one that would have given us the most detail of his activities over the last month, probably went down with him on the plane. But from what we've pieced together, that appears to be what he was doing."

"But . . . how?"

"And why," Jim interrupted. "They were divorced."

"The why is the easy part, so I'll start there. Actually, it's clearly documented in his journals, even the ones he left behind in his apartment. He blamed you for everything that went wrong in his life, starting with the . . . the drowning of your daughter. He was jealous that you had gotten over . . . "

"You never get over something like that," Sue interrupted.

There was a long uneasy silence before Jack, looking down at his notes, spoke up again. "He couldn't get on with his life the way that you had appeared to have done, then when he was diagnosed with cancer, that seemed to push him off the deep end. It was then that he devised his plan. One that would basically ruin your life. Make you as unhappy, or if he could, even more unhappy than he was."

Jack first stirred, then took a sip from his iced tea.

"The how part is not as straightforward and clear, probably because he never had the chance to finish what he had started."

"The plane crash?"

292

"Exactly. I think I said it once before. He was in the wrong place at the wrong time. He died months before he thought he was going to. We'll never know what his final plan was, but what we do know is, it had clearly been set into motion, and even his death did not stop it. In fact, it may have accelerated it. He had already set someone else up to carry out his plan, long after his death"

"Roger Stone?"

"That's right. As luck would have it, he found the perfect person to play his game with in Roger Stone. Dr. Lockwood used greed as the bait and Stone took it, hook, line, and sinker. We found an extensive file in Stone's car that he had kept on the whole episode. It totally corroborates the con."

"No matter how much he hated me, I still can't see the man killing me. That just wasn't in him."

"Maybe he never intended that either."

They both looked at Jack.

"Logic would tell you, if he had wanted you dead, he would have done it himself, for the satisfaction of it, knowing even if he got caught, he was going to die anyway. I don't think he wanted you to die. He wanted you to be miserable. But he died before he had a chance to put his entire plan, whatever it was, into place. Once he died, Roger Stone took over, and he was driven by other motives.

"Then, the same force, greed, probably mixed with jealousy, motivated Nikki Larson to carry on where Stone had left off. As I said, we will never know what he really had in mind for you."

"I've been sitting here listening to you," Jim spoke up, "but there's one thing that still doesn't make sense to me."

"The money?" Jack interrupted.

"Yes, the money. Where did it all come from?"

"That's the one issue that had us baffled too." Jack took another sip of his drink.

"Dr. Lockwood's plan would have you believe he intercepted the supposedly counterfeit money as part of a terrorist plot. The only problem with that scenario was, the money was real. So we had to ask ourselves where would someone come up with two million dollars in cash.

"Do you recall the gang-like slaying of three young men that took place in Syracuse two years ago?"

"There have been so many murders . . . "

"All three were shot in the head," Jim interrupted Sue, recalling the slayings.

"That's right."

"Didn't they determine that it was drug related, too?" Jim added.

"We initially thought the killings were part of the gang wars that were going on over the control of the drug trafficking in Syracuse. An informant came forward about a year ago who claimed that the three were killed by their own gang members, over a botched transfer of drug money.

"They were to have picked up the cash on the evening of August 8, at the Canastota rest stop on the Thruway. Supposedly, the money was delivered and the transfer took place, but when the three arrived in Syracuse, the cash was not in the trunk of their car.

"The informant, who supposedly spoke with one of the men before they were killed, said they may have forgotten to put the bag of cash in the trunk and drove away, leaving it lying in the parking lot. Someone probably pulled into the rest stop, saw the bag and . . . "

"Are you saying that someone was Dan?" Sue again interrupted, to which Jack sat motionless.

"Two years ago," Jim interjected, then looked at Sue. "That was the same time Dan started paying cash for everything. But it still seems like a huge stretch to me to say that he found the money."

Again, Jack sat there silent, letting the almost incredible story sink in some more.

"You have other proof, don't you?" Sue asked.

"On the evening of August 8, Dr. Lockwood entered the New York State Thruway at Albany, entrance 24 at 9:05 p.m. and exited at Syracuse, exit 36, at 11:55 p.m. This was documented on his E-Z Pass account. It put him passing by the Canastota rest area at the approximate time and day in question and gives him enough time to make one, even two stops along the route."

"Still seems too circumstantial to me."

"Except, at 11:38 p.m., he filled his car up with gas at the Canastota rest area Sunoco station, charging the purchase on his Visa card."

"You have something else, don't you."

"The money you found in Dr. Lockwood's apartment, the money Nikki took from your apartment, we had it analyzed for drug residue. If you randomly select a bunch of twenties, fifties, or hundred dollar bills in circulation in the US, about forty percent of them would show some kind of drug residue on them, mostly cocaine. Over eighty percent of the bills from Dr. Lockwood's apartment were contaminated.

"We think there is enough evidence, circumstantial evidence, to indicate that is where Dr. Lockwood got the money from."

"And I guess the drug dealer who lost the money to begin with thought so too."

"That's what we surmise."

"You know what's ironic . . . Dan really didn't need any elaborate plan to hurt me after he died. If he had just left the money for me to find, the drug dealer would have carried out a plan of his own."

EPILOGUE

"They make a great couple, don't they?"

"They sure do. They always have, though."

"I'm so glad the weather forecast changed. I guess you were right, the weather up here is so different than it is in Syracuse."

"Aren't you glad I made you bring your sunglasses!"

"Shhhhhh . . . ."

"Dearly beloved, we are gathered here today to join this man and this woman in the bond of holy matrimony. Do you, James Calihan, take . . . "

They had both decided that the perfect location for their wedding ceremony would be the gazebo that sat on a slight hill overlooking Market Square Park and the town dock in Sackets Harbor, New York. They knew they were taking a risk when, six months before, they reserved the gazebo for the first Saturday in August, twelve noon to be exact, for their ceremony. Although the Farmer's Almanac called for sunny skies, it had rained every day since Tuesday, and Friday's prediction for Saturday was for more of the same. But earlier in the morning the puffy gray clouds that rolled in off Lake Ontario slowly broke up and in short order the sun erased any evidence of the previous five days' deluge.

Sackets Harbor, located at the mouth of the Black River on the northeastern end of Lake Ontario, was just ten miles north of Henderson Harbor, where Jim had kept the Obsession. The town was a vital strategic center during the War of 1812, and several battles took place between the American forces based there and the British forces in Kingston. Although the town still had many of the old stone buildings that were built in the early 1800's, in recent years, the village had been turned into a major summer tourist destination. The small town gained worldwide notoriety in 2003 when Funny Cide, an unknown horse boarded at Sackets, almost became the first horse in twenty-five years to win the Triple Crown, when it won the Kentucky Derby and Preakness, but lost the Belmont Stakes.

"I now pronounce you husband and wife. You may kiss the bride."

A round of applause, not just from the hundred or so guests that were invited to the wedding, but also from the tourists who had stopped to watch the ceremony, erupted as the couple kissed.

"I would like to remind everyone that the reception line and cocktail reception will take place immediately, at Tin Pan Galley, one block that way," the man said, as he pointed up Main Street.

The Tin Pan Galley was one of a dozen restaurants located in the small town, and the most elegant. With no facility in Sackets large enough to hold a wedding reception of this size, they had planned an outdoor reception, in the tree and flower lined garden, bordering the restaurant.

"We really lucked out with the weather," Sue said, as they stood, champagne glasses in hand, waiting for the toast.

Finally the small three-piece band stopped playing and the crowd quieted.

"I would like to propose a toast." The crowd followed suit and raised their glasses. "May the dreams that Brandi and Trip see in each other's eyes today, all come true." The clanging glasses were followed by loud cheers from the crowd.

"Are you sorry that we eloped?" Jim asked Sue, as she watched the crowd of people re-surround the bride and groom.

Sue turned, looked into Jim's eyes, then answered with a long, passionate kiss.